THE MALLORCA CONNECTION

THE MALLORCA CONNECTION

Peter Kerr

ISIS
LARGE PRINT
Oxford

First published in Great Britain 2006
by
Accent Press Ltd.

Published in Large Print 2007 by ISIS Publishing Ltd.,
7 Centremead, Osney Mead, Oxford OX2 0ES
by arrangement with
Accent Press Ltd.

British Library Cataloguing in Publication Data
Kerr, Peter, 1940–
    The Mallorca connection. – Large print ed.
    1. Police – Scotland – Fiction
    2. Murder – Investigation – Spain – Majorca
    – Fiction
    3. Detective and mystery stories
    4. Large type books
    I. Title II. Kerr, Peter, 1940–. Bob Burns
    investigates – the Mallorca connection
    823.9'2 [F]

ISBN 978-0-7531-7844-7 (hb)
ISBN 978-0-7531-7845-4 (pb)

Printed and bound in Great Britain by
T. J. International Ltd., Padstow, Cornwall

CHAPTER
ONE

Here Lies
"BERTIE" McGREGOR *Died 13 July, 2000,*
Aged 77 Years
"DIXIE" McGREGOR *Died 13 July, 2000,*
Aged 5 Years
TOGETHER FOREVER

Bob Burns looked on as the workman put the finishing touches to cementing the tiny headstone onto its plinth, then stepped forward and laid a single red rose on the grave.

"Relation of yours, was he, mate?" the workman asked, gathering up his tools.

"No, I didn't even know Bertie all that well. Just came along to pay my respects at her topping out, sort of thing. Somebody had to."

"Did you say *her*?"

"That's right — although I think it's safe to say her father *had* been hoping for a son. Roberta Roy McGregor, her full name was."

"Hmm, it takes all kinds, and that's a fact," the workman muttered. He cast Bob a glance that was a mixture of puzzlement and wariness, then asked, "And what about Dixie the bairn? Grandchild, was it?"

1

Smiling to himself, Bob knelt down and propped the rose against the little headstone. "No," he chuckled, "Dixie was her cat."

With some urgency, the workman grabbed the handles of his wheelbarrow and trundled off to his van, mumbling, "Aye, they're not all bloody locked up yet, and that *is* a fact!"

Bob took one last look at the headstone. "So long, old girl. I'll try to drop by occasionally with a flower for you. Too bad it can't be a dram, eh?" He glanced at his watch. Eleven o'clock — opening time. Time for a quick pint before going back to work? Yeah, bugger it! Why not? He stuck his hands in his pockets and ambled out of the churchyard.

Dirleton was looking at its best, a picture postcard of leafy tranquillity, still half asleep in the warm glow of the late August sunshine. The most typically English village in Scotland, some called it, and it was a fair enough description, Bob reckoned — what with the village green, the little stone church, the whitewashed inn at the corner, the cluster of pantiled cottages all nestling snugly in roses-round-the-door serenity, and even the upmarket homeliness of the Open Arms Hotel, sitting in its understated elegance just over the road from the walls of the famous old ruined castle itself. Typically English, perhaps — yet to Bob Burns, Dirleton embodied the very essence of rural south-east Scotland.

"Maybe that's why the Highlanders used to call us folk from round here Sassenachs as well," he said absentmindedly, leaning his elbow on the bar.

"What was that, sir?"

Bob blinked at the barman. "Oh, sorry — just thinking aloud, friend. Pint of Belhaven Best, please." He nodded to two old codgers sitting with a collie dog over in the corner, then cast his eyes round the otherwise empty room. The public bar in the Castle Inn hadn't changed much in the twenty years since he left the village. The fruit machine was new, and the barman looked as if he was young enough to be playing truant from school, but otherwise everything was pretty much as he remembered it.

"Just passing through, sir?" the barman said as he placed Bob's brimming pint on the counter. "Just popping down the coast for a game of golf, are you? Nice day for it."

Bob eased himself onto a bar stool. "No, I've only come down from Edinburgh to pay someone a quick visit, as a matter of fact."

"Is that right? Got friends in the village, have you? Ah, well, I'll likely know them. We get them all in here, you know."

As much as he knew that the young fellow was only trying to make polite conversation, Bob couldn't resist an acerbic quip: "You won't get this one in here any more, son. She's pushing up daisies from six feet under the graveyard."

The barman was clearly taken aback. "No offence, all right? I mean, I didn't mean to be nosey, like. I was only —"

"Only trying to make conversation? Yeah, I understand. No offence taken, OK?" Bob took a long,

3

deep draught of the tawny brew. "Ah-h-h . . . bloody marvellous!" He dipped his chin and masked a burp behind his hand. "No, I was just having a wee look at old Bertie McGregor's gravestone, actually. Just sort of paying my respects to old Bertie."

"Old Bertie," the barman echoed, his tone as sombre as his look. "The village will take a long time to get over what happened to her. A terrible tragedy."

The two old boys in the corner nodded their acquiescence. "Aye, a terrible tragedy. Terrible . . . and that sudden, too."

"Suddenly" was certainly how the notice in the *Deaths* column of the local paper had described her passing at the time, as Bob recalled. And, true enough, death usually didn't come any more suddenly than via a belt on the side of the head with a garden spade.

Bob had been on duty at HQ in Edinburgh that evening, sitting with a Leith hooker, sifting through wads of mug shots in a forlorn attempt to identify some guy who had punched her in the chops after doing the business and then buggered off with the thirty quid he'd slipped her up front.

The phone on his desk rang.

"Let me speak to Detective Sergeant Burns," the voice on the other end said.

"You're speaking to him. What's your problem?"

"DCI Spiers here, Burns. Get yourself out here to Roodlands Hospital in Haddington at the double. There's been —"

"Ehm, excuse me, Chief, but I can't. I'm right in the middle of investigating an alleged GBH against a —"

"Screw your GBH, Burns! Delegate one of your coppers to look after that shit for you — that's what they're there for — and get your arse out here smartish! There's been a bloody murder, and as from right now *you're* on the case!"

Bob didn't have to be told a third time — not when his boss was in that kind of mood. He was a mean, arrogant bastard, Jack Spiers, but a bloody good 'tec who had clawed his way up the force from rock bottom and wouldn't think twice about booting any of his subordinates all the way back down there if they didn't cut the mustard.

Bob cleared the city and covered the twenty miles to the old market town of Haddington in as many minutes — blue lights flashing, siren wailing, the lot. He still got a schoolboyish kick out of that; a feeling of power, of unchallenged superiority, watching gobsmacked pedestrians stop and gape as he Silverstoned his white Mondeo through the scattering traffic. He'd even been known to employ the complete lights-and-siren dodge to carve through the rush-hour gridlock on his way home for his evening meal when he first made it into the CID. But time and eventual promotion had long since put paid to that caper. Now he usually didn't get home for an evening meal at all!

He pulled off the A1 and through the gates of the hospital just as the midsummer sun was starting to dip behind the topmost branches of the tall oaks that shaded the sprawling grounds. It was just after eight o'clock, and long shadows were already falling over the scatter of single-storey pavilions that housed the various wards. A clutch of panda cars and a milling throng of nurses and porters indicated the ward he wanted.

"In the gardens round the back, Sarge," said the picket bobby, taking a cursory glance at Bob's ID and gesturing towards a path at the side of the building. "And I'd step lively, if I were you. Your chief seems to be getting a wee bit edgy."

Jack Spiers was standing in the middle of a huddle of uniformed policemen and a few white-coated hospital staff by a clump of shrubs at the far corner of the lawn. He didn't even bother to introduce Bob to the others.

"Ah, the late Sergeant Burns. Good of you to favour us with your presence at long last."

Bob was tempted to tell him that he had violated every traffic regulation in the bloody book and then some to get there as quickly as he had, but he knew he'd be doing himself no favours by back-chatting Jack Spiers in public. He walked directly over to where a rubber sheet was covering the outline of a body lying hunched up beside a keeled-over wheelchair.

"Would you mind?" he said to the young copper who was standing by.

The constable bent down and gingerly folded back the sheet to reveal the ashen, wax-like face. A shock of white hair was matted with blood that had oozed from a gaping wound behind the ear and now lay in a congealing crimson pool on the grass. Bob swallowed hard and motioned the bobby to replace the sheet.

6

Even after twenty years, the stark spectacle of violent death still turned his guts.

"Bertie McGregor," he whispered. "The poor old bugger . . ."

"You know the victim, Sergeant?" DCI Spiers called out.

Bob paused for a moment to stare down at the lifeless bundle. "Used to," he said, sauntering back to join the onlooking group. "But that was a long time ago. She was one of the village characters. Swore like a trooper, drank like a fish, smoked like a chimney, spat like a bullfrog —"

"Fine," Spiers cut in. "You can enter all that fascinating background detail in your report, *if* you think it's really relevant. But right now you'd better get on with tying things up here." He half turned towards a lanky uniformed officer standing next to him. "This is Inspector, ehm . . ."

"Wilson. Jim Wilson," the Inspector muttered, his expression a blend of irritation and embarrassment as he offered Bob his hand.

"Yes, yes, yes," Spiers confirmed, with undisguised lack of interest. "Inspector Wilson from the local nick. His lads have already done all the dog work, so they'll fill you in on the basics. Then it's all yours, Burns."

"Wait a minute, Chief," Bob frowned. He drew his boss aside. "Aren't you taking charge of this case personally? I mean, we're dealing with a pretty horrific murder here, and while I mean no disrespect to the local fuzz, that surely calls for the full specialised treatment from our mob."

Jack Spiers took a deep breath, looked Bob squarely in the eye and announced in a voice that was intended for all to hear, "Look here, Detective Sergeant Burns, this case is so simple and clear-cut that any rookie fresh from police college could handle it. In truth, there's really no need for the CID to waste any more time here, but we have to be seen to be going through the motions. I'm expecting you to have our side of it all stitched up and your report ready for the Procurator Fiscal by midday tomorrow at the latest."

Bob resisted the urge to tell his Detective Chief Inspector that, if he cared to rustle up a broom, he'd be happy to stuff the handle up his own jacksy and sweep the hospital grounds while he was at it. Instead, all he came out with was a pension-saving, "Whatever you say, Chief — you're the boss," for which he instantly hated himself.

"Carry on then, Burns. The Inspector here will brief you fully on what's happened and what I want done about it. His men will help in whatever way you want. Now, if you'll all excuse me, I'll go and pay my wife a belated visit in surgical — which was my reason for coming here in the first place this evening."

"Oh, yes, I was forgetting that you live hereabouts," Bob remarked, continuing his pretence of not being niggled by his boss's slighting manner. "And how is Mrs Spiers? Nothing *too* serious, I trust," he added, almost gagging on the words, while thinking that, if the surgeon had any compassion for his fellow men, he would have stitched the big-mouthed, stuck-up bitch's lips together.

8

"Not at all serious," Spiers responded offhandedly. "Just a minor woman's problem, that's all."

"Ah, very pleased to hear it," Bob lied. He reflected briefly on the depths a man will stoop to in order to safeguard his mortgage repayments, before adding, "Please pass on my best wishes to her for a speedy recovery."

"A no-nonsense man, your Chief," the local Inspector remarked once Spiers had gone.

"That's one way of putting it, I suppose. But after a while, you get to know that his bite's a lot worse than his bark." Bob glanced at the setting sun glinting through the trees. "Anyway, sir, you'd better clue me up on all of this while we've still got some daylight left."

He ambled around taking mental notes while Inspector Wilson recounted the details of the evening's events; of how old Bertie, a resident patient in a geriatric ward, had come out of theatre at four o' clock after undergoing a small operation on an ingrowing toenail. She had then been wheeled by a porter to her favourite spot by the shrubbery, from where she could watch the cattle grazing in the nearby field. Shortly after, she had been taken a cup of tea by a nursing auxiliary, and had been discovered lying where she was now by the same auxiliary about twenty minutes later. DCI Spiers had been getting out of his car in the parking lot some twenty yards away when he heard the auxiliary's screams, and he'd immediately taken charge of things. The police photographer, fingerprint and forensic people had been called to the scene, and a senior staff doctor had confirmed his police colleague's opinion that the cause of death had been a single blow to the head from a sharp instrument.

"And that sharp instrument was?" Bob asked.

"A garden spade. It was found lying on the ground beside the body."

"Uh-huh? So where is it now?"

"The forensic boys took it away to match the traces of blood and bits of skin and hair on it with the victim's. But it's all pretty much a foregone conclusion. Just a formality, your Chief said."

"And the teacup?"

"As I recall, the auxiliary was allowed to take the tea things away and put them in the dishwasher."

"Why? They should have gone to forensic with the spade."

The Inspector laughed. "Come on, Sergeant, you can't be seriously suggesting that the teacup was really the murder weapon?"

Bob Burns stooped down and carefully picked up a shred of white cloth that was lying under the wheelchair. "I wonder how my friends from forensic missed this." He turned to the young constable. "Here, lad, put that in a plastic bag and label it."

Inspector Wilson gave a little laugh. "Do you really think that little scrap is going to make any difference? I mean, it seems as plain as daylight to everybody that the gardener did it."

Bob raised a cynical eyebrow. "Oh yeah?"

"Well, your boss was certainly convinced enough to have him arrested on the spot for questioning." Wilson nodded his head. "Yeah, and I think he was right."

"You'll be telling me next that you've even got witnesses."

The Inspector hunched his shoulders. "Not to the actual act, but we've got statements from several people — patients and staff — who saw the gardener turning over these rose beds here right up to the time of the crime."

"Motive?"

"That's the other thing. There appears to be no motive. No theft involved, no sexual interference — just an act of madness."

"But the gardener wasn't actually here when the nursing auxiliary found the body, right?"

"Correct, he was working with a knapsack sprayer over behind that next ward when my lads collared him."

"And how long after the event was that?"

"No more than ten minutes after your boss arrived on the scene and phoned us."

"And the gardener hadn't tried to make a getaway? He battered this old dear's brains in, then walked away casually and started spraying weeds or whatever across there until the bogeys arrived and nicked him? Is that what you're telling me?"

"That's how it happened, Sarge," the young copper piped up. "I was right there, and he just stood with a stupid grin on his coupon when me and the lads nailed him. A few sandwiches short of the full picnic, that one, if you ask me. Bloody weirdo!"

Bob scratched his head. "I've heard it all now," he muttered, his mouth twisting into a wry smile.

"Young Green's right in what he says," the Inspector affirmed, "even if his medical terminology is a bit unorthodox."

"I'm Doctor Bill Baird," a distinguished-looking member of the white-coated group said, stepping forward and shaking Bob's hand. "We haven't been introduced."

"My apologies, Doc. Bob Burns — Detective Sergeant. It's just that, well, I'm still a bit fazed. This is the first time I've arrived at the scene of a crime to find that it's been solved and the culprit arrested before I even got here."

"I appreciate your problem, Sergeant, but my colleagues and I have a hospital to run. We've already answered your Chief Inspector's questions, so is there any particular reason for us to be kept hanging about here any longer?"

"No reason at all. My apologies again. I hadn't been informed that you'd already made statements. Sorry, ladies and gentlemen," he called over to the others. "Thank you for your assistance. We didn't mean to detain you for so long. I'll talk to some of you again later, if necessary. Thank you." He waited until they were out of earshot, then snarled out of the corner of his mouth, "If Jack Spiers is trying to make an arse of me here, the bastard's doing a damned fine job!"

Inspector Wilson pretended not to hear Bob's derogatory aside about his superior officer. "I was about to tell you," he said, "that the gardener does have a mental health problem. He's schizophrenic *and* he has a past record of violence."

"So bloody what?" Bob barked, his temper rising. "That doesn't automatically mean he goes about melting old ladies on the head with his bloody spade, for God's sake! OK, I've got my doubts about some of this Care In The Community crap, but let's face it, this guy wouldn't be working in a place like this if he was considered dangerous, would he? I mean, they'll have him *well* doped up in any case."

"You're the expert," Inspector Wilson retorted, clearly nettled. "We're just country bobbies doing what we can to help out. But we've also got our own jobs to do." He pulled a sarcastic little smile. "You know, helping pensioners across the street, looking for lost dogs, rounding up stray cattle, that sort of thing. So, if you're about finished here, *Sergeant* . . ."

Bob fixed him in a steely stare. "I'm not finished here — not by a long chalk, *sir*. And just for the record, *I* didn't ask for your blokes to be dragged into this, so if you're not happy about it, you'd better take it up with the officer responsible." He gestured towards a nearby building. "He's probably still sitting over there in women's surgical taking a statement from his wife's varicose veins or whatever."

"OK, Sergeant Burns," the Inspector droned, "what do you want my men to do, eh? They're serving no useful purpose standing about here twiddling their thumbs while you try to create a mystery where, in my humble opinion, one doesn't exist."

"They can get a couple of porters who know what they're doing to help get the body sorted out, and then one of them can drive it to the police mortuary in

Edinburgh — *if* you can spare a van. I'll notify the morgue boys that it's coming."

Wilson shook his head. "DCI Spiers specifically said that the body was to be kept here in the hospital mortuary, and while I hesitate to pull rank on you, Sergeant, I suggest that —"

"Listen, Inspector Wilson," Bob snapped, "I don't give a monkey's shit what DCI Spiers specifically said. He's lumbered me with being in charge of this bloody case and *I* say that the body goes to our slab in town. *That's* correct procedure, and *that's* what's gonna be done!"

"Fair enough," Wilson shrugged. "It's your career. Anything else?"

"Yes, somebody can rope this area off and . . . wait a minute. What's in that plastic bag over by the wall there?"

"That's the cat, Sarge," young Constable Green volunteered enthusiastically.

"What bloody cat?"

"The old stiff's cat. The retard domed it with his spade as well. I'm tellin' you, that cat's face looks like it's come out on the wrong side of an argument with an express train."

Bob scratched his head again. "Murdered moggies now," he sighed. "What the hell next?"

"No probs, Sarge," Green breezed. "Your gaffer said just to bung it into the hospital incinerator, so I'll see to that for you right now."

Bob raised a hand. "No way, kid. The cat goes to the police cold store with the human corpse. Yes, and I'm holding you responsible for finding a biscuit tin to put it in, so that it arrives there intact — apart from its face, that is."

Constable Green was patently delighted. "You got it, Detective Sergeant!" he beamed. "Glad to help the CID out. Oh yeah, beats the shit out of helping lollipop ladies any day."

"And your further instructions, *Detective* Sergeant Burns?" Inspector Wilson enquired caustically.

"That's it. Once your lads have tidied up, you can detail one of them to act as a night watchman here, and the rest can go and round up a stray heifer or two." Then, as a sudden afterthought, he added, "All except young Green here, that is. If you've no objections, I'm deputising him as my Number Two. I like *his* attitude."

CHAPTER
TWO

It didn't take Bob too long to eliminate from his list of possible suspects the ten other patients in old Bertie's pavilion. Being a geriatric ward, many of the inmates (as a couple of the more lucid occupants described themselves) were well over eighty, and most of them incapable of raising themselves out of bed unaided, never mind wielding a garden spade to the permanent detriment of one of their cronies. As one bedridden worthy put it to an intrigued PC Green, "Most of us old boys in here can't even piss in the bottle without the nurse givin' us a hand. I tell ye, laddie, I used to be terrible embarrassed by it, but now it's the only pleasure I've got to look forward to every day. Aye, pour me a glass o' Lucozade, son. A large one!"

And enquiries at the five other wards proved equally barren. Every patient had a rock-solid alibi for the time of the murder — afternoon tea, taken either in the ward, or, if they were fit enough, in one of the TV rooms. The same applied to every member of staff — medical, administrative or otherwise. All could account for their whereabouts between the times of 4 and 4.30p.m., and all had verifying witnesses. So, unless there had been collusion between two or more people (and there appeared to be no obviously logical reason for that), Bob's stubborn repetition of the preliminary enquiries already undertaken at DCI Spiers' behest had resulted in his arriving at precisely the same conclusion. The finger of suspicion pointed squarely at Billy Thomson, the gardener, now sweating it out in a cell at Haddington police station.

Even Bertie's hospital record, explained in detail over a midnight coffee in his office by Doctor Baird, offered not one clue to Bob Burns as to why anyone other than a deranged psychopath would have wanted to take her life. She had been a patient in Roodlands for two years, since the creeping frailty of old age and a deteriorating lung condition had rendered her incapable of looking after herself adequately at home. And, although she had more rough edges than a lump of coal, she was everyone's favourite. They all loved old Bertie.

"So, she had no enemies — in the hospital, at any rate," Bob pondered, while Dr Baird returned the notes to his filing cabinet. "How about visitors — friends, members of her family?"

The doctor shook his head. "Bertie had no one. She never married, and she lived alone. As far as I know, the only visitors she ever had were the volunteers and social work people who go around old folks' wards as a matter of course. Mind you, she was never shy at buttonholing somebody else's visiting relation if she was in need of a chinwag. But, as I say, they all loved Bertie. I've never heard a bad word spoken about her by anyone."

Bob flicked through the pages of his notebook. "Yeah," he sighed, "every single person here says the same thing." He looked up. "And you say she had no money, Doc? No assets?"

"Nothing, apart from the two or three quid in her purse. Her financial status was gone into fully when she was admitted here. All part of the NHS rules. Even the bulk of her old-age pension went directly into contributing towards her keep. That's how it works these days."

"Any insurance policies?"

"The usual Sun Life job. You know the sort of thing — a few pounds a year to cover the eventual cost of her funeral, that's all."

"You mentioned something about a chest complaint."

"Yes, pulmonary emphysema. Enlarged air sacks in the lungs, resulting in ever-increasing difficulty in breathing. Bertie's condition was already fairly advanced when she came in here. Had a wheeze like a set of bagpipes. You see, she spent all of her working life in the market garden at Archerfield Estate outside Dirleton — near the coast, about nine miles from here."

"Hmm, I remember that from when I lived in the village."

"And she always reckoned that years of breathing in fungicides and insecticides in the greenhouses had done for her lungs." The doctor stroked his chin and chortled softly. "But I tend to believe that the major cause of her trouble was cigarettes. She said she started smoking when she was five or six, and she was still getting through more than twenty fags a day when she was admitted here."

"And this emphysema thing could have killed her eventually?"

Doctor Baird smiled indulgently. "Oh, yes, and I can see what you're getting at, Sergeant. But it *was* that blow to the head that killed her. She wouldn't have survived that, even with a perfect set of bellows."

Bob gathered his lips into a meditative pout. "Which brings us right back to Billy Thomson."

"Listen, I'm no sleuth," the doctor nodded, stifling a yawn, "but unless you can produce someone who crept unseen into the garden behind the geriatric ward, did the deed and then crept unseen away again, it would appear to me that Billy has got to be your prime suspect."

"You really think he's capable of having done it, Doc, do you? I mean, with his record of violence and all that."

Doctor Baird held up his hands. "Woah! I'm no more a psychiatrist than I am a detective. You'd have to put that question to a specialist who's familiar with Billy's case. But as far as his past record is concerned, he certainly did have a habit of clobbering six bells out of other kids when he was at school, although he claims he was only reacting to playground jibes about being some kind of loony. You know how cruel kids can be if they sense that someone's a little bit, well, *different*. But anyway, ever since his mental condition was diagnosed and he was admitted to a special establishment where it could be treated and monitored properly, there's been no further incidence of violent behaviour. And Billy's nearly fifty now."

"And he must have been considered totally harmless, or he wouldn't have been working unsupervised here, right?"

"Right. And I wouldn't be exaggerating if I said that my wife and I wouldn't have thought twice about letting Billy Thomson babysit for us . . . until tonight, at any rate."

"Ah, so you *do* think he might have flipped and staved old Bertie's skull in, then?"

The doctor took a deliberately deep breath and exhaled slowly through his nose. "Look, this is off the record, Sergeant Burns, and it's entirely up to you whether you follow it up or not, OK? Billy *was* put on a new regime of drugs — tranquillizers — on the instructions of his specialist a few days ago. That's quite normal, by the way — all part of the continuing therapy. If the experts consider that it would be to the patient's benefit to switch to an alternative drug, then that's what happens."

"So, you're suggesting to me that changing his pills or whatever might have made him — well, take a daft turn?"

"I'm suggesting nothing of the sort," Doctor Baird protested. He shook his head vigorously. "No, all I'm saying is that a change of chemical intake, if you like, can — very rarely — cause an unforeseen reaction in a patient." He studied Bob's expression for a moment. "Don't get me wrong, Sergeant. I'm not trying to put another nail in Billy Thomson's coffin. Far from it. I'm only trying to present you with the facts as I know them. For, no matter how much I like Billy, if he *is* guilty of killing someone in cold blood, I'd be very wrong to withhold any information that might be relevant to his eventual conviction."

Bob checked his watch. "I appreciate your frankness, Doc," he said as he stood up. "I think it's about time I went down to the local nick and had a word with this Billy Thomson chap myself. He's been in that cell for over six hours now, so he should be ripe for a nice wee session of questions and answers."

"Go easy on him, though," Dr Baird cautioned. "I mean that, Sergeant. What he's going through right now would be a big enough ordeal for anyone, but for somebody with his background of mental illness . . ."

Bob Burns paused at the door and gave a reassuring smile over his shoulder. "Don't worry, I'll handle him with kid gloves. Oh, ehm, just one other thing before I go. My boss's wife, Mrs Spiers — the sister in women's surgical was loath to divulge any information about why she's in here. All she would say was that she's in a side ward on her own." Bob inclined his head to one side and raised an eyebrow. "Got leprosy or bubonic plague or something, has she?"

Doctor Baird smiled knowingly. "Nothing quite so dramatic, I'm afraid. No, she's merely recuperating from treatment which your boss has asked us to keep confidential. But fear not, Sergeant Burns, I'm sure she's not your killer. Even a tongue as sharp as Mrs Spiers' would hardly be capable of inflicting a wound like the one which dispatched poor old Bertie McGregor."

PC Green's panda car screeched up alongside Bob Burns' white Mondeo in the yard behind the police station.

"Well, lad, that hasn't taken you long," Bob remarked, yawning down a great lungful of cool night air. "Don't tell me the auxiliary, Mrs Whatsername, wasn't in."

"Mrs Reynolds? Yeah, she was in — in bed."

"Well, you should've got her out of bloody bed! This is a murder enquiry, and at this moment in time Mrs Reynolds is only one short step behind the demon gardener in there in the suspect stakes." He hit himself on the forehead with the butt of his hand. "It's what I always say, if you want something done properly . . ."

Constable Green waited patiently until he was sure the Sergeant had finished, then declared with a boyish smile of self-satisfaction that he *had* got her out of bed. Or rather that he had interviewed her *in* bed. Well, not that he had actually been in bed with her, but sitting in her bedroom, like. Her daughter had taken him up, because her mother wasn't able to come down. On sedatives under the doctor. Widow woman. Bloody shame. Still traumatised from discovering the stiff and all that. A right belter of a daughter, though. Yeah, he wouldn't have minded taking her particulars down if he'd had a couple of minutes to spare.

Bob was struggling to keep his cool. "What's your first name, young Green?"

"Andy, Sarge."

"I might have known it. Randy bleedin' Andy! I mean, I don't want to rush you or anything, but when you're through fantasising about Mrs Reynold's daughter, do you think you could possibly let me know if you've managed to add anything of significance to the case, beyond what was on the statement the woman gave to my gaffer seven hours ago?"

"No."

"No what?"

"No, sir."

"No, sir, what, for Christ's sake?"

"No, sir, I haven't managed to add anything of —"

"Bugger me, boy!" Bob exploded. "What the hell have you been doing for the last half hour — sipping tea and nibbling biscuits?"

"Yeah, Shona — that's the daughter — brought some up to the bedroom. Except it wasn't tea, it was coffee. Oh, and a couple of Snickers. I could've had a Kit-Kat or a Bounty as well, like, but I just went for the Snickers because I really like the nuts."

"I'm sure you do, Constable Green," Bob responded in tones of great restraint, his hand lighting gently on his unlikely sidekick's forearm, "but unless you fancy this sleepy wee town of yours to be the scene of the second vicious murder within the space of twelve hours, you'll engage what little brains you've got hidden away under that black-and-white checked cap of yours and think of something, *anything*, that Mrs Reynolds might have said that could prove useful."

23

Andy pondered that one for a few moments. "Hmm," he hummed while nibbling meditatively on a fingernail, "there *was* Oor Wullie and The Broons."

"There was Oor *Wullie* and The *Broons*?" Bob echoed, his voice yodelling on the verge of hysteria. "What the *hell* have Oor Wullie and The Broons got to do with an old biddy getting her skull battered in?"

"*The Sunday Post*, Sarge," PC Green coolly elucidated. "Mrs Reynolds said that old Bertie always read Oor Wullie and The Broons and then did the kids' crossword in the magazine, and that's what she was doing when she got croaked."

Bob squinted incredulously at his young colleague's wholesomely-grinning features as he continued his discourse . . .

"When Mrs Reynolds said that old Bertie did the kids' crossword, she didn't mean that she actually *did* the crossword, of course. What she did, like, was see how many words she could get to fit into the spaces — but without bothering about clues or any of that stuff, if you see what I mean. Yeah, old Bertie only did it to keep her brain active, to keep herself from going senile, Mrs Reynolds said. But she usually only got about three words down before she forgot what she was supposed to be doing and dropped off to sleep."

"Fascinating," Bob groaned, glassy-eyed. "Absolutely bloody fascinating." He feigned a note of intrigue. "And tell me, Constable Green, where exactly is this crucial item of evidence now?"

"Ehm, what item would that be, Sarge?"

Bob conjured up a voice of sardonic calm. "Why, *The Sunday Post* magazine, which the victim was using as a senility stopper when a person or persons unknown quietly sidled up behind her and switched out her lights with a shiny Spear & Jackson, of course."

"Oh, *that* item! Yeah, Mrs Reynolds said she lobbed it onto a bundle of other old papers for picking up by the rubbish wagon in the morning."

"Well, well, well, our Mrs Reynolds certainly knows how to get rid of the evidence. First the teacup, now *The Sunday Post* magazine . . ."

Andy's face lit up. "Hey, right enough, Sarge! I never thought about that." He then attempted an American accent. "OK, get yer blue lights flashin', pardner," he drawled at Bob. "We'll shoot off and collar the broad right now!" Then, reverting to his normal speech, he said, "But give me a go at reading her rights to her, eh? Yeah, I've always wanted to have a bash at that since the good old Kojak days on telly."

"Better keep your lollipop wrapped for another time," Bob grunted. He hustled his hyper-keen assistant back towards his little panda car. "Just get yourself back up to that hospital and tell whoever's in charge that you want unlimited access to the trash cans. Oh," he added as he slammed the panda's door shut, "and if you're not back here with that magazine before I've finished questioning the prime suspect, I'll come up there and stuff you head first into a wheelie bin myself!"

Billy Thomson wasn't at all what Bob Burns had imagined. Instead of the squat, clumsy clodhopper he'd expected to find lying quivering and sniffling on his bunk when the duty sergeant opened the cell door, Bob was greeted by a relatively urbane chap (if you ignored his gardener's clothes) who looked more like a Sunday-afternoon-at-home accountant than a homicidal maniac. But then, as Bob mused, homicidal maniacs very often did.

Billy looked up from the tiny table where he was sitting reading a book. "Hello there, Inspector Burns," he said with a relaxed smile. "They told me you'd be along sometime. And, uh, pardon me if I don't stand up. But if I do, my trousers will fall down." His accent was more yuppie than yokel and his laugh more mellow than manic as he quipped, "They took my belt away, you see. I suppose they were afraid I might hang myself — being a nutcase and all that."

"Nah, they do that with everybody," Bob instinctively replied. He pulled up a chair at the other side of the table. Then, realising that he had put a patronising foot right in it, he swiftly appended, "And it's Detective *Sergeant* Burns, by the way. The elevated rank of inspector has so far managed to elude me."

"Ah well, I guess they'd have sent an inspector if they'd thought I was worth one," Billy shrugged. "*C'est la vie, non?*" He laid the palms of his hands on the table, leaned forward and smiled openly. "Now then, Sergeant Burns, how can I help you?"

This guy was cooler than a fridge full of bloody cucumbers, Bob said to himself, opening his notebook.

"That's the benefit of being on tranquillizers," Billy said, as if reading Bob's thoughts. "One tends not to get one's knickers in a twist as readily as one otherwise might. As they say," he chuckled, "keep taking the tablets, Thomson."

Bob already found himself making a conscious effort not to appear unnerved by Billy's air of quiet self-assurance. "Have you seen a lawyer yet?" he asked.

"What would be the point? At this stage, all a lawyer could do would be to apply for bail, and we both know, Sergeant, that there's about as much chance of that being granted as there is of you being promoted to Chief Constable of Lothian and Borders Police by breakfast time."

Bob tapped the flap of his case file, which he had placed on the table between them. He raised his eyebrows and looked directly at Billy. "You do realise that things are stacked pretty heavily against you here, don't you?"

That wide-eyed, open smile returned to Billy's face. "All I realise is that I'm innocent. Everything else is now beyond my control, so there's nothing I can do but sit here — or wherever else they choose to lock me up — and wait until you have *proven* me innocent."

"Or guilty," Bob said. He fixed Billy in an eyeball-to-eyeball stare.

But Billy didn't flinch from it. "You have an honest face, Sergeant," he remarked matter-of-factly, "and I've no reason to believe that you're anything other than a very diligent policeman. So," he shrugged again, "I have nothing to fear. The truth will out, I know."

Bob Burns allowed a few moments of silence to pass before asking: "How well did you know Bertie McGregor?"

Billy Thomson's eyes moistened and he looked down at the table. "I knew her as well as anyone at the hospital, and better than most, I think. I used to spend hours with her when she felt up to sitting out in the gardens and talking about the flowers and things. You see, Bertie had forgotten more about gardening than I could ever hope to learn." A little laugh escaped his lips. "Oh yes, and she never tired of reminding me of that, either."

"Cats!" Bob blurted out, leaving the word hanging in mid-air.

Billy rested his head between his hands. "Like a carrot in front of a donkey," he muttered, clearly unimpressed by the crudeness of Bob's interrogation technique. "I happen to be a cat lover, Sergeant — to the extent that I'll make a point of looking after any stray that comes along. Anyone at the hospital will tell you that."

"That's as may be, but cats have been known to do some pretty unsociable deeds in flower beds. I mean, you wouldn't be the first gardener to lose the rag at some scabby old moggie that had been shi—"

"Dixie was *my* cat!" Billy snarled, his self-control appearing to waver at last. He began to massage his temples with his fingertips, as if striving to recover his composure. "And she was not some scabby old moggie."

"Funny," Bob continued casually, "I was under the impression that she was Bertie's cat."

With a slow shake of his head, Billy murmured, "Hospital patients are not allowed to keep pets, for obvious reasons, of which you must be aware." He cast Bob a condescending glance and hunched his shoulders. "However, if you feel that it might be central to your investigations, I'll be happy to tell you all about Dixie the cat."

He went on to explain how, about five years earlier, he had found her as a tiny kitten, apparently abandoned in the hospital grounds, and how he had helped the little creature survive by painstakingly feeding it warm milk from a pipette until it was able to lap from a saucer. Whereas all the other strays that he fed with scraps from the kitchens would come and go at will, the way cats do, Dixie decided to make his tool shed her permanent home. He had even installed a cat flap in the door for her. Then, when old Bertie came along, Dixie had inexplicably adopted her, the way cats do, and soon became her constant companion, sitting curled up on her lap in the garden on nice days, or — under the blind eye of the duty sister — in the ward's TV room when the weather wasn't so good. They were inseparable, until evening, when Dixie would return to the tool shed for Billy to feed her.

"Very touching," Bob commented at length, patently untouched. "However, a cynic might suggest that you resented the affection your cat showed towards someone else."

Billy raised a hand to stroke his closed eyelids, then answered in a whisper, "Bertie McGregor was like a mother to me, Sergeant." His voice broke slightly. "And none of you can ever have any idea of just how much I'll miss her."

There was a note of genuine sorrow about the way Billy Thomson had spoken these final words. So convincing had he been, in fact, that Bob had to remind himself that he'd seen and heard it all so many times before.

Then, as if trying to make light of the situation, Billy forced a smile and said wistfully, "Who else but a character like Bertie would leave everything to her cat?"

"What's the difference?" Bob scoffed. "She had nothing to leave anyway."

"I wouldn't know anything about that, Sergeant, but I can tell you that she did go to great pains to have a proper will made. I know, because I had to write it all out for her. In the event of her death, all her wordly possessions would be bequeathed to Dixie, it said. She was deadly serious. Even had it properly witnessed by two people."

"And who were they?"

"I've no idea. Bertie simply handed me a sealed envelope one day, saying that it was her will — all duly witnessed — and would I look after it for her. I was to be her executor, you see."

Bob shook his head in disbelief. "Nothing personal, but it sounds to me as if the old dear was going a bit doolally. Anyhow, where's this last will and testament now?"

"It's in a tin in the cupboard at the back of my tool shed."

"Anyone else know about it?"

"No. It didn't even come to mind when your Detective Chief Inspector Spiers was grilling me earlier. To be absolutely frank, I'd forgotten all about it until now." Billy's eyes glazed over again. Caressing his chin with trembling fingers, he let out another little melancholy laugh. "Poor old Bertie. What a dreadful shame . . ."

Bob lifted his file, stood up and walked over to the door, where he turned and asked flatly, "Did you kill her, Billy?"

Billy raised his head and met Bob's stare.

"No," he said without a trace of emotion, "I did not."

PC Andy Green was already sitting down at the table with a mug of coffee when Bob Burns entered the rest room.

"Hiya, Sarge! Here's that item of evidence you wanted." He slid the magazine over the table. "Fancy a cuppa?"

Bob stretched his arms, yawned and collapsed into a chair. "I'd murder for one."

"In that case, I must caution you, sir, that anything you say may be taken down and used in evidence." Andy ignored Bob's groan of tedium. "And anyway," he continued in his usual bright and breezy way, "you surely didn't spend much time squeezing the truth out of the prisoner through there. Doesn't take you long to scare the shit out of 'em — eh, Sarge?"

"Cut the crap and pour the coffee, Constable. And when you're about it, you can let me into the secret of how you got to the hospital, rootled through the garbage and got back here with the necessary in less time than it probably takes you to tie the laces of your Doc Martens in the morning."

"Easy! The evidence in question was still where Mrs Reynolds had dumped it — on top of a heap of old newspapers behind the sluice room door in the wrinklies' ward."

"Solid detective work, Green," Bob mumbled. He picked up the magazine and flicked through the pages. "Mm-hmm, scintillating stuff, *if* you're into exclusive interviews with personalities like the seamstress who stitched up Andy Stewart's original 'Donald' troosers in 1961. Now, where's this bloody kids' crossword?"

"Second last page, Sarge. I've checked it out."

"And what case-cracking discoveries have you made?"

"None, except that old Bertie only managed to fill in one word this week."

Bob scanned the page with a look of weary indifference. "So I see. Never mind, let's have a butcher's at the clue. Let's see . . . Three Across . . . Hmm, very apt . . . *An Aberdonian Police Chief Could Be Expected To Protect His Carefully*. Uh-huh, and what did old Bertie write down?" He ran his forefinger over the page, then gasped, "*Grass!* Would you believe it, she's actually put the answer down as *grass!*"

PC Andy Green clapped his hands together. "Yeah, brilliant that! I'd never have got that in a month of Sundays. Brilliant!"

"Brilliant?" Bob droned, closing his eyes and rubbing his forehead. "Just what prompts you to think it's *brilliant*, Constable?"

"Come on, Sarge — it's obvious, intit? A good copper would never divulge the identity of his informant, would he?"

"But *grass* has only got five letters."

"So?"

"There are seven spaces in Three Across."

Constable Green craned his neck to peer at the page. "Aw yeah, so there are. Well, there you go." He raised his shoulders. "Maths was never my strongest subject."

Bob heaved a sigh of despair. "The correct answer — if my brain can still manage to match the deductive power of a ten-year-old's — would appear to be *Coppers*, no?"

"Yeah, yeah," young Green concurred, frowning and clueless, "so it is, right enough."

Sinking low into his chair, Bob took a sip of his coffee and loosened his tie. "Tell me, PC Green, what exactly made you decide to join the police force?"

"My father told me to." A delighted grin spread over his youthful features. "He said I was too fuckin' thick to do anything else."

"And what does your good father do for a living himself, as a matter of interest, Andrew?"

"He's a policeman an' all."

Bob stuck out his bottom lip and nodded sagely. "Yes, well, he would know, boy. He would know."

Andy got up and wandered over to a wall cupboard above the cooker, where he began to rummage amongst some boxes of edibles. "Hey!" he yelled, wheeling round suddenly. "It doesn't matter what the old stiff wrote on the crossword, because Mrs Reynolds said she never bothered about the clues anyway. Remember?"

Bob drummed his fingers on the open magazine. He stared at that solitary word. "I wonder," he said under his breath. "I wonder . . ."

Constable Green sat down again and threw a round packet onto the table. "What time are we knocking off, Sarge?" he yawned. "It's past two o'clock. I mean, I'll keep going all night if you want, but — ehm — isn't it about time you were getting back home to Edinburgh for some kip?"

Bob wasn't listening. "There's something not right about all this," he mumbled into his coffee cup. "Something stinks."

"Tell me all about it, Sarge. Two heads are better than one."

Bob's fingers continued to beat a slow tattoo on the magazine. Through heavy eyes he glanced over at his young aide, but appeared to look straight through him. "My head says guilty," he mumbled drowsily, "but my guts just don't agree."

Constable Green grabbed the packet off the table and thrust it at him. "Have a digestive biscuit, Sarge. That should do the trick." Then, inspired, he added brightly, "Here! Fancy an Alka-Seltzer?"

But his question fell on deaf ears. Even as he spoke, the first purring snore was already rising from the gaping orifice of Bob Burns' upturned mouth.

CHAPTER
THREE

"What do you mean, there isn't gonna be a bloody autopsy?" Bob yelled down the phone.

DCI Spiers' response was somewhat less blunt than might have been expected, but very much to the point, nonetheless: "Simply because I'm not prepared to tie up already hard-pressed police resources and waste taxpayers' money on a totally unnecessary exercise. Not only does the circumstantial evidence of this case appear very conclusive to say the least, but the forensic people have confirmed that the murder weapon was as identified at the scene. And the fingerprints chaps have established that the suspect's dabs — and no-one else's — were all over it." Before Bob could respond, he continued: "Now, for your information, Sergeant, I happened to have dinner with the Procurator Fiscal last night, and — pending receipt of our final report, of course — he's perfectly happy, on having listened to my verbal account of events, to go along with my recommendation of having the suspect Thomson charged with this crime without undue delay."

"I'm sorry, but I can't agree to that, Chief. There are one or two things that I need more time to look into. So —"

"You haven't been listening, Detective Sergeant Burns." The tone of DCI Spiers' voice was now giving off clear warning signals. "This case, apart from the usual formalities, which will be attended to in due course, is effectively closed. The accused will face trial in the fullness of time and, I'm certain, will be convicted by the jury of callously killing that old woman."

Bob could contain himself no longer. "Nobody gives a damn, do they? Just one worthless old crone less for the State to support, and a nice handy patsy with a mental problem to take the rap, without even being given the chance to have his innocence proved." Bob was fuming now. "Take it from me, boss, we're gonna look no better than the lynch mob of local ghouls who've been swarming outside this nick since seven o' clock this morning, baying for Billy Thomson's blood!"

There were a few seconds of gravid silence at the other end of the phone before Jack Spiers said with surprising constraint, "I'm going to pretend you didn't say that, Burns. But I won't tell you this again — I expect your report to be on my desk by midday today. Unfortunately, I'll be leaving for a meeting in a few minutes, but Detective Inspector Blackie here will be looking after things in my absence. He'll be expecting you."

The line went abruptly dead.

"You look as if somebody just stuffed a weasel down your Y-fronts, Sarge," PC Green commented, while breezing into the police station munching a bacon roll.

"Your missus been giving you blazes on the blower for not coming home last night?"

If looks could have killed, Bob Burns would have been up on a murder charge himself. "I hope your mammy gave you a hearty breakfast, sonny boy," he growled, "because you've got one helluva busy day ahead of you!" The young constable hovered in mid-munch, astounded. "Hold on, Sarge. I thought we only had to write up the report and that would be it — back on school crossing patrol for me by lunchtime."

Ignoring that, Bob took his unofficial apprentice by the elbow and shepherded him outside and into the car park. He glanced about furtively. "Now, this is for your ears and for your ears only, OK?" he hissed.

Slack-jawed, Constable Green nodded his head.

"Right, I'm assigning you to the type of mission that's known in the CID as Clandestine Research And Probing, or C-R-A-P for short."

Constable Green mouthed the letters silently, a frown of confusion wrinkling his brow.

"That said," Bob quickly continued, "I have to tell you it's highly irregular for a junior officer to be entrusted with such hush-hush duties — particularly when he's not even a detective . . . yet."

Constable Green was all ears.

"Your extended secondment to the CID will have to be squared with your boss, Inspector Wilson, of course. But leave that to me. I'll make up some excuse that I need you for a few mundane mop-up jobs. No sweat."

Constable Green winked a conspiratorial wink. "Got it, Sarge. Your secret is safe with me." Agog now with bewildered enthusiasm, he then enquired, "So, eh, what exactly do you want me to handle on the, ehm, C-R-A-P front?"

Bob grabbed him by the lapels. "Don't ever let me hear you uttering those initials out loud around here again, boy!" he snarled. "What the hell do you think clandestine means, for Christ's sake?"

The corners of PC Green's mouth dropped into a facial shrug of transparent mental darkness.

"It means," Bob rasped, "you keep shtum, right? You say *nothing* about what you're doing or what you find out to anybody except me."

Andy Green nodded his head like a budgie on speed. "Yeah, yeah, got that now, Sarge," he whispered. "Yeah, have no fear — you're looking at Mr Candlestein himself."

Bob gave him an encouraging pat on the shoulder. "I know that, lad. I know that. I had you sussed as one from the word go. Now then, here's what I want you to do. First you go to the farmer who owns the cattle in the field next to the hospital, and you find out if he or any of his men were there checking on the animals around the time of the murder yesterday. And don't forget to write it all down. Then you check to see if any of the houses near the hospital have upstairs windows that overlook the shrubbery. Ask the occupants if they noticed anything suspicious going on there between 4 and 4.30 yesterday."

"Wow, that should keep me busy! Should I tell my mum I won't be home for lunch?"

"Better tell her you won't be home for dinner either, 'cos I haven't even started yet!" Bob had dispensed with the need to talk in hushed tones. "Now then, Randy Andy," he went on, "would there be, by any chance, a nice young nurse in the women's surgical ward at Roodlands Hospital that you're intimate with?"

PC Green's eyes sparkled and his lips contorted into a lopsided grin. "We-e-ll, there's that trainee Nurse Golightly," he drooled. "I mean, to be honest, I haven't *actually* got as far as slipping her the truncheon yet, but given half a chance —"

"OK, OK, spare me the smutty details! As long as you're on familiar terms, that's all I need to know." Giving PC Green a stern look, Bob lowered his voice again. "Now, here's your mission. Tell your Nurse Golightly not to let on to anyone that you asked, but I want you to pump her for any info you can get on why my gaffer's wife is in Roodlands, all right?"

"Any excuse to pump Nurse Golightly will do me, Sarge," Green chuckled. "Oh yeah, I fancy her strongly!"

Bob jabbed a finger in his chest. "Just remember you're on urgent CID business, Green, and don't bugger about. Savvy?"

"You bet, chief!"

"Right, I'll be radioing you with further instructions later, so better make sure you never stray too far from your panda car. Now get weaving!"

★   ★   ★

40

Bob had asked the police lab to telephone him the results of their analysis of the scrap of white cloth before putting their findings on record . . .

"Is that Detective Sergeant Robert Burns?"

"Yeah, yeah — Bob Burns here."

"Hello, my name's Julie Bryson from forensic, Sergeant Burns."

"Hi. So what have you got for me?"

"Well, there's not an awful lot I can tell you that would be of much use, I'm afraid. All pretty much as you might have expected."

"What do you mean, darlin'? I didn't know *what* to expect."

"Fair enough, then. Here's the highlights. The cloth's a bit of coarse cotton of the type most commonly used in the manufacture of gardening gloves — more often than not imported from China. That particular scrap had a splinter of wood snagged in it, and I won't offer any prizes for guessing where that came from."

"The handle of the murder weapon?"

"Clever boy."

"Yeah, but that still doesn't prove that the cloth came from Billy Thomson's gloves. Let's face it, we don't even know if he's got a pair like that."

"That's your problem, Dick Tracy. Why don't you have a snoop about his potting shed, and if you can find gloves that look the part, let me have them and I'll give them the once over for you."

"I'm on my way. Oh, Julie — before you hang up, just one other wee favour, eh? I mean, you sound like a nice obliging sort of lass . . ."

"Mmm, well, as long as it's legal and doesn't cost me anything."

"OK, any chance of you keeping the gen on this gardening glove thing up your sleeve for a couple of days? You know, delay the report due to pressure of other work — that kind of thing?"

"But, Sergeant, that *is* illegal."

"Only very slightly, and the main thing is that it isn't gonna cost you a penny. As a matter of fact, if you do this little thing for me, I'll stand you a slap-up feed at the restaurant of your choice."

"Oh yeah? And, uhm, where would you recommend, Sergeant?"

"Well, uh, let me see." Bob wasn't too clued up on Edinburgh's swanky eateries. "OK, there's Karen Wong's place out near Meadowbank Stadium, for instance," he finally blurted out, hoping for the best. "Yeah, Karen's. I know it well. Used to get takeaways from there when I lived out that way. Great Cantonese grub."

"You drive a hard bargain, Sergeant Burns."

"So you'll do it?"

"We-e-ell, just this once — and only because you're such a smooth-talking devil. And before *you* hang up, I'd better mention that there were traces of the victim's blood on that piece of cloth, as well as a smidgen of weedkiller and oil."

"What kind of weedkiller and oil?"

"Is that important? It seems to me that you've already got enough on this guy to put him away for life."

"Just answer the question and leave the Dick Tracy stuff to me, pet, OK?"

"OK, if that's the way you want it. The weedkiller was paraquat, and the oil was one of those vegetable derivatives."

"Like *Mazola* or something?"

"No, like *Castrol R* or something."

"Racing oil? You're joking!"

"When did you ever know someone with a sense of humour working in a forensic lab? No, seriously, if you find a grand prix lawn mower parked behind that potting shed at the hospital, I'd say your gumshoe work on this case will *definitely* be over."

But the cogs in Bob's head were already turning in a more practical direction. Reminding Julie that an autopsy had been ruled out, he asked her: "Off the record, if you were provided with a swab or whatever from the victim's mouth, could you analyse it for traces of paraquat?"

"Anything's possible in this game, Sergeant, but I'm not saying that we'd necessarily come up with anything conclusive."

"How do you mean?"

"Well, obviously, a lot would depend on the extent of dilution of the chemical in the first instance, then you have to take account of any depurative agent that might have been consumed later."

"Depurative agent?"

"Water, tea, coffee — any liquid that could have flushed the toxic deposits from the mouth — assuming that there were any there in the first place."

"OK, so it's a long shot. But I won't beat about the bush. If the boys at the mortuary can fix me up with a suitable sample, could you do the business on it?"

"Would this be a sub rosa bush that you're not beating about, perchance?"

"It's seventy-five percent unofficial and it's gotta be kept a hundred percent shtum, if that's what you mean. But it might just help save an innocent guy from languishing in the slammer until his Alberts rot off."

"His Alberts?"

"Rhyming slang. Just think of the Last Night of the Proms, right?"

"My, my, you do have such a poetic turn of phrase, Sergeant Burns," Julie replied, suppressing a snigger.

"Yeah, well, it comes with the name."

"Hmm, but tell me something — if I were to see my way to doing this extra favour for you, am I to take it that there would be an extra portion of Prawn Alberts in it for me?"

"You never know your luck, Julie darlin'."

"Done, then! But, uhm, just a couple of final points before you slink off with your cloak and dagger . . ."

"Uh-huh?"

"Uh-huh. One, it's *Doctor* Julie darlin'. And two, I don't like Chinese food!"

The gardener's store, as it was referred to at Roodlands, was in reality a small outhouse attached to the hospital boiler room — in all probability a redundant stoking bunker from the old pre-oil-fired days when the hospital's hot water system had been coke generated. Jock King, the laconic old caretaker, unlocked the door for Bob, who quickly took stock of the cramped interior of the little shed.

"Did any of my mates have a squint around in here after the murder yesterday?"

Jock waited until he had completed the sombre ritual of lighting his pipe, then muttered, "Plain-clothes bloke — middle-aged — big-heided bastard."

"Yeah, that'd be my gaffer. Did he make a thorough inspection?"

With a callused thumb, Jock firmed down the glowing tobacco in the bowl of his pipe. "In and oot quicker than that!" He snapped his fingers. "Never even touched nothin'."

Bob lifted a knapsack sprayer off the floor behind the door. "Is this the one Billy was using when the local bobbies nicked him?"

"That's it. Only one there is."

Bob gave the reservoir a shake. "But it's empty. Surely the rozzers didn't give him time to finish what he was doing before they ran him in?"

"Nope. I emptied it, cleaned it, brought it back in here. Cannae stand untidiness."

Bob flipped open the lid and took a sniff. "Doesn't smell like chemicals to me. Too sweet. What is it?"

"*Fairy Liquid.* Good as ye'll get for cleanin' them oot."

"What had Billy been doing with the sprayer? Killing weeds?"

"Nope. Sprayin' plants for aphids — greenfly."

"Billy told you that, did he?"

Jock nodded. "The minute the wind dropped — came into the boiler house there — said he was away to blooter them."

"Why would he go to the trouble of going in there to tell you first? Sounds a bit strange, doesn't it?"

Jock didn't like the smack of that. "Been watchin' *Columbo*, have ye, son?" He raised a hoary eyebrow and locked his inquisitor in a beady-eyed stare, his stubby pipe clenched firmly between his teeth at the corner of his mouth.

"Just doing my job, mate," Bob sighed. "So, I'll ask you again. Why do you think Billy went into the boilerhouse and told you what he was planning to do next?"

"'Cos that's where the fuckin' chemicals is kept — locked in a metal cabinet." Jock pulled a bunch of keys from his pocket and dangled it in front of Bob's face. "And it's *me* that keeps the bloody key. Ask Doctor Baird."

Bob shook his head in exasperation. "OK, now that we've got that out of the way, maybe you could tell me if you keep paraquat weedkiller in that locked cupboard of yours."

After puffing contentedly on his pipe for a moment or two, Jock pursed his lips and cocked his head to one side. "D'ye mean *Gramoxone*?"

"Same thing," Bob nodded, growing impatient. "So, have you got any?"

"Nope. Billy used the last of it in the autumn. Never asked for any more yet."

"You do the ordering, then, do you?"

"Nope. Doctor Baird."

He was getting nowhere fast with this cantankerous old bugger. "What about gloves? Did Billy wear gloves when he was spraying?"

Jock puffed his pipe and thought a while. "Aye, sometimes."

"How about yesterday? Was he wearing any yesterday?"

"Aye. They're hangin' up there by the windae."

Bob turned towards where Jock had gestured. "Right, there's two lots of gloves there — a rubber pair and a cloth pair. Have you any idea which ones Billy Thomson was wearing yesterday, by any chance?"

"What the hell kind o' stupid bloody question is that supposed to be?" Jock exclaimed in an uncharacteristic burst of verbosity, the pipe plucked from his lips so as not to impede the flow of words. "He might be a shitso, but he's no a fuckin' heidcase!"

Bob's strenuously-maintained air of calm was starting to fray at the edges. "Meaning?" he asked.

"Meanin', what kind o' pea-brained eejit would wear cloth gloves to work wi' chemicals? If he was as daft as that, he'd have been in the bloody polis!" Jock stuffed his pipe back into his mouth and grunted his disgruntlement amid a string of mumbled expletives.

"OK, I'll take these for forensic examination," Bob said, stepping over to the window and taking the cloth gloves off the hook, while purposely leaving the rubber pair hanging.

"Christ almighty!" Jock muttered. "Deaf as well as bloody daft!"

"Excuse me," Bob said as he edged his way past the old caretaker, who had resolutely stationed himself squarely in the middle of what little floor space there was, "but I want to have a look in that cupboard while I'm here."

Sure enough, tucked behind a pile of gardening magazines and nurserymen's catalogues on the top shelf was a square shortbread tin, and, inside, a miscellany of nuts, bolts and washers and a solitary sealed envelope. "I'm taking this as evidence," Bob advised the intently peeping Jock. He then slipped the envelope into his inside pocket. "All right?"

"I'll be needin' a receipt — for that *and* the gloves."

Crouching down, Bob had a quick rummage through a platoon of tin cans that were arranged in a neat line under the window. "Ever known Billy to use a lubricating oil like *Castrol R* at any time?" he asked offhandedly.

His question was greeted with a loud snort of derision. "If ye take a gander in the corner yonder, ye'll maybe just manage to ascertain that the lawnmower's an Atco, not a fuckin' Ferrari!"

Bob counted silently to ten. "That's about it for the moment at any rate, sir," he sighed, standing up and brushing the dust off his trousers. "But just as a matter of interest, did you know Bertie McGregor at all?"

Jock tamped down his pipe tobacco again — this time with the butt of his penknife. "Used to go oot wi' her," he chortled, his eyes glinting like little black marbles, his pipe-worn graveyard of teeth exposed in a delighted grin. "Could go like a bloody rabbit when she was a lassie . . ." Suddenly, his features darkened into a wary scowl. "But I've never had nothin' to do wi' her since I left Dirleton, mark you, if that's what ye're thinkin'."

Bob made to open his notebook. "And when was that exactly?"

"1940 — joined the Royal Scots — wounded at Normandy — got medals to prove it." Whatever defence old Jock was conducting on his own behalf, he was in deadly earnest. "Cannae pin nothin' on me, son. Wasnae even there. Got ma war service record in the hoose to prove it!"

Bob put his notebook away and scratched his head despairingly. "No, I'm looking for somebody who knew Bertie a wee bit more recently than that."

Conspicuously relieved that the heat was off, Jock grabbed Bob by the arm and eagerly blurted out, "Jimmy! He'll help ye!"

"Jimmy?"

"Aye! Jimmy, the old cattleman at Archerfield!"

"Fine. Thanks," Bob grimaced as he struggled to prize his arm free of the old man's iron grip. "I'll go and see him right now. This Jimmy a friend of yours, is he?"

Shaking his head determinedly, Jock removed his pipe from his mouth and spat a symbolic spit cleanly through the open door. "Nope," he grunted, "he's ma twin fuckin' brother!"

Bob couldn't remember how long it had been since he last drove from Haddington to Dirleton. Ten years,

49

maybe fifteen. But it still struck him as about the most serenely beautiful six or seven miles that anyone could wish to travel. The stunning view all the way over the Forth Estuary as you clear the ridge of the Garleton Hills and descend towards the broad, fertile fields of East Lothian's coastal plain never failed to take his breath away. Knowing that Dirleton, his native village, lay hidden behind a gentle rise somewhere away down there towards the sea was all it took to send a warm glow surging through his veins.

He'd already instructed PC Andy Green on his car radio to interrupt his enquiries and rush Billy Thomson's gardening gloves, which he'd dropped off at Haddington police station, to Julie Bryson at the forensic lab in Edinburgh. And having studied Bertie McGregor's will just as soon as he was away from old Jock King's prying eyes, he had made up his mind to restrict all knowledge of its existence to himself and Billy for the present. Not that the terms of the will appeared particularly vital to the case. Being just as Billy Thomson had described them, they seemed more eccentric than important. But the identity of one of the two witnesses to Bertie's signature *did* intrigue him. Choosing the geriatric ward's Sister Ramage to be a witness seemed logical enough, but Bertie's selection of the other struck Bob as puzzling in the extreme, so he had decided to keep the name under wraps until some other pieces of the jigsaw had fallen into place.

The long driveway through the grounds of Archerfield Estate was just as he remembered it from childhood days, when he and the other village kids would sneak into the walled gardens on summer evenings to pinch plums. Even then, there had been an air of creeping neglect about the place, but the present state of dilapidation of the once-elegant mansion house was not something that he had been prepared for. It had always been said around Dirleton that the Polish servicemen who had been billeted there during the war had left the interior of the house in a bit of a mess, but now the entire structure had been allowed to degenerate into little more than a ruin, a sorry skeleton of its former grandeur.

"I hope ye realise ye're trespassin'," a voice behind him said. "Did ye no see the *Private Property* sign at the gate?"

Bob turned round to face a burly young chap in gamekeeper's clothes. He was carrying a shotgun in the crook of his arm, and was accompanied by a brace of perpetually-mobile springer spaniels.

"I presume you've got a licence for that firearm," Bob joked as he flashed him his police ID.

"Detective Sergeant, eh? They're no still tryin' to find out who ripped the lead off the big hoose roof, are they?"

"No, nothing as exciting as that. Just a murder enquiry. Where can I find an old guy by the name of Jimmy King? Ex-cattleman here, I believe."

"Fame at last for Jimmy! Who's he bumped off?"

"I only want to ask him a couple of questions, friend," Bob smiled. "Just routine. Do you know where he lives?"

"The first cottage ye come to at the farm. Just go along that road there until —"

"It's OK. I know where it is. Thanks for your help all the same." Bob climbed back into his car and gave the 'keeper a salute. "Happy hunting!"

Jimmy King turned out to be the spitting image of his brother — literally. Squirting a jet of saliva from one corner of his mouth while still gripping a metal-lidded pipe between his teeth in the other, he squinted suspiciously at Bob from under heathery brows. "Even if I did ken Bertie McGregor, what are ye tryin' to prove? I wasnae even here in 1944, and I've got a picture taken wi' Montgomery at Tobruk to prove it!"

"Wasn't that 1942?"

"I'm sayin' nothin' without ma lawyer," Jimmy mumbled, ducking back inside his front door and preparing to slam it in Bob's face.

Bob stuck an expert foot in the way. "Hold it, Mr King!" he said. "I'm really not interested in what you did or didn't get up to during the war, believe me. All I want to know is if you can tell me anything about Bertie's life latterly. For instance, I believe she still lived on the estate here until a couple of years ago. Is that right?"

Peering round the door, Jimmy screwed his eyes into a glower of deep mistrust. "I might need that in writin' about the war, mark you."

"Whatever you say, Jimmy," Bob replied wearily. "If you'll just cooperate a wee bit, I'll be glad to give you a written pardon, even if it turns out that it was you that shot Hitler."

"Aye, well, I never fuckin' done that either," he grumped, slinking out reluctantly from behind the door. "Now then, what d'ye want me to tell ye?"

"Where Bertie lived would do for a start."

"The wee cottage built into the wall o' the gardens behind the big hoose."

"I remember it well," said Bob as he ushered old Jimmy towards the car. "Come to think of it, it must have been Bertie who used to come out and chase us when we were pinching plums all those years ago."

"I thought I kent yer face." Jock made himself comfortable in the front passenger's seat. "You'll be one o' the Burnses that used to live in Halliburton Terrace in the village?"

"The very same."

A little smirk crept over Jimmy's weather-gnarled face. "Aye, I kent yer mother fine as well."

Drawing a prudent veil over that one, Bob promptly enquired, "Would there be any chance of me seeing inside Bertie's cottage?"

Jock shrugged his shoulders. "Why no? It's only the fuckin' pigeons that's likely to object!"

He wasn't far from the truth. When they had finally trampled a swathe through shoulder-high nettles to the cottage door, not only pigeons exited the broken windows in haste, but also a couple of swallows, a robin and a whole family of sparrows. And once through the unlocked door, it became obvious from the rat and rabbit droppings on the rotting floorboards that the feathered mob were not the only squatters who had moved in since Bertie's departure.

Bob swiped a tangle of cobwebs away from his face. "They say she lived here alone. Is that right?"

She had, but only for the final three years or so, Jimmy explained. Up until then, her lifelong friend, Pinkie Dalrymple, had shared the place with her. Some local gossips had had them tagged as a couple of old dykes, needless to say, but Jimmy knew better. That same little smirk lit up his face again. "Aye, they could fairly put it aboot in their younger days, that pair. Never mind a pair o' dykes — bikes would be nearer the mark!" His ensuing guttural chuckle was cut short to solemnly point out: "No that I speak from personal experience, like. Nah, nah — never let it be said . . ."

Bob stuck his head into the living room, empty now except for a spectacular show of dry rot sprouting from one wall, and a woodworm-riddled sideboard covered in bird droppings. "Pinkie Dalrymple died, I suppose."

"Nope. Went away to look after an invalid sister. Up north somewhere, if I mind right."

Gagging at the stench of ammonia and dampness, Bob tiptoed through the turds to the sideboard. He raised the toe of his shoe to the guano-caked handle of the drawer and pulled it open. Inside were what appeared to be a couple of mice-nibbled electricity receipts and a similarly-disfigured picture postcard showing a view of the River Tay at Perth. Taking a pair of tweezers from his top pocket, he picked up the postcard and read aloud the hand-printed scrawl on the reverse:

SETTLING IN NOT TOO BAD. MISS THE OLD PLACE. COME UP AND VISIT SOON. P.

The postmark was dated 7th February, 1995.

"She never had a phone in here, then?" Bob asked.

Jimmy shook his head.

Bob slipped the postcard into a small plastic bag and put it in his pocket. Emerging with a gasp of relief into the fresh air, he said to Jimmy, "Putting two and two together, I think we can safely say that Pinkie must have sent Bertie that postcard shortly after she moved away from here."

Jimmy nodded his assent, while simultaneously putting his thumb to his nose and blasting out each nostril in turn. "Fuckin' bird shite. Enough to make ye spew!"

Bob was deep in thought. "Pinkie. I don't suppose that was her real name, was it?"

"Nope — Effie. Got the name Pinkie after the highfalutin way she held her teacup. More patter than bloody Al Jolson, that one."

"Effie. Hmm, that'd be short for Euphemia." Bob strode over to his car and grabbed his mobile phone through the open window. "Hello, Directory Enquiries? The number of Tayside Police Headquarters in Perth, please. Yeah ... OK ... Got it. Many thanks." Whistling to himself, he tapped the number out on the handset. "Good morning. DS Burns, Lothian and Borders Police here. Could you put me through to Sergeant Moran, if he's on today, darlin'? Thanks ... Hi, Johnny! Listen, can you do me a favour? Can you get on to Perth Town Hall and ask them to check their electoral roll for a Miss Euphemia or Effie Dalrymple, usually known as Pinkie . . . Yeah, that's right, there won't be too many around with a handle like that . . . Uh-huh, there's a chance she may have moved to your area about five years ago . . . OK, I'll hold on."

"Why d'ye want to find Pinkie anyway?" Jock said in the meantime. "She cannae bring Bertie back to life."

"No, but she may know something that could save an innocent man from *getting* life."

"The paper this mornin' says the gardener done it. Some kind o' loony. Should hang the bastard!"

"Whatever happened to innocent until proven guilty?"

"Load o' shite!"

"Is that the way you thought in 1944 as well, Jimmy?" Bob teased, poker-faced.

Jimmy's expression was a picture of antagonism. "Hey, ye slimy bugger! You promised me that ye —"

"Sh-h-h! Hi, Johnny . . . OK, let me just write that down . . . 'The Rowans', Scone Loan, Perth . . . Lived there until two years ago, you say . . . Never mind, Johnny, it's a start. I'll meet you for a pint some time and explain it all. Thanks, mate. Cheers!"

Bob hustled Jimmy back into the car and started back towards the farm. "Better get you home again, then." He nudged the old fellow with his elbow and winked. "Unless you fancy a trip to Perth on the off chance of seeing your old girlfriend Pinkie Dalrymple, that is."

"Away an' stuff yersel'!" Jimmy was resolute. His eyes were blazing. "I've never been further than ten

56

miles out o' Dirleton since I was demobbed in '46, an' I'm no gonny start now!" He slapped Bob on the thigh with the back of his hand. "And another thing! Don't you swallow anything that old hoor tells ye aboot me in the wartime. I'm warnin' ye in advance. She's a fuckin' liar!"

CHAPTER
FOUR

Bill Blackie and Bob Burns had joined the Edinburgh police on the same day, and they'd quickly become the best of buddies — two country lads enjoying their first taste of city living, and even sharing a room during their time at Tulliallan Police Training College. For a number of years their professional and private lives progressed in parallel, too — both diverting from the uniformed branch to the CID while still keen-as-mustard young constables, then marrying two sisters in a double wedding and buying their first little flats less than a hundred yards from each other in the same street off Leith Walk. A lot had changed since then, though . . .

"Nearly an hour late, Bob," Bill grinned, darting a glance towards the clock on his office wall after they'd exchanged the usual hail-fellow-well-met salutations. "Jack Spiers wanted that report of yours here by twelve o'clock, but better late than never, I always say." He nodded in the direction of a chair at the side of his desk. "Grab a pew."

"I may as well come straight out with it, Bill. There's no point in sitting down, because I haven't done the report."

"Tut, tut!" Bill kidded. "Been sleeping on the job, eh?" He reached over his desk towards the intercom. "Not to worry. You can dictate it off your notes to one of the girls. She'll rattle it out for you on her computer in a matter of minutes."

Bob gripped his friend's wrist. "Don't bother, Bill. What I'm saying is that I won't be submitting my report right now, and I don't intend to until I've completed the line of enquiry I'm following."

Bill took a deep breath and stroked the bridge of his nose while contemplating the dour look on Bob's face. "Found another suspect, have you?"

"Not exactly, but —"

"Come on, Bob, you can come clean with me." Bill's tone was ostensibly genial, but Bob could detect an underlying note of irritability. "What's the problem?"

"The problem is that I'm not convinced that this bloke Billy Thomson is the killer, and until I *am* convinced —"

"That's not the way it works, pal, and you know that as well as I do." Bill wasn't one to mince his words. "Jack Spiers is satisfied that we've got enough on this Thomson guy to make it stick, and he wants your report on the PF's desk by this afternoon. How much longer do you think we can hold Thomson without charging him, for God's sake?"

"What's the hurry? Give the poor bugger bail and give me some time to check out the things that are bugging me. That's the way it *should* work."

Bill leaned back in his seat and began to tap his pen impatiently on the desk. "If that report hasn't been submitted to the PF by the time Jack Spiers gets back, your arse is going to be in a sling and there's bugger all that I or anybody else will be able to do about it."

"That's nice and reassuring," Bob countered. "And just between ourselves, are you telling me that as a friend or as my superior officer?"

Bill slapped his pen down on the desk. "What the hell's got into you?" he snapped. "I don't clap eyes on you for weeks, and then you wander in here with some vague bee in your bonnet that's only going to create problems for everyone concerned. Just do it by the book, and if there are any loose ends that you're really bothered about, you can sort them out before the guy goes up for trial." He looked Bob coldly in the eye. "And I'm telling you that as a friend, so do yourself a favour and get that bloody report done!"

"I think you know me too well for that," Bob said flatly. "And don't worry, I won't create any problems for you. I'm well used to carrying the can for my own actions, and I'll be doubly careful not to saw through any of the rungs on your ladder . . . pal."

This unexpectedly acerbic remark from his long-time friend had the effect of jarring Bill Blackie into a more conciliatory frame of mind. He lowered his voice. "Come on, Bob — please take a seat. We won't work anything out by jumping at each other's throats like a pair of scrapping schoolboys."

Holding up the palms of his hands, Bob accepted the invitation this time. "You're right — and I'm sorry," he said quietly. "I shouldn't have said —"

60

"No, no, it's better out than in," Bill cut in, attempting a smile, "as you used to tell me when we got back to the room at Tulliallan after the occasional pub crawl round Alloa and I was trying not to part company with my last fiver's worth of beer."

"Yeah," Bob chuckled wistfully with a little sideways cant of his head, "you'd never get a decent puke for that kind of money nowadays."

There was a tense silence for a few seconds, then they both spoke at once.

"Sorry, Bill — on you go . . ."

"No, no, please — you go ahead . . ."

Another uncomfortable little interval followed before Bob said, "How's Connie — the kids — all keeping well?"

"Oh, aye, all keeping well, thanks." Bill couldn't disguise his feeling of awkwardness. "In fact, Connie was saying only the other day that it's been so long since she saw you that an invitation to dinner at our place was long overdue, and, ehm . . ."

It was Bob who broke the ensuing silence again, a certain edginess in his voice as he said, "And Sally — do you see much of Sally these days?"

Bill shifted uneasily in his chair. "Yes, oh yes," he replied with contrived indifference. "She's always popping in. Every two or three days, I suppose. Well, being sisters and all that, you know . . ."

"And what about her lawyer friend — Roddy, or whatever his name is?"

"Rory, you mean?"

"That's him. Got his feet well under the table by now, has he?"

Bill raised his shoulders. "Look, Bob, I honestly don't know what Sally's personal life is all about now. I mean, it's really none of my business, is it? After all, since you two broke up —"

"We didn't break up, Bill. Sally left me, remember?" Bob took a cursory look round the comfortable trimmings of his old friend's office, then added cynically, "Still, I'm not the first mug who's picked up that particular award for unstinting devotion to the force, and I don't suppose I'll be the last."

"Some wives can take, some can't. It's as simple as that — a police cliché. And if you didn't have that worked out before you tied the knot, you were living in fairyland." Bill detected what he thought was an uncharacteristic element of self-pity in his friend's attitude, and he didn't like it. "Hell's teeth!" he rasped. "What's up with you these days, man?"

Bob prepared to stand up.

"No, I think you should just sit where you are, Bob! It's high time you heard this, and it's better coming from me now than from upstairs when it's too bloody late!"

"Be my guest, boss," Bob muttered moodily. He slouched down into his chair, his head resting on one hand.

The telephone rang and Bill picked it up. "Yes . . . OK, put him on . . . Hello, Jack . . . Yes, Bob Burns is with me right now . . . Uh-huh, it's all in order — just making one or two final amendments before it's

62

re-typed . . . No problem, Chief . . . Yep, I'll see to that personally. 'Bye."

Bob looked directly at Bill and shook his head gravely. "That wasn't very clever, mate. You just stuck your head in a noose for nothing."

Bill carried on regardless. "As I was about to say — everybody, including myself, knows that you've always been twice the copper I am, or that most of the blokes we started out with are, for that matter. But, own up, you've always had this bloody huge chip on your shoulder that you know best, that your way's best, and stuff anybody's opinion if it doesn't tally with your own. Fair enough, but the fact is that there's a lot more to getting on in the force than just being a good cop — if only you'd get off your high horse for long enough to see it."

"Oh yeah? Tell me about it. You should know."

"That's right, I *do* know! That's why I made it to inspector in quick time, and that's why I'm on the way up, while —"

"While I'm stuck down here as Sergeant Plod?"

"Exactly! And the sooner you stop feeling sorry for yourself and get in there among the movers and shakers the better."

"You forgot to include arse-lickers in that short list of high achievers, Bill, and you're beginning to make me feel sick."

"Vomit away, if that's how it grabs you. There's a bucket over there. But before you stuff your fingers down your throat, just take a look at yourself in the mirror! Look at the state you've let yourself get into since Sally left. Look at your suit. Hell's bells, man, you'd think you'd bloody slept in it!"

This time Bob did stand up. "The suit's in this state because I *did* sleep in it," he said matter-of-factly. "In a lumpy heap of a torn leatherette armchair in the bobbies' rest room at Haddington nick, to be precise. Yeah, and all endured willingly in the execution of my duties, naturally. Sleeping on the job, if you like. And just for the record, Sally had bugger all to do with it. It was only me, slumped there with my chip firmly on my shoulder, my high horse tethered to the chair leg, and a coil spring trying to worm its way up my hole for four luxuriant hours." He started to walk towards the door. "But don't let it bother you, Bill. Just regard it as an amusing little conversation piece to share with the other movers and shakers when you pop into the lounge of the police club for a quiet G&T on your way home to Barnton for dinner tonight. Have one for me. I'll most likely still be dragging my jacksy around the countryside somewhere trying to do things by the book. *My* book!"

Realising that he had probably gone too far, Bill began to apologise. "Wait a minute, Bob. I was out of order there, and I'm sorry, OK? All I'm trying to say is that I hate to see you grinding yourself down for nothing. What's the point of digging yourself an early grave? All you'll get out of the bastards is a posthumous medal, if you're lucky." He forced a laugh. "And a lot of good that'll do you where you're going, eh?"

"The only place I'm going is Perth," Bob retorted dryly, reaching for the door handle.

"Listen to me, Bob, for heaven's sake," Bill pleaded. "Think what you're doing. I mean, just look at things realistically. You're pushing forty now. All you've got to do is play the game the way we all do. Look out for number one. Act smart. Get those inspector's pips. Shit! The chances are they'll offer you early retirement in a few years, anyway, so the higher your salary when the time comes . . ."

"You can spend the best years of your life sitting there with your head in the sand, giving yourself piles trying to hatch the biggest pension egg possible, if that's what turns you on, Bill, but count me out. I've got too much respect for my conscience . . . as well as my arse." He checked the time. "Now, if you'll excuse me, I've got work to do."

Bill Blackie stood up and thumped his fist on the desk. "The report, Bob!" he barked, his face livid. "I want that bloody report, and I want it *now*! You heard me on the phone to Jack Spiers. I promised him! Can't you understand I'm trying to save your fucking bacon?"

Bob opened the door and paused. "I told you when I came in what the score was regarding the report, Bill. So," he shrugged, "maybe you'd better concentrate now on saving your own fucking bacon!"

"O wad some Power the giftie gie us To see oursels as others see us!"

Bob Burns was mulling over these immortal lines from the pen of his venerated namesake as he parked his car on the double yellow lines outside the Raeburn House Hotel in Stockbridge, and much as he tried to tell himself that he didn't give a toss for Bill Blackie's opinion of him, he had to admit that there was one thing he *had* been right about — he looked a total mess. After sticking his police pass on the inside of the windscreen, he crossed the street, unlocked the tenement door, and climbed the steep, winding staircase to his third floor flat.

Mrs Jamieson, his diminutive but robust charlady, was on the point of leaving when Bob staggered in, gasping for breath. She looked him up and down and declared, "I only ever seen one thing that was a bigger midden than you, and that was the state of this flat when I come in this mornin'!"

"I kid you not, Mrs J, those bloody stairs are gonna be the death of me yet," he panted, brushing past and pretending not to hear.

But Mrs Jamieson was not that easily put off. "Don't you talk to me about bloody stairs, my lad. I can give you a good quarter of a century and I can still nip up and down a dozen o' them stairs every day without endin' up soundin' like a candidate for Medic One like you."

Bob sifted through the pile of bills and junk mail that she'd placed neatly on the hall table. "Yeah, yeah," he mumbled, "you're a credit to your generation, Mrs J."

"Never off the stot, that's your trouble. And it'll take its toll, if you don't get a grip and sort yourself out. Just you mark my words!"

He threw his jacket through the open bedroom door, muttering, "You never spoke a truer word, Mrs J."

"And far be it from me to complain — you know me — but I've got to say this. I'm fair scunnered wi' comin' in here every week and findin' this place lookin' as if it's just been ransacked by a gang of starvin' vandals. Nothin' but crumpled clothes lyin' everywhere. Half-eaten pizzas and stinky milk cartons on the kitchen table. Bloody flies and bluebottles. The place is mingin', maukit! Without a word of a lie, I can truthfully say that there's not one person that you'll come across that's more long-sufferin' than me. I had to be, livin' wi' Archie Jamieson for well nigh fifty years, God rest his useless hide. But I am *not* puttin' up wi' this another minute. It won't do. It just will *not* do. There is no way, no *way*, that I am prepared to keep actin' as a bloody skivvy in a pigsty like this any long—"

"Now, now, don't you get yourself overexcited, Mrs J," Bob interrupted, while shepherding her out the door. "Remember Medic One. And, ehm, how would you feel about an extra tenner in your envelope next week?"

Mrs Jamieson's magnified eyes blinked pensively behind the thick lenses of her specs. She hesitated only momentarily, then declared, "Aye, well, if ye put it that way, like. See ye next week, Mr Burns."

Bob was soon Perth-bound, feeling refreshed, relatively spruce, and with a renewed sense of wellbeing. Amazing, he smiled to himself, what a shower, shave, a change of clothes and a satisfactorily-concluded annual round of pay negotiations with the redoubtable Mrs J could do for one's self-confidence. If there wasn't quite a bright golden haze on the meadows of Fife as he gazed across to them through the flickering tracery of suspension cables while speeding northward over the Forth Road Bridge, the world did appear decidedly less depressing than it had an hour ago.

For all that, he knew only too well that his little set-to with Bill Blackie was sure to have been but a mild forerunner of the unholy row that would erupt once word of his recalcitrance reached Jack Spiers. There could be no doubt that he was taking one almighty gamble on the strength of what was, at this stage, little more than a hunch. But he'd crossed the Rubicon just as surely as he was now crossing the River Forth. There was no turning back. He switched on the car radio just in time to catch the end of the local two o' clock news bulletin . . .

"And now an update on yesterday's brutal killing of a female geriatric patient at Haddington's Roodlands General Hospital. A spokesman for Lothian and Borders Police has just announced that a man arrested near the scene of the crime yesterday is expected to appear in court tomorrow morning, charged with the murder of the woman, who has now been named as Miss Roberta McGregor, aged seventy-seven."

Either Jack Spiers had got back from his meeting already, or Bill Blackie had flapped and taken matters into his own hands, Bob surmised. Something told him he was about to find out as he turned off the radio to answer his car phone.

The voice at the other end, however, was only that of PC Andy Green, sounding more confused than ever. "I'm on the way back to Haddington from the forensic lab, Sarge," he yelled, "and I've just had Inspector Wilson on the horn telling me to report back to him pronto. What's happening?"

"Your guess is as good as mine, kid. But forget about that for now. What's the news from forensic?"

"The news is that Doc Bryson is a right belter. Maybe only an eight out of ten in the thrup'ny bits department, mind, but a right wee stotter all the same."

"Never mind all that Randy Andy crap, Constable Green! What about the damned gloves?"

"Yeah, I delivered them safe and sound, and the Doc says she'll do the business on them a.s.a.p. She also said to tell you that she got the samples from the morgue. Said you'd know what she meant."

"OK, well done. What else have you got for me?"

"First of all, I drew a blank with the farmer. He was through west at a farm sale all day yesterday and he had his two workers with him, so nobody went to the hospital field to check the cattle yesterday at all. They were all too pissed when they got home, and their wives confirmed that."

"Hmm, well, it was worth a try. And how did you get on with the voluptuous Nurse Golightly?"

"Nah, drew a blank there an' all."

"How do you mean?"

"I mean she's already got a steady lumber. Big bugger called Quinn. Works in the slaughterhouse over at —"

"So help me, Green, I'm not bloody well interested in her love life! What I wanted was some info on why my DCI's missus is in that side ward at women's surgical, that's all!"

"Aw that? Yeah, well, it's all a bit mysterious, like."

"OK, but tell me all about it anyway, and be bloody quick about it!"

"Right you are, Sarge. Turns out she shouldn't even be in surgical, 'cos she's never even had an operation, as far as Dolly Golightly knows. They call her Dolly, by the way, 'cos she's got a fantastic pair of —"

"Cloned sheep?" Bob shook his head in despair.

"No, no, Sarge. You miss the point. It's 'cos she's got big —"

"GREEN!"

"OK, boss, sorry about that. Right, so Nurse Golightly says it's all very hush-hush, but the rumour on the ward is that your gaffer's wife has been sneaked in there for a spell of rehab after a stint in some detox unit in Edinburgh. Not the first time, either, Dolly reckons."

"Detox? You mean she's been getting dried out? Funny, I never had her figured as a piss-artist."

"Search me, Sarge. I'm just repeating the ward gossip the way I heard it."

"Fair enough. Did you get anything else on her?"

"Only that she's one of them voluntary welfare workers in her spare time. You know — hospital visits to the oldies and all that do-gooder stuff. Yeah, she's well known around Roodlands for that, it seems."

70

"Well, well, well, that *is* interesting. What about the houses near the hospital? Did you have time to check them out?"

"Just one, Sarge. But it's the only one that you can see the murder scene from in any case."

"So, anything of interest to report from there?"

"Zilch! The owners are in Tenerife on holiday. Have been for the past week."

"Right. Not to worry. It was a long shot anyway. Now listen — did your Inspector Wilson ask you where you are and where you've just been?"

"Certainly did, and I told him I've just been in at forensic getting a copy of their report on the murder weapon for you."

"Good thinking, Batman. What did he have to say about that?"

"He said I was a bigger fuckin' idiot than he thought I was, 'cos forensic had already faxed a copy down to Haddington nick for you this morning."

"Excellent! If he asks you what else you've been up to today, you can tell him about calling on the farmer and checking out that house, if you like, but keep your lip buttoned about the DCI's wife, whatever you do."

"You got it, Sarge. But what happens next?"

"At a guess, I'd say you'll be back on lollipop duty when school comes out this afternoon."

"Aw, shit! No more CID secondment work?"

"Not by the looks of things right now, lad. But there'll be other cases, never fear."

"Hey! You mean you'll put a word in for me with the top brass?"

"Not unless you want your police career to come to an abrupt end, I won't," Bob laughed.

There was a bamboozled silence at the other end.

"But thanks for your help all the same," Bob added. "And don't forget what I told you about the C-R-A-P, right?"

"Ehm, yeah . . . shtum, right?" There followed another silence — a pensive one this time. "Here, wait a minute, Sarge!" PC Green finally blurted out. "I've just rumbled it. C-R-A-P! That spells . . . crap!"

"Good for you, Constable. You've got a natural bent for detective work. You'll go far."

"Aw gee, thanks, Sarge."

"You're welcome, Kojak. And that's a big ten-four. Over and out!"

CHAPTER
FIVE

Bob's acquaintance with the Fair City of Perth was more of a passing than an intimate kind, though not due to any aversion to the place on his part. Quite the contrary. On any occasion when he'd had the good fortune to stop in the town — usually en route to or from somewhere farther afield, like Aberdeen or Inverness — he had always found Perth to be one of the more pleasant and quietly spectacular of Scottish county towns. In truth, it had always seemed to him more of a large village than a small city, nestling on the banks of the River Tay, with its wide, grassy haughs fanning out beneath the rugged beauty of Kinnoul Hill. Perth was a fine town and a prosperous one, steeped in history and somehow reflecting the very essence of the stolid Scots flair for trade and commerce. Bob liked it.

He had no idea what Pinkie Dalrymple looked like now, although he had probably seen her countless times in and around Dirleton during his childhood and youth. But he knew at a glance that the woman who answered the door of "The Rowans" in Scone Loan couldn't be her. Sarah Thorn, as she introduced herself, was no more than thirty and had, as was becoming increasingly common in these northerly parts, an accent that was unmistakably Home Counties English.

She and her husband, Sarah Thorn readily volunteered, had bought the little terraced stone house from a widow called Mathieson almost two years earlier, when Paul, her husband, had taken up his new post as an analytical chemist with Bell's, the local the whisky distillers. Mrs Mathieson, as she recalled, was a victim of Alzheimer's disease, and had eventually become too much for her younger sister Pinkie to look after. Pinkie herself was in her seventies. The house had been sold in order to raise sufficient capital for the two elderly ladies to retire to the Gowrie Nursing Home in the village of Scone, just a couple of miles up the road, where proper medical care would be provided for Mrs Mathieson, while still allowing her the comfort of her sister's company in her twilight years.

And approximately how much, Bob hoped she wouldn't mind his asking, had Mr and Mrs Thorn paid for the property? This, he assured her, was an item of strictly confidential information, which might prove crucial to his investigations.

The guide price had been only a hundred-and-forty thousand pounds, Sarah Thorn revealed almost apologetically, and her husband's offer of just a few hundred pounds over that amount had been accepted by the sisters without quibble. The little house, she stressed, had been in need of extensive modernising and upgrading. Hence the modest price — by Home Counties standards — for such a desirable residence in that idyllic location.

74

While picturing in his mind's eye the cramped flat in some featureless block in Slough that the Thorns had probably swapped for this bijou des. res., Bob thanked the young woman profusely for her kind co-operation, and pointed his Mondeo in the direction of Scone.

Fairly predictably, the Gowrie Nursing Home turned out to be an elegant, stone-built Victorian villa that had been built, perhaps, as a spacious family residence by one of the many enterprising Perth merchants of the time, who had made his fortune trading, via the River Tay, the area's rich and varied produce with his counterparts on the Continent a century or more before the European Common Market had been dreamed of.

Bob thought of Scone's legendary Stone of Destiny as he tugged the polished brass bell pull, and he reflected on how his own fate might depend upon whether Pinkie Dalrymple still lived there, and on what potentially vital information she might be able to come up with.

"Detective Sergeant Burns, Lothian and Borders Police," he said to the rather serious-looking girl who opened the door. "I wonder if I could trouble your principal for a few minutes of his time?"

"I'm afraid Mrs Boyd is on the phone at the moment," the girl replied, ushering Bob inside and showing him to a solitary couch in the lobby. "But if you care to take a seat, I'll tell her you're here as soon as she's free." She half turned to leave, then added, "Would you like a coffee while you're waiting?"

Bob said he wouldn't, thanks all the same, the quiet rumbling in his stomach serving as a reminder, if he needed one, that he'd had nothing to eat since the handful of digestive biscuits he'd stuffed into his mouth and washed down with stewed tea that you could have raced spiders on in Haddington police station at seven o'clock that morning. He was sorely tempted to ask the girl if it would be out of the question for her to substitute a jumbo steak pie with mashed tatties and all the trimmings for the cup of coffee, but thought better of it. He'd heard what the food in some of these establishments was like.

He looked around the austere decor and furnishings of what must once have been a graceful and welcoming hall. "So, this is how it all ends up," he thought to himself, "*if* you can afford it." Through a glass partition opposite, he could see a handful of the residents sitting slouched and semi-comatose in a row of chairs laid out along the back wall of a bleak conservatory. The only visible concession to plant life was a straggly, yellowing, grapeless grape vine, which appeared to be even nearer to God than some of its human companions. Hell, he had been in more welcoming jails than this!

Bob's spiralling plunge into depression was checked by the reappearance of the girl.

"Mrs Boyd will see you now, sir." She guided him through a door at the side of the stairs and along a dingy corridor, which led to what may originally have been a maid's room, but was now the principal's office. The overwhelming doominess of the cramped interior had Bob comparing it instantly with the funereal lair of a skinflint Dickensian lawyer.

Mrs Boyd, on the other hand, had quite the opposite effect. "Come away in and sit you down, Sergeant," she beamed, as bright and breezy in her flouncy floral frock as a bumblebee in a petunia patch.

She was a jolly, roly-poly soul — in her mid-forties, Bob guessed — and she radiated an aura of bubbly good humour that was the absolute antithesis of everything else he'd seen inside the place so far.

"And what have I done this time?" Mrs Boyd asked while making a token attempt at tidying the happy clutter on her desk, then plopping her comfily-upholstered bottom onto an old leather swivel chair. "Don't tell me we got two urns mixed up and sent the right ashes to the wrong families again. Honestly, I've already done that once since we started this business, and once was more than enough, believe me. The embarrassment of it! Really, I thought I was going to die!" She let out a peal of jingling laughter that was so infectious that even the serious-looking girl ventured a prim smile.

Bob cleared his throat. "Nothing quite so traumatic for you as that, I hope," he said, "although I suppose dying *is* a common denominator. You see, I'm here in the course of a murder investigation."

"How exciting!" An impish twinkle glinted in Mrs Boyd's eye. "But none of *our* residents could be the culprit, *surely*."

Through force of habit, Bob flipped open his notebook and intoned, "Perhaps not, but I've reason to believe that you do have someone here who may be able to assist me in my enquiries."

Mrs Boyd leaned closer and clasped her hands in anticipation. "Who ever would have thought it!" she declared, wide-eyed and fascinated. "You're not about to tell us that we're actually harbouring an accessory before or after the fact or something as Machiavellian as that, are you, Sergeant Burns?"

"No, no, I'm quite sure the person I want to interview isn't involved in any sinister way," Bob assured her. "Just an old friend of the victim — a Miss Pinkie Dalrymple."

Looks of genuine shock spread over the faces of the two ladies.

"Pinkie's been murdered?" they gasped in concert.

Apologising for his unintended ambiguity, Bob hastened to explain that no, Pinkie wasn't actually the victim. She was the old friend.

"Oh, thank heavens for that!" Mrs Boyd warbled. She fanned her face with a handful of papers from her newly-tidied desk, then gave the serious-looking girl a few soothing pats on the hand. "Dear me, I came over all wobbly for a wee minute there — didn't *you*, Brenda?"

"Phew!" Brenda puffed, mirroring her principal's face-fanning movement with her other hand, her secretarial poise slipping briefly as she exclaimed, "No half!"

Bob allowed them a few moments to pull themselves together, before calmly saying, "I don't want to create any unnecessary upset to your routine, Mrs Boyd, but if you could arrange it for me, I'd like to have a word with this Pinkie Dalrymple — uhm, in private, right away."

Mrs Boyd pursed her lips and shook her head solemnly. "Sorry Sergeant, but no can do. Pinkie left here shortly after her sister died, just a few months back. I can check the exact date, if you want."

"That would be useful, thank you," Bob said, then offered up a silent prayer of gratitude to the god of Detective Sergeants for at least having kept the old dear alive. A wistful smile crossed Mrs Boyd's chubby features. "As Pinkie herself used to say, the scene in here wasn't buzzing enough for a livewire like her. Hmm, she only endured it because of her sister, I'm sure, because as soon as Mrs Mathieson passed away, Pinkie flew the coop."

"And where did she go?" Bob urged, anxious to get on with the job. He turned to Mrs Boyd's assistant. "I'd appreciate a note of her new address, if you'd be so kind. Her telephone number would be handy, too, if you've got it."

Mrs Boyd was quick to intervene. "Aha, but it's not as simple as that, Sergeant. You see, we haven't the foggiest where she is. She just packed the few worldly posessions she had into a suitcase one day and took off in a taxi. No forwarding address, phone number or anything."

Bob felt his short-lived sense of relief being replaced by one of mounting frustration. "But that's crazy! An old woman of almost eighty just doesn't up sticks and bugger off — if you'll pardon the French — without telling someone where she's going. That just doesn't happen. It's not *normal*, for heaven's sake!"

Mrs Boyd smiled a patient little smile. "You obviously don't know Pinkie Dalrymple, Sergeant Burns." Then, as if soliciting some form of corroboration, she looked towards young Brenda, who wasn't slow to oblige . . .

"It's right enough what Mrs Boyd says. Pinkie just sort of disappeared . . . in a taxi."

Bob clapped his hand to his forehead. "OK, I'll buy all that for the moment. But let's face it, there can't be that many taxi companies in a place the size of Perth, so —"

"Phoning the taxi office was the first thing I did after Pinkie left that morning," Mrs Boyd butted in. "Surprising as it may seem, Sergeant, some of us in this profession do actually *care* about the elderly people in our charge, and I was worried sick about Pinkie setting off on her own like that."

"Yes, I appreciate that, I really do. But right now, all I'm concerned about is tracing Pinkie Dalrymple, so just tell me where the taxi driver delivered her, if you don't mind, please."

"To the railway station. And before you ask . . ." Mrs Boyd raised a calming hand, "I spoke to the taxi driver when he came back here later that day to take a couple of our old ladies into town, and all he remembered Pinkie saying was that she was looking forward to her holiday, because she'd never had a proper one before. And before you ask again, no, she didn't let on to him where she was going."

80

"But hadn't she mentioned this holiday to you or anyone else in the home here?"

"Not a word."

There was a short interlude of meditative hush before young Brenda said, rather timidly, "I don't suppose it's important, but there was a woman at the door this morning asking about Pinkie as well. She said she was a relation, just visiting the area, and wondering if we could tell her where Pinkie lived now. You were out, Mrs Boyd, so I just told her we didn't know, but I would make an appointment for her to see you, if she wanted."

"And what did this woman say to that?" Mrs Boyd asked, her brows knotting into a perplexed frown.

"She just went all sort of grumpy and mumbled that she didn't have time to hang about here all day. Then she stomped off."

"Did she tell you her name or give you a contact number or anything?" Bob enquired.

Brenda shook her head. "No, nothing. And I didn't bother to ask." She darted an appealing glance at Mrs Boyd. "I'm sorry, I just didn't think it was important enough to —"

"It's all right, dear," Mrs Boyd said. She gave Brenda another reassuring pat on the hand. "There's probably nothing in it." The puzzled look returned to her face. "Although, now I think about it, I don't remember Pinkie ever mentioning a female relation."

"Well, at this stage, everything's worth following up, I suppose," Bob shrugged. He pulled a pen from his inside pocket. "So, I'd better take a note of whatever details you have on Pinkie's family and friends."

His request was met once more by Mrs Boyd's ominous pout and shake of her head. "No can do again, I'm afraid. Pinkie and her sister didn't have one single visitor during the entire eighteen months or so they lived here, and the only family that she ever spoke of was some distant nephew or other that she couldn't abide the thought of. I do recall him phoning her a couple of times, mind you, but she always gave him short shrift. The conversation never lasted more than a few seconds."

"And I don't suppose there's any point in asking if you happen to know this distant nephew's name or his whereabouts, is there?"

Mrs Boyd's reply was an apologetic raising of her shoulders.

"OK," Bob went on, "but can you at least tell me the last time he phoned?"

Mrs Boyd didn't have to think about the answer to that one. "Yes, I can remember exactly. It was on the day of Mrs Mathieson's funeral. Pinkie was sitting right where you are now, Sergeant. She was talking to me about the financial implications of her sister's death and so forth. I went out and waited in the corridor while she took the call, naturally."

"And did you manage to catch anything of what they were talking about?"

"Not a sausage. But I can tell you that it sounded anything but a pleasant little chat. I could hear by the way Pinkie was shouting at him that she wasn't best pleased, but I couldn't make out what she was actually saying . . . until her parting shot. And they could have heard *that* in Perth!"

"Her parting shot?"

Mrs Boyd held up two fingers, and her face opened into a blushing grin. "The first word began with the letter *F* and the other word was *Off*."

While the ladies indulged in a polite little giggle, Bob concluded, "I think we can safely assume that Pinkie didn't take that holiday at her mysterious nephew's place, then."

Mrs Boyd nodded her agreement. "I don't think there's *any* doubt about that," she smiled.

Bob was still professionally suspicious, however. "But, just as a matter of interest, how long after that phone call was it that Pinkie decided to leave?"

"Only a few days," Mrs Boyd replied, "but I'm sure the phone call had nothing to do with her decision, if that's what you mean. I'm absolutely certain that the nephew, or whatever he is, would've been the last person that Pinkie would've been influenced by."

"How much," Bob asked bluntly, "was Pinkie worth, Mrs Boyd?"

"I honestly can't tell you exactly, but it couldn't have been a lot," said Mrs Boyd, patently unfazed by the question. "She certainly inherited the residue of the money her late sister had received from the sale of her house, but that capital would have been eaten into quite considerably already by the cost of living in a home like this. In fact, the question of whether she could afford to live here for much longer without applying for DSS assistance was precisely what I was trying to get Pinkie to address on the day she received that phone call."

Bob turned to young Brenda again. "I take it that you answered the phone when this nephew character called?"

"I did the last time, anyway. Can't remember if I did before or not. Probably did, though."

"So, what can you tell me about his voice? You know — what age you'd put him at, that sort of thing."

Brenda gave the matter careful consideration for a moment, then said, "Nothing really. It was just an ordinary voice — not too young, not too old, not too deep, not too high. Just, well . . . ordinary."

"Accent?" Bob prompted. "What about that?"

Brenda's face went blank. "How do you mean, like?"

"Well, for example," Bob sighed, trying to control his growing impatience, "did he sound local, or English, or maybe Irish, or foreign even?"

No, he hadn't been foreign, Brenda decided after due deliberation. She was pretty sure about that. No — Scottish, definitely Scottish — but not local, though. She was pretty sure of that, too . . . she thought.

"OK, but can you maybe be a *wee* bit more specific? Did it sound like Edinburgh? Glasgow? Aberdeen?"

Brenda freely admitted that she wasn't too hot on accents, but said that if she had to plump for any of those, it would be the Edinburgh one. Yes, she affirmed with a cautious note of confidence, the caller had definitely sounded like an Edinburgh bloke . . . but maybe with a touch of Glasgow . . . she thought.

"Thanks a million. A description like that's as good as a voice print," Bob muttered under his breath. "Lucky for him he's not a bloody suspect!"

Mrs Boyd had read Bob's mood of frustration. "I shouldn't worry too much about it, if I were you, Sergeant Burns," she advised. "As I said, I'm certain that the chap wouldn't be of any use to you in tracing Pinkie, anyway."

But Bob was still concentrating on young Brenda. "This woman who turned up at the door this morning — can you describe her, please?"

Brenda was quick off the mark this time. The woman had reminded her of her Auntie Isa from Arbroath — a right old dragon — so she could conjure up a mental picture of her no bother. Elderly — tweedy — frumpy — grey, permed hair — National Health glasses — hairy legs. A real torn-faced old pain in the neck!

"With a relation like that on the loose," Bob mumbled through a wry smirk, "I'm not surprised Pinkie did the sudden off without trace." Turning his attention once more to Mrs Boyd, he asked, "If Pinkie had booked this holiday of hers through a travel agent, is there one in particular she might have gone to, or am I gonna have to slog round every one in Perth?"

A smug smile dimpled Mrs Boyd's cheeks. "I think I can save you some legwork there, Sergeant. If she'd gone to any travel agent, it would have been to W. A. Main in South Street. Mr Main used to visit his mother here several times a week until she died. He got on like a house on fire with Pinkie. Same zany sense of humour. They were great pals." Mrs Boyd's face took on a more serious look. "But to be quite frank, I'm certain that Mr Main would have let me know if Pinkie had booked a trip through him. I mean, I've bumped into him on more than one occasion recently, and I'm sure he would have said *something*."

"All the same, I'd like to check it out with Mr Main. Do you mind if I use your phone?"

"Be my guest." Mrs Boyd lifted the receiver. "I'll get him on the line and do the introductions, shall I?"

Bob checked his watch as Mrs Boyd punched in the number. Almost five o'clock, and no farther forward than he had been when he set out that morning. He listened impatiently to Mrs Boyd's excited banter with the travel agent (being caught up on the periphery of a murder enquiry was clearly a huge thrill for someone who spent her life minding people who only snuffed it of natural causes), then accepted the phone from her with a courteous nod of the head.

"Believe this or believe it not, Sergeant," Mr Main enthused, "but you're the second person to ask about old Pinkie this afternoon. Aye, there was a woman in here just over an hour ago, asking if Pinkie had booked a holiday here before she went away. Imagine that!"

Bob described young Brenda's Auntie Isa lookalike to him.

"That's her, Sergeant! Brilliant! You've got her off to a tee. And pain in the neck is right. Believe this or believe it not, I went to all the trouble of phoning round the other Perth agents that she hadn't already tried, and after I was done she just stormed out without as much as a word of thanks. Pain in the neck? Pain in the arse!"

"Do I take it that you didn't book a holiday for Pinkie, then?"

"Correct! And neither did any of the other local shops." There was a slight note of inspiration in Mr Main's voice as he added: "Hey, Sarge, something tells me old Pinkie's been pulling that taxi driver's leg. She used to do that all the time to me, you know. You can believe this or believe it not, but there was actually one time when the old besom even —"

"Look, I'm greatly obliged to you for taking the time to speak to me, Mr Main, and you'll excuse me if I appear a bit abrupt. But, like you, I'm a busy man. Just before you go, though — did that woman tell you her name, by any chance? . . . No? . . . No, I didn't really think she would've done. But thanks again, sir. 'Bye now."

By the time Bob hung up, Brenda had already left the room, and Mrs Boyd was standing somewhat agitatedly by the door.

"I don't want to chase you away, Sergeant," she said, "but I'm afraid it's all hands on deck at this hour of the day. Chimps' Tea Party time, as some of our old folk like to call it. But please feel free to come back and resume your enquiries later. You're *more* than welcome, honestly."

Apologising for taking up so much of her time, Bob shook her hand and thanked her, assuring her that he didn't think he would need to trouble her again. "There *is* only one last thing, however . . ."

Mrs Boyd cocked her head expectantly.

"You wouldn't happen to have a photograph of Pinkie Dalrymple, would you?"

A spirited rummage through the papers on her desk resulted in the total restoration of the original happy clutter and in the discovery of a dog-eared picture album. "Here we are, Sergeant," she announced brightly after a quick thumb through. "Pinkie and her sister taken at last year's Christmas party. Here," she said, detaching it from the page, "it's all yours. Oh, Pinkie's the one with the pink hair and bamboo spectacles, by the way."

"You're a gem, Mrs Boyd. I won't bore you with the details, but right now, this snapshot is the only thing that stands between one very desperate man and oblivion — and I'm not talking about the accused."

Confused, Mrs Boyd accompanied Bob to the front door, where she suddenly piped up, "It's just come back to me! I *knew* there was someone — an old friend that Pinkie used to talk about at times. Perhaps she could help you find Pinkie. Now let me see, her name was something like . . ."

"Bertie McGregor?"

"The very one!" she beamed. "What's more, I'm sure she lives down your way. Find her and your troubles could be over!"

Bob pursed his lips and shook his head solemnly. "No can do, Mrs B. As my immortal namesake might have put it . . .

> Old Bertie, you see,
> Just happens to be
> The poor murderee!"

CHAPTER
SIX

Bob had passed the stage of being hungry. He had that old feeling in his solar plexus that seemed to be trying to convey the message to his otherwise-occupied brain that his stomach was attempting to digest itself. He swung off the M90 at the Kinross exit and pulled into the Granada services complex, not with the primary intention of having a bite to eat, but rather because his car was getting low on petrol and he needed to get back to Haddington. He had an idea that Mrs Reynolds, the nursing auxiliary who had found Bertie's body, knew more than PC Andy Green had managed to wheedle out of her between mouthfuls of Snickers and eyefuls of her daughter's vital statistics.

But the smell of food wafting from the Granada kitchens proved too much even for his iron-willed policeman's nostrils, and besides, he reckoned it was about time he took a few minutes to quietly review the happenings of the past twenty-four hours. In the event, he only allowed himself a mug of hot chocolate and a sticky bun, having concluded that the consumption of anything more robust might not be too conducive to positive investigative reflection. That steak pie would have to wait.

Choosing a window table well away from the family dining area, which was teeming with harrassed holiday-making couples and their squawking infants, he opened his file and began sifting through the few bits and pieces which had been found in Bertie's bedside cabinet at the hospital. There were a couple of comic birthday cards from the staff and a Basildon Bond writing pad containing an undated, unpuctuated, unfinished letter to P, whom Bob now took to be Pinkie. In the letter, Bertie said that it had been right nice speaking to her on the phone the other day and she was fairly looking forward to her visit but as scunnered as she was she couldn't go away with her because her lungs were fair buggered now and she would be no decent company for anybody in her knackered state and she was about ready for the midden anyway and what with this damned big toe of hers giving her nanty and everything . . .

If only she had mentioned *where* she couldn't go away to, Bob mused. The only other items of Bertie's in the file seemed equally unhelpful — a couple of yellowed cuttings from the *Haddingtonshire Courier*, in which her name was included among the lists of winners at Dirleton Flower Shows of yesteryear, and a slimline Gunsmoke Western paperback, entitled *Return To Tombstone*. Bob flicked idly through the well-thumbed pages of the latter until they fell open at a place where Bertie had inserted a postcard, presumably as a bookmark. He quickly scanned the two facing pages of the little book on the off chance that the text might contain something of significance. It didn't. The postcard, however, most certainly did.

The sixty peseta postage stamp was franked *Palma, Mallorca* and dated *18 abril* — just a couple of weeks, according to Mrs Boyd's records, after Pinkie had quit the nursing home. Bob ran his eyes over the now-familiar block capitals of the written message:

THIS IS THE LIFE. COMPANY AND NIGHTLIFE MAGIC. SO IS WEATHER. YOU SHOULD HAVE CAME. LOVE P.

So, now at least he knew where Pinkie had gone on holiday. OK, Mallorca was a big place, but . . . He turned the card over to see if the picture might help pinpoint her exact destination on the island. To his further frustration, however, the scene depicted was the familiar night shot of Palma with the floodlit cathedral and the lights of the city mirrored on the limpid water of the bay. He held the card up to the window in the somewhat forlorn hope that Pinkie might have left one of those X-marks-the-spot clues as to the location of her hotel. But there was none.

Under normal circumstances, a quick phone call to HQ would have had half-a-dozen telephone girls chivvying the various tour operators to check for Pinkie's name on their manifests for the week in question. However, he was only too well aware that these were now far from normal circumstances. He would have to think of another way. Bob slipped the postcard into his breast pocket and dolefully considered his options, while eating his bun and absentmindedly reading the thoughts of the ageing Wyatt Earp as he rode tall-in-the-saddle into town.

A hefty tap on the shoulder jolted him out of his musing, and he looked up into the enraged face of DCI Jack Spiers.

"What the bloody hell are you doing here, Burns?" he snarled.

"I could ask you the same thing," Bob countered automatically, realising too late that it was scarcely the type of answer that his chief would have been expecting.

Jack Spiers looked as if he was about to have a seizure. "It's got bugger all to do with you, Sergeant, but as it happens, I've been attending a meeting with colleagues from other constabularies at Gleneagles Hotel. Now, I repeat, what the bloody hell are you doing here?"

Bob had known all along, of course, that he would have to face the notorious Spiers wrath sooner or later, but this was a mite sooner than he'd hoped. "Just stopped off here to pacify the old ulcer whilst proceeding in a southerly direction in the course of my duties . . . sir," he replied through a thin smile, his deliberate use of ham copper-speak unfortunately sounding rather more like sarcasm than the mollification intended. He was off to a bad start, and things were about to get worse.

DCI Spiers sat down opposite him and, leaning threateningly across the table, growled, "I distinctly remember telling Bill Blackie on the telephone at one o'clock this afternoon — and you were in his office at the time — that as soon as you finished your *overdue* report for the Procurator Fiscal on the Haddington murder, you were to get yourself down to Dalkeith double quick and help out with mopping up the inquiries into that botched armed robbery."

Knowing that there would be more to come, Bob elected to make no comment at this stage.

"But now, Burns, I bump into you five hours later, sitting about drinking cocoa, scoffing a cream cookie and reading some asinine cowboy comic, not only thirty-five miles north of where I intended you to be, but twenty-five miles outside your own bloody turf as well! For the third and last time, what the hell are you doing here?"

It was now obvious to Bob that Bill Blackie had made no further contact with Spiers since their one o'clock telephone conversation, so it followed that his chief was still blissfully unaware of the stark truth regarding his precious report for the PF's office. But precisely whose bacon Bill's holding back of that information was intended to save was, for the moment, purely academic.

"I've been following up a lead on the Bertie McGregor case, Chief," Bob said, taking the bull firmly by the horns and bracing himself for a goring.

"You've been doing WHAT?"

"It was more of a gut feeling than anything," Bob went on instinctively, though knowing full well that any attempt at justifying his actions would prove totally futile. "But I felt I wouldn't have been doing my job properly if I'd ignored it."

Jack Spiers lowered his voice in unison with his eyebrows. "And where exactly did this gut feeling of yours lead you?"

"Ultimately, to an old folks' home outside Perth."

A look bordering on the homicidal contorted Jack Spiers' already menacing features. "And resulting in *what*?"

Bob figured that the time had probably come to box clever — to duck and dive a bit in the hope of buying himself enough time to maybe put some meat on the bones of that hunch of his. "Resulting in an absolute dead end, chief. It was a total waste of time — a complete wild-goose chase. You were right from the beginning. This Thomson guy's got guilty written all over . . ."

DCI Spiers was already tapping out a number on his mobile phone. "Hello . . . yes, Spiers here. Detective Inspector Blackie, please . . . Bill? Glad I caught you. What's the latest from the Procurator Fiscal's office on the McGregor case? . . . In court tomorrow morning — charged as accused. OK, well done . . ."

Bob watched his boss's expression grow darker with every word of the lengthy spiel that he was now being given by Bill Blackie. Clearly, bacon-saving was finally in progress, and Bob had a feeling that it wasn't his which was being preserved.

At the end of an unusually one-sided conversation, Jack Spiers stood up and looked Bob coldly in the eye.

"My maxim has always been that nobody disobeys my orders and gets away with it, and you've seen fit to try it on *twice* in one day. What's more, if Bill Blackie

95

hadn't had the initiative to write *your* report from my own provisional notes on the case, your indiscipline may well have resulted in that prisoner being released from custody, and *I* would have been left with a large amount of egg on my face." He reached out and picked up Bob's case file. "You won't be needing this any more." There was an ominous pause before he added, "I don't know what your game is, Burns, but whatever it is, it's up. Be in my office tomorrow morning at eight-thirty — sharp!"

CHAPTER
SEVEN

There was only one message on Bob's answering machine, and he was pleased in more ways than one to hear Julie Bryson's voice telling him that she had some interesting information for him. Luckily, she'd also left her home phone number on the tape — just in case he got back late, she said.

Bob called her right away. "Hi, *Doctor* Julie darlin', and *please*, I don't want to hear that interesting information of yours over the phone. So, before we go any further — have you eaten yet?"

"Do I detect a detective's invitation to dine in the offing?"

"Look, I know you don't fancy Chinese, but how does an Italian grab you?"

"I've never been grabbed by one, but if he happened to look like Al Pacino, the answer to your question would be, any way he wants."

"Well, there's a little place I know in Antigua Street called *Mamma Roma*. And OK, admittedly the proprietor doesn't look too much like Al Pacino, but he's the best I can do on a sergeant's wages. I mean, I've got to own up that I've been dreaming about a big, juicy steak pie with all the trimmings all day, but what the hell, I'm game to settle for you and a pizza instead. So, what do you say?"

"Wow! How could a girl resist that romantic turn of phrase of yours, Sergeant?"

"Great! If you tell me where you live, I'll pick you up in half an hour."

"Thanks for the offer, but I live only just round the corner from Antigua Street, so I'll meet you outside the restaurant."

"Magic!"

"Just one thing, though — how will I recognise you?"

"Easy. I'll be the guy with the flat feet and the unmarked police car parked on the double yellow lines right outside. But in any case, I reckon I should be able to clock you no problem from the detailed description young PC Andy Green gave me. *Ciao!*"

Yet it was despite, rather than because of, PC Green's sketchy verbal portrayal of her that Bob recognised Julie Bryson the moment he saw her walking towards him down the gentle gradient of Leith Walk. And it could only have been the sound of her voice on the phone that had implanted this exact image of her in his mind's eye. Fair enough, PC Green had hit the nail on the head when he said she was "a right wee stotter", but then, that somewhat crude stamp could have been applied equally to any of half-a-dozen girls who had passed by during the few minutes that Bob had been waiting there.

No, Julie Bryson had that special *something* that made her stand out from the rest. And it wasn't just her pretty face, softly framed in flowing dark brown hair, or even her petite but (as far as Bob could ascertain) perfectly formed figure that set her apart. It was a kind of unaffected vivacity which just seemed to radiate from her. It was the understated elegance of her clothes, her quiet self-confidence, her poise, and that infectious, ice-melting smile as she approached him. Julie Bryson had class.

"And just how *did* young Constable Green describe me?" she asked as she sat down with Bob at a quiet corner table, while still going through the mental process of sizing *him* up herself.

"Sorry. Classified CID material, that."

"Hmm, and X-rated, too, if your PC Green's wandering eyes were anything to go by."

"Yeah," Bob laughed. "Randy Andy, I call him. But he's young yet. He'll grow out of it . . . if he has any sense."

"Oops! Do I note a touch of cynicism there? Have Cupid's little arrows left a few open wounds in the tough lawman's hide, perchance?"

Bob had a quiet chuckle to himself. This little lady certainly didn't believe in messing about when it came to getting down to brass tacks. "And do I note the analytical mind of the forensic scientist working overtime, perchance?" he parried.

Their little bout of exploratory verbal sparring was interrupted by the waiter asking if they would care for a drink while studying the menu.

"A glass of the house white wine — *if* it's dry — would suit me just fine, thank you," Julie said without hesitation.

Bob was impressed. Not only had Julie Bryson more than lived up to young Andy Green's assessment of her appearance, but she was no slouch in the drinks-ordering stakes either. No frumpy, teetotal boffin, this one. He smiled at the waiter. "And a beer for me, please. *Peroni*, if you've got it." Turning back to Julie, he willingly volunteered, "My wife and I are divorced, if that's what you wanted to know. And, yes, it was painful having the arrows extracted."

Julie arched her eyebrows. "And it still hurts?"

An impish grin lit Bob's face. "It did, but it's getting better by the minute."

Lowering her eyes coyly, Julie smiled, "You're only saying that to please me . . . or maybe it's just the smell of pizzas acting as an anaesthetic."

Bob's stomach rumbled bang on cue. "What more can I say," he laughed, patting his midriff, "except, pardon me. It's only my ulcer complaining that he's been in there too long on his own today. Tends to get a bit lonely after a while."

"When did you last have a decent meal, for heaven's sake?"

"That's the way my mother used to look at me if I hadn't eaten up all my Brussels sprouts. Well, not *exactly* the way my mother looked at me." His stomach rumbled again.

Julie shook her head while making an effort not to smile. "You're digging yourself an early grave, you know. And the only thanks you'll get is —"

"Is a posthumous medal, if I'm lucky?"

"Precisely."

Bob nodded his head. "That's the second time I've been told that today, as it happens."

"There you are, then. Whoever told you that obviously has your best interests at heart."

"Mmm, if you'd said that yesterday, I might almost have believed you, but . . ."

Much to his own surprise, Bob suddenly found himself pouring out the whole story of his relationship with Bill Blackie, right from the day they both joined the force until the moment he stormed out of Bill's office that very afternoon.

When he was through, Julie hesitated for a moment, then said, "I know it's none of my business, and I'd be the first one to stand up for the *I Did It My Way* principle, but first your marriage, then your best friend, and next — unless you can prove them all wrong about this Billy Thomson bloke — possibly your career prospects as well. Is it really worth it?"

"I'd probably say it wasn't, if I were the one who was doing something wrong. But I'm not. I mean, the way I see it is that I'm only trying to do the job I'm paid to do, but I'm being told to put a poor sod's neck on the block without a proper investigation. And for what? For the sake of police expediency, that's all. That kind of thing stinks, and everybody knows it happens too often these days." Bob took a gulp of his beer. "And they wonder why the police get a bad name? Nah, at times like this, I'd rather go back to driving bloody tractors!"

Julie smiled and sipped her wine. "Is that what you did before you became a policeman?"

Bob didn't answer right away. He was more immediately concerned with looking through the window at a young beat bobby who was walking over the street towards his illegally-parked car. The constable gave Bob's Mondeo a cursory once-over, checked the police pass on the windscreen and, with a knowing smirk, ambled on his way.

"Sorry, Julie, I just wanted to make sure that young copper didn't go all promotion-conscious and call in the tow truck."

There was a mischievous glint twinkling in Julie's eye. "But even if he had," she reasoned, "wouldn't the young constable only have been doing the job he's paid to do . . . Sergeant?"

"Touché," Bob conceded, an approving smile on his face as he raised his glass. "Cheers!" She was as sharp as nails, this one.

At that, the waiter returned to take their order.

They agreed to share a plate of *Bruschetta* to start. Julie chose *Canneloni Ripieni* to follow, while Bob opted for *Pizza Marinara*.

"And to drink, *signore*?"

"Please, Julie, you go ahead and have whatever you want." Bob gestured towards his car. "I'll have to take it easy, unfortunately."

Julie gave the waiter a melting smile. "In that case, another glass of the house *bianco* will be fine for me . . . *per favore*."

"Yeah, uhm — and just a bottle of mineral water for me . . . please." Bob handed the menus to the waiter, then turned back to Julie. "Driving tractors? Yes, that's right. I did that from when I left school until I was old enough to join the police. Happiest couple of years of my life, in many ways." He sensed Julie watching him closely as he toyed with the stem of his glass.

"Funny," she said at length, "you didn't really strike me as the farmer's boy type."

Bob raised his eyes to meet hers. "Well, I am. Or a farm *worker's* boy, to be exact." He shrugged his shoulders. "But, hey, you've listened to enough about me for one evening. Let's talk about you for a change."

"Nothing much to tell, really. I was born and bred in the south side of Glasgow. All very *poash* and genteel. Dad's a lecturer in biology at Glasgow University, and Mum seems to spend her entire life being in the chair of the women's committee at Whitecraigs Tennis Club. I'm an only child. Never again, Mum said. So, I was spoilt rotten as a kid, was the original smart-arsed brain box at school, followed Dad into science as expected, got the first-class honours degree as predicted, then shattered the entire dream by getting a job in the Strathclyde Police forensic lab. Dad did his nut and said it was a waste of a good scientific education, and Mum pulled a face, said 'How *seedy!*', then poured herself a large G&T and switched on *Coronation Street*."

"But your mum was right. Why a police forensic lab of all places, for Pete's sake?"

"Why not? OK, a seedy job it may be, but life's seedy, so why hide from it?"

"Just roll up your sleeves and get stuck in there, eh?"

"You bet! Otherwise I'd have ended up just like Dad — droning on like an automaton day after boring day to lecture rooms full of crotch-scratching, acne-spattered students whose main concern in life is working out how many more times they can afford to get stoshious before the next instalment of their student loan comes through, and when the hell they're ever gonna get laid. Come on, get a life! But even at that, I couldn't be myself, do my own thing. You know, still living with your Mum and Dad and all that when you're nearly thirty. I just couldn't take it any more. So, that's why I applied for this job in the Edinburgh lab a month or so back. And, thank heavens, I got it!" A pleased-as-Punch grin spread over her face. "I just moved into my own little flat round the corner there last week, and for the first time in my life, I can really be ME. Yippee!" Julie downed the last of her wine and discreetly held up her empty glass to the waiter at the bar, that same melting smile flashing across her face like a light being switched on, and off, just as soon as the waiter got the message.

It was the nearest thing to instant telepathy that Bob had ever seen. Fascinated, he watched her as she skilfully munched her way into her first slice of *bruschetta*. Not a drop of the golden-green olive oil that oozed from the bread was allowed to dribble onto her chin, not one solitary piece of slippery chopped tomato was permitted to escape onto her lap.

"It's bad manners to stare," she said, looking askance at Bob whilst raising her napkin to delicately dab a non-existent smudge of oil from the corner of her mouth. "Didn't your mother tell you about that as well as about Brussels sprouts?"

"I'm sure she did, but she wasn't to know that I'd ever come face-to-face with a *bruschetta*-eating virtuoso. A jeely-piece-gobbler was the nearest we ever got to that in our house."

Julie acknowledged his off-handed compliment with a surprise outburst of extremely convincing Rab C. Nesbittesque. "Jeely piece, is it? Heh, get tore in, well. Ye're up against the Glesca jeely piece-eatin' champion here, boy!"

Although trying to put it to the back of his mind, Bob was beginning to realise that he had never felt so at ease in any woman's company since Sally. Hardly surprising either, he then told himself, since this was the *only* woman he'd been out with since his marriage hit the rocks. And, come to that, what the hell had taken him to ask out someone he'd never even met before? After all, he could easily have taken all the forensic information she had for him over the phone, could have gulped down a quick microwave dinner at the flat, and could still have made it down to Haddington, as intended, in time to put in a good hour or two of questioning, which just might have turned up something to make his meeting with Jack Spiers the following morning something less of a nightmare than it promised to be. That particular best-laid scheme had gone well a-gley now, however. Yet he hadn't even known of the existence of this girl before she phoned that morning. And that was less than twelve hours ago. God, she must think him a real presumptuous bastard!

But on the other hand, what the hell had induced her to *accept* his invitation, anyway?

Perplexed, Bob took his first tentative bite of *bruschetta*. This resulted in a dribble of tomato-laced olive oil oozing through his fingers and plopping like bloated raindrops onto his side plate, which had been thrust under his chin not a second too soon by an alert and giggling Julie.

She took her napkin and leaned over the table to wipe his chin. "Hmm, extra virgin," she said, looking him in the eye, "Ye cannae whack it, son!"

Bob's laugh was spontaneous and uninhibited. He was no scientist, but he could recognise the chemistry that was at work here. And he liked it, despite a nagging voice in the back of his mind that kept repeating all the old once-bitten-twice-shy clichés. "I presume you're referring to the olive oil," he said, returning her glance.

Julie merely smiled a little coy smile, sat back in her seat, and took another immaculate nibble of *bruschetta*.

They ate in silence for a while; an easy, comfortable silence, with neither feeling any need to impose idle conversation upon the other.

"So why *did* you give up driving tractors?" Julie eventually asked, shamelessly licking the last succulent smudges of the *bruschetta* juices from each of her fingertips.

"First, I'd have to tell you why I *started* driving them, and I'm sure you're not really interested in all that old —"

106

"Listen, china," Julie interrupted, "I wouldn't have asked if I wasn't interested. So, come on — spill the beans!"

Bob had never talked about this part of his life to anyone before — not even to Sally, who had always seemed more interested in her tomorrows than his yesterdays. But now, here he was with a virtual stranger, effortlessly unburdening himself of details about his youth, some aspects of which had always been too saddening to even think about all that much.

Julie listened intently, sipping her wine and watching the changing expressions on Bob's face as his story unfolded.

He recalled how he had spent the first ten years of his life on one of the large farms outside Dirleton, where his father was grieve, or farm foreman, and where he and his younger brother and sister had been part of a family which, although not rich in financial terms, could hardly have been happier or more content with its lot. The farmer was a good and considerate employer, entrusting the day-to-day practicalities of running the farm to Bob's father, whilst ensuring that the equipment and machinery that his men worked with were the best available, and always maintained to the highest standard of safety. Similarly, the farm workers' cottages were kept in immaculate condition, with every reasonable modern convenience provided at the farmer's expense. In addition, it was only a short walk to the village, with its little school and close-knit community of friends. And at weekends and on long summer evenings, when the farm kids tired of their idyllic but over-familiar surroundings, the unspoiled and often deserted expanse of Yellowcraig beach was no more than an easy bike ride away.

But the mainstay of that simple Utopia was suddenly to be torn from Bob's family for ever . . .

"It's your Rab, Mrs Burns," the farmer had said, his voice breaking, his eyes filled with tears as he stood ashen-faced at their kitchen door on that bright July morning. "His tractor slid off the top of the silage pit where he was working. Just slid off as easy as that and overturned. Old Dod and I managed to get him out of the cab. I mean, we were right there as soon as it happened, but . . ." His voice faltered and the tears began to roll down his cheeks.

Bob was only nine years old, his brother seven, and his little sister barely five. His mother, although only just turned thirty herself, seemed to age before their eyes during the months that followed her husband's death, her hair turning grey almost overnight, her bonny, strong features becoming lined and careworn as the tribulations of bringing up three young children on her own began to exact their toll.

Meantime, the farmer and his wife couldn't have been more supportive, finding paid work for her whenever possible — on the platform of the mechanical potato digger in the autumn, perhaps, or sitting guiding the steerage hoe behind a tractor when it was time to weed the fields of young vegetables, occasionally looking after the electrical controls of the bulk grain drier at harvest time, even seeing to odd jobs in the farmhouse or in the garden when there wasn't much doing on the farm.

Then came the inevitable day when the farmer, in order to accommodate a new full-time tractorman and his family, was obliged to reclaim vacant possession of the Burnses' tied cottage. A seemingly harsh, but nonetheless necessary, fact of life on the farm had finally caught up with them.

The local council re-housed them in the village, of course, and although young Bob, his brother and sister took to the change well enough, the trauma of the move from the house that had always been their home had a telling effect on their mother. Exacerbated, perhaps, by the cold and damp conditions that so often prevailed in the farm work that she continued to undertake, she began to suffer from arthritis — first in her fingers, then her legs, shoulders and neck. She struggled on gamely for as long as she could, but by the time Bob was approaching his sixteenth birthday, so severe had his mother's condition become that it was impossible for her to continue working any more. She was now left with three teenagers to support and educate. And with the insurance compensation which had been paid following her husband's death all but gone in trying to make meagre ends meet, she was faced with the prospect of having no income other than the statutory State handouts. It was a depressing and demeaning situation for a hard-working woman of fiercely independent nature.

Bob's academic prowess at North Berwick High School had singled him out as a pupil almost guaranteed to qualify for a university place, with very real prospects of going on to realise his ambition of gaining a degree in law. But, before even sitting the first of his "Highers", prevailing circumstances at home made him decide to leave school to take up an offer of employment from a local farmer.

He interrupted his narrative for a moment to take a sip of beer and stare wistfully through the window. "But there's no use in wondering what might have been," he murmured, almost to himself. "*Che será será*, as Giovanni the boss in here is wont to say."

Bob paused while the waiter served them their main courses.

"Still," he went on when they were alone again, "at least it helped young Gilbert and Mary to get on with *their* education without the bailiffs coming knocking on the door."

"Gilbert and Mary — your brother and sister?"

"Yeah, and they've done OK for themselves. My folks would have been proud of them." Bob was making a brave attempt to put a cheery face on things. "They were a pair of bright kids at school, so they deserved to be given every chance. Gilbert's in Australia — chartered accountant — making a bloody fortune. And wee Mary's in the States — ex-interpreter at the UN — married an up-and-coming senator." He chuckled quietly. "Future First Lady, if I know her!"

"But your teachers at school," Julie frowned, "— didn't they try to persuade you to carry on with your *own* education? Surely there must have been some way . . ."

110

"Oh aye, the teachers, the headmaster, they all ranted and raved and came up with their tuppence-ha'penny worth of advice. But the decision was mine, and I did what I thought was best for the family at the time."

Julie cast Bob a look that was a mix of reproach and admiration. "Hmm, the *I Did It My Way* syndrome again, huh?"

"Unfortunately," Bob went on, his expression becoming reflective again, "the person it hurt worst of all was the person it was intended to help most."

"Your mother?"

"Right. I'm afraid she saw my decision to jack in school as a sign of some kind of failure on her part. It wasn't, of course. Hell, no woman could've done more for her kids under the circumstances." Bob's eyes glazed over. "But she was a proud woman, and by her way of thinking, she had somehow let me down."

"But what about picking up the threads of your studies later on? Couldn't you have done that?"

"Oh, that was my master plan, all right. Join the police, poke the old finger into the legal pie, so to speak, then hit the formal education trail again once Gilbert and Mary were safely into uni, but . . ."

"But the best-laid schemes o' mice and men, as the other Robert Burns so perceptively put it?"

"That's right. You get caught up in your job, you meet someone, you get married, take out a mortgage, and wham! Before you know it, you're past it."

There wasn't anything Julie could say to refute that, so she prudently redirected the conversation back to the present. "From what you say about this Haddington murder case you're embroiled with, it would appear that this DCI Spiers guy is hardly your number one fan. Again, none of my business, but maybe —"

"But maybe I should join the Masons?" Bob laughed.

"No, seriously, I was going to say that maybe you should bypass him, go above his head, take the whole thing to *his* boss, the Superintendent, or whoever he is."

Bob laughed again. "I appreciate what you're saying, but to try that one on, I'd probably have to be the Master of their lodge, and even then it would be doubtful if I'd get away with it. No, I know what's eating Jack Spiers, and there's damn all I can do about it, except press on regardless and hope for the best. You see, the Spiers situation goes back a long way . . ."

He proceeded to tell Julie of how, some years earlier, he had been assisting Jack Spiers — then still a detective sergeant himself — on what was being treated as a serial child-molesting case involving five police forces the length and breadth of Great Britain. A coordinating centre for the investigation had ultimately been set up at New Scotland Yard, and Jack Spiers and Bob had been obliged to commute weekly between Edinburgh and London, gathering relevant information from the Lothian and Borders Police area, then collating and assimilating it with the wider findings of the operation.

It was during this period that Bob first recognised Jack Spiers' qualities as an investigating officer — his blunt, no-nonsense manner being reflected in his approach to the job, and blending very effectively with his sharp and imaginative line of thought. It appeared that his tough upbringing in an orphanage had given him an edge and determination that many of his colleagues from more fortunate backgrounds lacked. And his will to succeed was paramount. If reaching his goal meant cutting corners and stepping on toes, then so be it. Then, as now, whatever Jack Spiers may have lacked in schooling and sophistication was more than compensated for in sheer ruthlessness.

What had originally been looked upon as merely a routine wrapping-up operation in London, perhaps lasting three or four weeks at most, eventually dragged on for six long months. It was less than halfway through this time that Sally first began to show signs of disillusionment with marriage — at least to Bob. Admittedly, she now lived in a stylish bungalow near Duddingston village on the eastern outskirts of Edinburgh, a much sought-after suburb that Bob had stretched his resources to the limit to buy into. And this was the reason for his regarding as most welcome — despite his deep dislike of being parted from his young wife for five days every week — the overtime pay and away-from-home allowances that came with the period of semi-exile in London. But it wasn't enough for Sally.

One Friday night, after flying up from London on the last shuttle of the day, Bob had arrived home to find Sally entertaining a rather dapper-looking, middle-aged man to drinks in the lounge. She'd introduced him as Rory Armstrong, a senior partner in the firm of George Street solicitors where she'd worked as a legal secretary before marrying Bob. She and Rory had just happened to bump into each other in Jenner's food hall in Princes Street that evening, she'd explained. Then, as it was threatening to rain, Rory had insisted on driving her home.

"But I must confess that I did have an ulterior motive," Rory had volunteered with that studied sort of amicable delivery that Bob had seen lawyers use so often in court and which he knew to be about as trustworthy as the welcoming smile of an alligator with worms. "You see, we're in the process of expanding the practice at present, and the long and short of it is that there's a staff vacancy for which I think your lovely wife here would be ideally suited . . . if I can coax you into letting her out of your sight for eight hours a day, that is."

Only too well did the smarmy rat know that there was bugger all anyone could do to stop Sally from doing whatever she bloody well wished, Bob had told himself. So what the hell, he'd thought. If that was what she wanted, then why not! It would give her something positive to do with her time, and God knows they needed the money.

As it turned out, though, a job was not the only thing that Rory Armstrong was able to give Sally. Long before Bob's London stint was over, Armstrong had also given her a taste for relaxed lunches and intimate dinners in some of Edinburgh's most discreet — and expensive — eateries, had encouraged her to become accustomed to driving his Porsche 911 Cabriolet between the office and the Law Courts, and even to using it for little shopping trips to one or other of the out-of-town hypermarkets of a sunny afternoon. In those, and countless other little ways, he had cunningly given Sally a glimpse of a luxury lifestyle which he knew she craved, and which her husband, humble Detective Bob Burns, would never be able to provide. And although he was more than twenty years her senior, the chances were that Rory Armstrong had also proved himself perfectly capable of providing Sally with the more physical necessities of life of which she had been deprived during her husband's regular absences on duty.

Rory Armstrong, Bob soon found out, had long been renowned as one of Scotland's leading divorce lawyers, and it was not to be long before he was preparing to add personal experience to his considerable professional know-how. Within a few days of Bob completing the London job, Sally had left their mortgaged-to-the-hilt Duddingston bungalow and had been installed in an upmarket Georgian flat in Edinburgh's New Town, there to reside in comfort until such time, no doubt, as Armstrong considered it prudent to have her replace his wife of twenty-five years in his luxury villa overlooking the River Forth at Crammond.

Although Bob had sensed the approaching break-up of his marriage for some time, it came as no less of a kick in the teeth when the crunch eventually came. For all the self-seeking traits which he had failed (or, perhaps, refused) to recognise in Sally before they married, and despite her infidelity with Armstrong, Bob's feelings for her had been as strong on the day she walked out as they had been on the day of their wedding ten years before.

"For a while after that, everything seemed pointless," he admitted to Julie. "The job, seeing friends, going to the shops, the pub, meeting people, all the normal things of life seemed unimportant, empty. It was as if she had died. Worse, in fact, because I knew she was still there, but with someone else. At first I really wanted to kill the bastard who'd taken her from me. But as time passes, you start to own up to yourself that, if it hadn't been him, it would eventually have been someone else. It was over. A chapter ended. But life goes on, and if you don't want to go under, you just have to get a grip of yourself and get on with it."

Realising that it was doing Bob good to get all this off his chest, Julie sat quietly, leaving him to gaze pensively into his glass until he was ready to continue.

After a few moments, he let out a little laugh. "The ironic thing is that it was making that decision to get on with my life that led to the bad blood being spilled with Jack Spiers. You see, I decided that the best way to keep my mind off Sally would be to concentrate all my thoughts and energies on my work."

"But surely Jack Spiers couldn't have taken exception to that!"

"Not as such. No, it was the specific thing that I set my mind to that bugged Jack. The point was that, at the end of that London stint, which had resulted in a sales rep from the Midlands being sent down for ten years, I still had a nagging feeling that something didn't quite add up. I couldn't quite put my finger on it, but there were a couple of details which bothered me in the case of one of the kids who'd been interfered with in our area. I'd mentioned it to Jack Spiers at the time, but, typically, he said that the case had been wrapped up, everyone who mattered was happy with the result, so don't make waves. Jack was already in line for promotion on the strength of the work he'd done in London, so it was obvious he didn't want anybody rocking the boat."

"But couldn't he see that it would have been another feather in his cap if he'd followed your hunch and it had resulted in something important being turned up?"

Bob smiled knowingly. "Oh, yeah, Jack was well aware of that, all right. And ninety-nine times out of a hundred he would have claimed the hunch as his own, if he'd believed it might do his career a bit of good. But he had bigger fish to fry this time. He'd been assigned to a case that had stardom-for-Jack-Spiers stamped all over it, if it turned out right, and he just was *not* interested in being sidetracked."

Julie listened closely as Bob went on to recount how, in the wake of Jack Spiers' brush-off, he had taken his thoughts on the matter to his then DCI, only to have them dismissed in similar fashion. No one had any inclination to dredge up superficially insignificant details of a case that had already been put cosily to bed. So, with no Sally to spend his non-working hours with, Bob had finally resolved to fill his spare time by making some discreet enquiries of his own into the aspects of the case that had been worrying him.

The result was his identifying an Edinburgh truck driver, who he was convinced could have been responsible for at least one of the incidents — that of the attempted abduction of a child on the city's south side. But to take it as far as making an arrest would have required the employment of much more concentrated investigative resources than Bob could ever have hoped to improvise on his own. Anyway, his request to have the case re-opened was turned down flat, both by the newly-promoted Inspector Jack Spiers and by his DCI, a man in the twilight of his career, named Adam Lindsay.

Julie was astonished. "Surely that should have been the time for you to go direct to the top banana, whoever he was!"

"And that's exactly what I made up my mind to do. But I knew I had to be bloody sure of my facts before I went dropping my guv'nors in the deep stuff, so I spent another fortnight of my spare time checking and rechecking everything I'd dug up so far. Then I submitted a full written report to the Super."

"Hey, you're not going to tell me that he binned it as well!"

"No, but he didn't exactly get the finger out to set the appropriate wheels in motion either." Bob took a deep breath, his brows knotting into a rueful frown. "And during the week that he was sitting on it, a five year-old kid was found floating in the Water of Leith behind Powderhall Greyhound Stadium. She'd been strangled and sexually assaulted — though probably not, they reckoned, in that order . . . the poor, wee mite."

Julie grimaced. "And the bastard who did it was the truck driver that you'd already fingered for being involved in the other case?"

"I'm afraid so," Bob shrugged. "The stuff in my report fitted the killer exactly. All the Detective Superintendent had to do was hand my file down the line to Jack Spiers and they had their man right away. They nailed him while he was stalking another youngster on her way home from school over on the south side."

"So, Jack Spiers was hauled over the coals for ignoring your hunch in the first place, and he's had it in for you ever since, right?"

A philosophical smile crossed Bob's face. "I wish," he murmured, "but instead of Spiers and his gaffer Lindsay being booted up the backside, the whole lousy episode was covered up, and the three brass hats involved came out smelling of roses."

Julie could hardly contain herself. "But that's incredible!" she gasped. "That little kid would still have been alive today if they'd followed your hunch in the first place. Spiers and his two bosses were guilty of gross professional negligence and should have been made the subject of an independent enquiry, surely!"

"And risk having the truth about the avoidable murder of a child being made public?" Bob gave a little laugh. "That's the last thing the people at the top of the tree wanted, you can be sure of that. No, the whole thing was swept smartly under the carpet. Lindsay and his Super took early retirement shortly afterwards, and Jack Spiers was recommended for further promotion for masterminding such a rapid arrest of the killer. And all that on the back of what he'd done by simply following up that report that *I* had done off my own bat and in my own time." Bob heaved a shrug of resignation. "My report was unofficial, you see. It was never logged in the computer, so it never really existed."

"And there was *nothing* you could do to expose these swine?"

Bob shook his head. "Think about it. Who could I report them to, outside the self-interested clique upstairs at HQ? My MP? Nah, even if he'd believed me, which is highly unlikely, I'd probably have found out that he did the same funny handshakes as the buggers I was trying to knock down. But most importantly, there was the family of the murdered kid to think about. What would an exposé of the facts of this particular instance of high-ranking police shenanigans have done for them? It would only have caused them even more hurt. But it wouldn't have brought their bairn back."

Julie tutted indignantly. "I don't know how you brought yourself to go on working with a character like Spiers. Honestly, if I'd been in your shoes, I'd have demanded a transfer out of his team pronto!"

He had considered that, too, Bob assured her. He'd even thought about chucking the job completely — maybe going to college as a mature student to get the

"Highers" he needed to go to law school. But, at the end of the day, he'd reckoned that quitting the force would only have been playing into Jack Spiers' hands, would only have been letting him off the hook. For, as long as Bob was around, he would be a thorn in Spiers' flesh. Sooner or later the bugger would slip up again. His preoccupation with his own advancement would see to that. Except, this time, Bob would be ready for him.

Julie nodded her head. "And you think that maybe that opportunity has arrived — the way he's trying to tie up this present murder case so fast?"

"Who knows? All I can say is that I'm getting those same old gut feelings, and come what may, I'm going to go through everything with a fine-toothed comb until I settle it one way or the other." He raised a disconsolate eyebrow. "Trouble is, Spiers has taken my working file from me, so I think it's a foregone conclusion that I'll be booted off the case in the morning."

"So, what now?"

"So, now we enjoy our meal," Bob replied brightly, before standing up and making for the door. "Excuse me for just a moment, though," he called back. "I've spotted that young beat policeman out there again, so I'm going to ask him to do me a little favour."

Bob was back in a trice. "A bottle of champagne, please, Giovanni," he shouted towards the bar. "We're celebrating!"

"We're celebrating what, for heaven's sake?" Julie hissed, somewhat taken aback by the attention Bob's sudden flamboyance was attracting from the other diners.

"For starters, we're celebrating the fact that I'm not driving any more tonight. That young copper is going to park my car for me at Gayfield Square police station round the corner. I'll pick it up there in the morning." He gave Julie a mischievous wink. "And I'm sure we'll find something else to drink to if we really try!"

So far, both Bob and Julie had purposely avoided broaching the rather unsavoury subject of why they had actually met there that evening, and it wasn't until they'd reached the stage of swapping mellow pleasantries over late-night *cappuccinos* and glasses of *Strega* that Julie casually asked, "Don't you think it's about time we got down to business, Sergeant?"

With a look of pretend astonishment, Bob exclaimed, "Puh-leez! I know I may look like the nearest thing to Al Pacino in here, but that doesn't mean I'm game for doing my Italian Stallion bit in the middle of a restaurant!"

"Trust me to come on too strong," Julie kidded. She gave herself a chastening slap on the wrist. "A plate of stuffed pasta tubes and a coupla glasses of bubbly and I'm anybody's!"

"I should be so lucky," Bob countered, then quickly cleared his throat, adopting an appropriately more serious manner, albeit reluctantly. "You're absolutely right, ehm, Doctor Bryson. This *is* a murder enquiry, after all, so we really should get down to business. Now then, this interesting information you've got for me. What's it all about?"

"Paraquat weedkiller, remember? The gardener's gloves? The oral swab from the victim?"

"OK, so what have you come up with?"

"First of all, there were no traces of paraquat or vegetable-derived lubricating oil on the gardener's gloves. Just about everything on them could be classified as organic — grass or plant stains, soil, compost, that sort of thing. *Plus*, the gloves' cotton fibres were of a considerably coarser texture than those of the scrap of material found near the body. Secondly, there were no traces of paraquat on the first swab." Julie looked enquiringly at Bob. "Does that tell you anything that you didn't know before?"

Bob shook his head. "It only confirms what the old caretaker at the hospital said — that Billy Thomson didn't wear those cotton gloves for spraying weedkiller. It also confirms that the scrap of material I found at the scene of the crime didn't come from Billy's gloves, whether he was wearing them or not, right?"

"That's the way it looks."

"And yet, the scrap did have traces of the victim's blood on it," Bob thought aloud, "*and* it was snagged on a splinter of wood from the murder weapon. But without evidence of the victim having consumed paraquat . . ."

"Look, I don't want to stick my nose in where it's not wanted," Julie ventured, "but if I knew what you were on about, I might just be able to help."

Bob waved a dismissive hand. "Nah, it was only a wild notion I had — not even worth bothering about now. I'll just mark it off as another inspired Burns theory that went down the pipes."

"Never mind, tell me about it anyway. I'm interested. Honestly I am."

While having an innate aversion to sharing any of his more private thoughts on a case with anyone, Bob was forced to admit to himself that, in this instance, the process of bouncing his ideas off an unbiased pair of ears like Julie's might prove mildly therapeutic, if nothing else. After all, she'd sat patiently through a deluge of all his most closely-guarded personal confidences already, so if she really wanted to be subjected to all this investigative dross . . .

"Bertie suffered from emphysema," he submitted as an opener. "Does that mean anything to you?"

A glint of enthusiasm flickered in Julie's eyes. "Lung disease. And I'm beginning to get your drift already!"

Encouraged by her positive response, Bob pressed on. "So, when you told me on the phone that you'd found signs of paraquat weedkiller on that shred of cotton —"

"You thought, emphysema — paraquat — eureka! Maybe the apparently violent cause of death had only been a cover for something a bit more subtle. Something even more diabolical than an unpremeditated wallop on the head with a garden spade could have been involved here, correct?"

"That's what crossed my mind at the time," Bob affirmed, Julie's immediate tuning in to his wavelength giving him reason to proceed with even less inhibition. "And you obviously don't need me to tell you that the

124

potentially fatal aspect of ingesting paraquat is the detrimental effect it has on the lungs."

Julie nodded her head rapidly, indicating a definite professional familiarity with the subject. "Pulmonary oedema, congestion and consolidation."

"Which means, in layman's lingo?"

"A one-way ticket to stiff city for the price of little more than a gram of the stuff."

"In a nutshell. And if old Bertie had croaked after sipping a drop or two of it, the symptoms of her death — terminal shortage of breath, in layman's lingo — would more than likely have been put down to the relentless march of her emphysema." Bob pursed his lips in an I-rest-my-case sort of way.

"Bingo!" Julie called out, puckering in concert, and oblivious to the consternation that her sudden shout had caused a prudish-looking elderly couple sitting at the next table. "The perfect murder!"

"Mmm, except for the minor detail that no paraquat showed up in your oral-swab analysis." There was a moment of pensive silence before Bob added, "I thought it was a cute idea at the time, I must admit. But, on reflection, maybe it was just a bit too cute to be true."

Julie wagged a finger at him. "You weren't listening, Sergeant. What I said was that there were no traces of paraquat on the *first* swab." She noted the look of puzzlement on Bob's face, then continued. "You see, for some reason best known to himself, your mate Alex in the morgue sent me two swabs — one labelled with the victim's name as usual, the other simply marked 'Dixie'."

"Go on." Bob said. He was giving nothing away.

"Well, the 'Dixie' swab was predominantly blood, but blood mixed with a liberal quantity of milk, of all things, *and* a discernible dose of paraquat." It was Julie's face that displayed puzzlement now. She released a tense little laugh. "I mean, if I'd had time, I'd have run a test on the blood groups, because my instinct just couldn't reconcile the two samples as having come from the same body. They were just so . . . *different*."

Bob's smile was one of amusement tinged with intrigue. "Maybe that wicked old bugger Alex only sent you the second swab as a kind of sick joke. I don't know, but I wouldn't put it past him. The main thing, though, is that he may well have helped lend my theory an even more cute dimension than I could have imagined."

Julie frowned over the froth of her second *cappuccino*. "Elucidate, mate. We scientists aren't noted for our expertise in cuteness assessment, you know." She looked Bob up and down with deliberate exaggeration. "Not in relation to sleuthery theories, at any rate."

Prompted by a sense of mounting elation, Bob signalled to the barman for another couple of *Stregas*, before turning back to Julie and whispering over the table in cod confidentiality, "Dixie was the victim's cat, my dear. Banjoed on the bonce in like fashion to her mistress with Exhibit A, would you believe!"

Stifling an involuntary giggle, Julie whispered back, "You don't mean to say that who done it not only felled the old dear, but wasted her pussy too?" She could contain the inevitable snigger no longer. "Hey!" she giggled, "just think yourself lucky that she didn't have a dog, a budgie and a pair of goldfish as well. Talk about your mass murders!"

Bob assumed an air of mock admonishment as the waiter recharged their liqueur glasses. "A little decorum, Doc, *please*," he muttered to Julie. "Death isn't a laughing matter, you know." Then, turning to the waiter, he asked, "Wouldn't you agree, Franco?"

The waiter pulled a one-shouldered Italian shrug. "I gotta uncle back in-a the old country who's-a in the undertake business. For him, he's-a always say, 'Where there's-a death, there's-a hope.' So, for-a him, is always a laughing matter. Capeesh?" With a sinister chuckle, he replaced the top on the *Strega* bottle and wheeled back towards the bar. "*Salute, eh!*"

"I'm sorry," Julie said to Bob, cringing slightly at the attention the starchy pair at the next table were paying them. "I didn't mean to appear flippant. It's just the wine and the champers and the *Strega* and the idea of someone going bonkers outside an oldies' ward with a garden spade and — and . . ." She started to giggle again. "Sorry, it's the cat bit." She was wiping the tears from her eyes now. "It just reminded me of that Tom and Jerry cartoon where Tom gets clobbered so hard on the kisser with a shovel that his whole head goes shovel-shaped." Covering her face with her hands, she dissolved into a fit of tittering.

Bob was grinning. "Heavens above, madam," he exclaimed theatrically, "I do believe you're quite tiddly!" With a nonchalant nod of the head, he then acknowledged the flagrant gawping of the two nearby prigs. "It's all right," he smiled comfortingly, "she's from Glasgow."

Bob was enjoying himself. He couldn't remember the last time he'd indulged in such silly banter. Although the effect of the evening's drink consumption on a metabolism so long deprived of solid nourishment had to be responsible in part for his frivolity, it was evident that the empathy that had been established between himself and Julie Bryson was a significant contributory factor as well. At that moment, it would have been all too easy to dismiss from his mind all thoughts of the Bertie McGregor case.

In the event, it was Julie who reverted to practicalities by giving her nose a composure-restoring blow and announcing in a businesslike voice that was pitched for the benefit of the ear-flapping occupants of the next table, "Anyway, Detective Sergeant, you were about to explain to me how the possible augmentation of poisoning to the ostensible battering to death of her dear pet may have added a dimension of cuteness to your theory regarding the modus operandi of the horrible homicide of poor Miss Thingmy. Do go on, please." She glanced sidelong at the *zabaglione*-supping pair of eavesdroppers. "And spare me no details of the gallons of snot and phlegm involved. You know how I *love* it when you talk disgusting."

128

The attentions (and *zabaglione*-supping) of their dining neighbours thus summarily terminated, Bob continued his theorising.

"It's an attractive enough hypothesis, in a gruesome sort of way," Julie conceded when he had finished, "but it still begs the question as to how the murderer managed to get poison into the cat's milk, and how Bertie rumbled the fact at the crucial moment, prompting the culprit to resort to basic spade work — pun intentional."

Bob tapped the side of his nose. "Aha, but I've got a theory for that too." He held up a hand. "But don't ask what it is — not just yet. I've got a bit more work to do on that one."

"Well, far be it from me to side with the enemy," Julie said bluntly, "but I've got to say that, the more I think about it, the more I'd probably have been inclined to go along with Jack Spiers and plump for the gardener as well. OK, there's the bit of cloth with the weedkiller and the splinter from the spade handle, but unless you can identify the actual gloves that the cloth came from *and* link their owner with the crime *and* establish a motive, it seems to me that you've got precious little to go on. Let's face it, even the smudges of blood on the cloth could have been picked up on the ground where you found it. The cloth might simply have blown into the shrubbery after the event."

Bob smiled patiently as Julie continued to wrestle with the facts.

"And the same could apply to the paraquat," she suggested after a brief moment of contemplation. "The

129

cat could have drunk contaminated milk anywhere — not necessarily in the shrubbery and not necessarily poured by the hand of the spade-wielder."

"All very true," Bob freely conceded, his demeanour exuding a degree of calm self-assurance, which Julie found difficult to square with the serious predicament that she knew him to be facing. "Very true, except that there was no wind yesterday evening — not even the slightest breeze. But I take your point."

"Right, so how do you reckon Jack Spiers is going to take all this gardening gloves and weedkiller stuff when you put it to him tomorrow morning?"

"I think it's a dead cert he'll bin it before I get to the end of the first sentence. That's if I do put it to him tomorrow morning. Which I probably won't."

Julie massaged her brow. "I don't get it. I mean, surely the only way you can hope to justify what Spiers sees as your maverick way of handling the case is to come clean about all these little thoughts and suspicions of yours. Otherwise, you're only putting yourself in the wrong by withholding information."

Bob shook his head and gave a quiet chuckle. "With anyone else but him, probably. But Jack Spiers has already made up his mind, and I've learned from experience that the best use I can make of these little thoughts and suspicions of mine is to keep them to myself until the time's right." His lips twisted into a foxy smile. "Besides, the forensic reports on the swabs, on the scrap of cloth and on Billy Thomson's gloves don't officially exist yet, do they? So how can I discuss them with Spiers?"

130

"Ah, so that's why you asked me to do the tests on the q.t., is it? Dealing yourself a few up-the-sleeve aces, huh?"

"Or jokers. Depends how the game goes."

"You're taking a bit of a chance, aren't you?" Julie teased. "Let's face it, I could blow the gaff at any time just by revealing to your boss — as I really should — that one of his detective sergeants has sweet-talked me into doing a few under-the-counter forensic tests."

"I realise that well enough, believe me," Bob acknowledged, "and don't think I'm not grateful."

Julie gestured to their candle-lit table and the cosy surroundings of the little trattoria. "Say no more. What's a secure job for life and an index-linked pension compared to all this?"

"True — and anyway, even if you did feel you were duty-bound to pass on your findings to Spiers right away, you could bet your last test tube that he'd keep them just as shtum as I'm doing — but for very different reasons."

Julie made a vague swatting motion with her hands. "All too foxy for a simple scientist like me, I'm afraid." She looked Bob straight in the eye. "But I *will* have to record those analyses and the results sooner or later, you know."

"Do it tomorrow," Bob shrugged. "As I say, I doubt if it'll make a blind bit of difference to Jack Spiers' attitude."

"Just as well," Julie sighed, a noticeable note of relief in her voice, "because I wasn't planning on doing anything about it for the next couple of weeks anyway."

131

Bob tilted his head inquiringly.

"Why do you think I left my home phone number on your answering machine and then accepted your invitation to come out tonight?" Julie asked, her face expressionless.

Bob tried to appear unfazed by the bluntness of her question. "Because you fancied the sound of my voice on the phone?" he ventured, unable to disguise the optimistic inflection in his words.

Julie maintained her deadpan look. "Because, as from now, Sergeant Burns, I'm on a fortnight's holiday, and I was under the impression that the results of my tests were likely to be crucial to this case. But now I'm informed that they're only to be used as bottom-of-the-deck cards in a vindictive poker game you're playing with your gaffer."

Bob could only admit the truth. "You're right on both counts, and I really can't say any more than that at this stage."

Leaning over the table towards him, Julie contorted her face into a menacing glower and grunted in an overdone Gorbals accent, "See you, polisman — if you drap me in the keech, Ah'll hing wan right oan ye!" She grabbed his lapel and mimed a Glasgow kiss. "Get ma message, pal?"

Bob drew back into his chair and raised his hands in submission. "Don't worry, I've grown accustomed to my teeth, so just trust me, OK?" He gave her a sly wink. "Maybe more will be revealed when I put old Bertie's crossword solution to the test."

"Crossword solution? What are you on about now, for heaven's sake?"

"I won't bore you with the details right now, but the clue was, *An Aberdonian Police Chief Could Be Expected To Protect His Carefully.*"

Julie didn't even have to ponder that one. "*Coppers, right?*"

Shaking his head, Bob mimicked her previous deadpan expression. "Nope — *Grass!*"

"*Grass?*" she gasped incredulously, then stared closely into his eyes in the manner of an examining doctor. "Huv you been puffin' the wacky baccy yersel', boy?"

Bob had to laugh. Deep down, Julie must have had a few nagging doubts about bending the rules of her job to oblige a total stranger like him, yet she didn't appear to allow such material considerations — no matter how professionally sacrosanct — to get in the way of her sense of humour. Bob liked her style.

"You were damned lucky to get a fortnight's holiday so soon after starting the job through here," he said by way of diverting the conversation away from his own mundane career problems.

"No, as it happens, your mob were quite happy to roll over my leave arrangements for this year from Strathclyde. It wasn't any big deal — just one of the wee perks of working for the great brotherhood of Scottish polis constabularies, I suppose."

Bob's immediate inclination was to ask if her old man just happened to be a Mason, but exercised a modicum of polite discretion in favour of: "Going somewhere exotic, are you?"

Julie jerked her head in the general direction of the door. "Up a communal stair round the corner there in Forth Street, if that's classed as exotic here in Edinburgh. That flat of mine was rented out to a bunch of art students before I bought it, so apart from getting rid of the ingrained exotic hum of half-dollar spliffs and carry-out Rubies, which is enough to give you the boak every time you open the front door, I'm gonna have to paint over those mauve walls and tangerine ceilings before I go totally Hare Krishna in my sleep."

Feeling relieved that she wasn't about to disappear into the wide, blue yonder for the next two weeks, Bob said, "There you are, I told you we'd have something else to drink to before the night was over." He raised his *Strega* glass. "Here's to a fortnight of doing it yourself!"

Julie smiled that coy little smile of hers again, sat back in her chair and fixed Bob in a smouldering stare. "DIY is *not* my bag, big boy," she cooed in a sultry drawl that was straight out of the Mae West Seduction Manual. "Why don't you come up and see for yourself sometime?"

"Gee thanks," Bob grinned. "I'll — ehm — I'll bring my paintbrush."

CHAPTER
EIGHT

Detective Chief Inspector J. A. Spiers, the sign on the door read. A gruff holler of "Come!" was the response to Bob's knock. He entered the office to be greeted by a view of the back of Jack Spiers' head — his best angle, Bob always reckoned. Spiers was on the phone, the swivel chair behind his desk turned through 180 degrees, his feet resting crossed on the window sill.

The room was almost a mirror image of Bill Blackie's across the corridor. The same spartan, standard-issue furniture; the same typically-stale office smells of musty records permeating from metal filing cabinets; the same drab paintwork and naked windows; the same bloody charmless career-policeman's sty, in fact. Bob's thoughts involuntarily returned to the long-relinquished charms of tractor-driving, and at that particular moment they could hardly have seemed more appealing.

He surveyed the room again, trying to close his ears to the heavy-duty bollocking that Spiers was dishing out to some poor bastard on the phone. Hell, at least Bill Blackie's Connie had fixed him up with a few framed Ikea prints and a sprinkling of artificial flowers to humanise his dreary workplace a bit, but this dump of Jack Spiers' ... Still, you'd scarcely expect a torn-faced pain in the neck like Lauren Spiers to waste any of her precious social-climbing time on lending much thought to the home comforts of her husband's office, even if he wanted her to — which he probably didn't.

"Torn-faced pain in the neck." Not for the first time, Bob turned the phrase over in his mind. That was exactly how the secretary lass at the old folks' home in Scone had described the strange woman who had been snooping around Perth yesterday, trying to find out where Pinkie Dalrymple had gone. Trouble was, though, that none of the other details of her description matched Lauren Spiers — except, maybe, for the hairy legs. Disguise? Possibly. Nah, too far-fetched. Besides, as far as he knew, Mrs Spiers was still cooped up in her side ward at Roodlands Hospital in Haddington. Bob banished the whole notion to the back of his mind.

His eyes lighted on an old black-and-white press photograph, framed a touch over-extravagantly, and purposely positioned on the otherwise barren wall exactly opposite Jack Spiers' desk, so that, every time he raised his head, he would be obliged to look at it. Bob had noticed it many times before, but had never paid it any attention. He sauntered over to take a closer look. It was a shot of two men in dinner suits, presumably taken at some formal police function or other. He recognised one of the subjects as a youthful Jack Spiers, his face in profile as he grinned awestruck at the stocky figure beside him. This was a well-groomed man of maturing years, whose natural but controlled smile, aimed directly into the camera, suggested that he was no stranger to media attention.

"Chief Constable William Merryfield of the old Edinburgh City Police," DCI Spiers boomed, clashing the phone down and jabbing a finger in the direction of the photo. "Finest damned copper that this country has ever produced. Started at rock bottom and clawed his way to the top by sheer hard work . . . *and* exceptional talent."

"Your hero, I take it, Chief?" The note of sarcasm in Bob's voice was entirely spontaneous, and he instantly wished he'd kept his trap shut. "Yeah, I know all about Willie Merryfield," he quickly added as an attempt to cover up. "I met him once myself, as a matter of fact — just after I joined up. Well, I didn't actually *meet* him — just had a pee about three bowls along from him in the gents' bog at Tulliallan Police College when he was there taking a passing out parade of rookies. Great man, though. A shining example to us all."

Spiers was buying none of this blarney. "You're full of shit, Burns," he snarled. "In my book, people like you aren't even fit to have a run-off in the same room as a man of Wullie Merryfield's calibre."

"Ah well, Chief, that's what made wee Willie stand out from the rest, for want of a better expression. Always remembered his humble beginnings, didn't he? No matter how high up the ladder he climbed, he didn't mind who he pissed beside — as opposed to on, like certain of his would-be emulators have done since."

Every time Bob opened his mouth now, his tongue was digging him into a deeper hole. He couldn't help it.

137

It just was. Must have been all that bloody *Strega* he consumed last night, he guessed. *Strega* was Italian for witch. That much he knew. And as if making his head feel like it had been walloped by the business end of a broomstick wasn't enough, it now seemed that a spell had been cast on his mouth as well. And the spell spelt "trouble".

Spiers was glaring daggers at him. "You're in deep enough shite as it is without trying to be a comedian, Burns," he muttered through his teeth. From a desk drawer he pulled out the file which he had taken from Bob at the Kinross service station the previous evening. "While you were swanning about the countryside chasing red herrings yesterday, young DC Bain had to stand in for you at that Dalkeith incident, and do you know what happened?"

"He did such a fine job that you've decided to promote him direct to detective inspector?"

Spiers thumped his fist on the desk and snapped, "He stopped a bullet in the leg when he entered a flat to question one of those pieces of human trash suspected of being involved in that bungled robbery, that's what happened!" His face was livid, his lips trembling. "That damned bullet had your name on it, Burns!"

Bob bowed his head in a show of simulated self-reproach. "Sorry about that, boss. I'll do my utmost to get myself shot — at least in the leg — at the first opportunity, if it'll make you feel any better." The *Strega* was working well.

138

Jack Spiers was on the verge of going nuclear. He lifted Bob's confiscated case file and spilled its contents onto the desk. "And *this* is all you've got to show for a whole day of buggering about yesterday." He scattered the sundry items with a sideways sweep of his hand. "Not one bloody iota more than I had already gleaned with the assistance of a bunch of hick bobbies before you even turned up at the murder scene the evening before!"

Unruffled, Bob lifted a tubular chair from a stack of three by the door, trailed it over to the desk and slumped onto it. "There's plenty more info, if you're really interested."

Spiers snapped his fingers in Bob's face. "Your notebook, Burns," he growled. "Give it here!"

Bob dipped into the breast pocket of his jacket. "Be my guest," he said, lobbing the notebook onto the desk.

Jack Spiers snatched it up and thumbed impatiently through the pages. "There's bugger all in here, except . . ." He peered at the scribbled writing on the very last page, then rasped, "Who the hell's Andrew, for Christ's sake?"

"Not who — what. It's Andrex. Toilet roll. Bumph. It's the stuff we lesser mortals, who haven't got brown-nosed minions like DI Blackie to call upon, use to wipe our arses." Bob grabbed the notebook back. "You're reading my shopping list!"

Just as Jack Spiers was about to blow his stack completely, Bob stuck his hand into his inside pocket again and produced a folded piece of paper. "Another small iota that my buggering about unearthed, sir." He shoved the paper across the desk. "You wouldn't want me to withhold anything, no matter how trivial, would you?"

If Jack Spiers discerned the irony loaded in Bob's last remark, he made no sign of it. He unfolded the paper, his expression turning from pent-up rage to open mockery as he quickly scanned the script. "The old bint wanted to leave all her wordly posessions — fuck all, in other words — to her *cat*?" His face a study in derision, he rapped the paper with the fingernails of his right hand and frowned at Bob. "What sort of puerile crap is this?"

"The sort of puerile crap that your wife saw fit to put her name to as a witness, sir."

Spiers reaction was predictably dismissive. "That's the kind of twisted aspersion that only a mind like yours could come up with, Burns. For your information, my wife and her volunteer social work colleagues are asked to witness dozens of these worthless documents for senile cretins every year."

Bob elected to make no comment on that remark, but said instead, "You'd better put this in the file as well." He passed Spiers the small plastic bag containing the picture postcard of Perth which he had found in Bertie's old cottage at Archerfield Estate.

Jack Spiers gingerly fished out the dirty, mouse-nibbled card with the tips of his forefinger and thumb. "Is this what you were gaping at when I spotted you in the Granada café yesterday?"

Bob pulled a noncommittal shrug.

140

Spiers responded with a scowl of suspicion, then raised the card to the light. "And what the hell did you expect to see when you were holding this filthy abortion up to the window?"

"I was checking to see if there were any clues written in the bluebottle shit, sir. It's a hereditary gift I got from my granny. She used to read tea leaves, you know."

That did it. The *Strega*-fuelled bluebottle shit finally hit the fan.

"Right, Burns," Spiers erupted, "if that's the way you want it —"

"I haven't finished," Bob interrupted, his assertive manner taking the wind out of Jack Spiers' sails. "There are a few more little iotas that you should know about, and the most important is that the postcard was written by a lifelong friend of Bertie McGregor's, called Pinkie Dalrymple." He didn't give Spiers a chance to get a word in. "I traced her to that nursing home in Scone that I told you about, but it turns out that she checked out of the place a while back and hasn't been seen since. Nobody knows where the hell she is. I'm telling you, Chief, something about all this stinks."

Spiers was still fuming. "And what precisely do you think this Pinkie person's got to do with the McGregor murder, may I ask?"

Bob spread his hands. "Something. I don't know exactly what yet, but something. And the fact that she simply disappeared off the face of the earth suggests to me that —"

"Has she been reported missing to Tayside Police in Perth?" Spiers butted in.

"No, but I think we should suggest to the principal of the nursing home up there that she does just that, and bloody smartly, too. I wasn't the only one asking about Pinkie's whereabouts in Perth yesterday, by the way."

Jack Spiers settled back in his seat, arms folded, his expression suddenly benign, in one of those apparent changes of mood that he seemed able to turn on at will. "Would it surprise you to learn that we already know all about this Pinkie Dalrymple and that she's in no way regarded as someone relevant to this case?"

Bob was stuck for words, and it showed.

"You appear surprised, Burns. As usual, you'd have made life easier for yourself if only you'd had the savvy to follow orders." There was a slightly less-than-convincing smile of self-satisfaction on Spiers' lips as he added, "Just for the record, though, did you come up with anything at all that might have pointed to the whereabouts of the Dalrymple woman?"

Bob could almost feel Pinkie's Mallorcan postcard burning a hole in his jacket pocket as he lied, "No, sir. Nothing at all." Spiers was up to something, of that he was now certain. And if the devious bastard wanted to play funny games, Bob was happy to join in. The Mallorcan postcard and the snapshot of Pinkie would now be added to his up-the-sleeve stash of playing cards that Julie Bryson had half joked about over dinner the night before.

Bob Burns and Jack Spiers sat looking at each other, stone-faced and emotionless. The poker game had started.

"You thought you were going to be able to put one over on me at last, didn't you, Burns?" Spiers opened. He stroked his top lip slowly, his eyes cold and penetrating.

Bob held his stare, but didn't answer.

"It's the old Scotland Yard needle, isn't it?" Spiers goaded. "You still haven't come to terms with the fact that you made an arse of yourself after that job, have you?"

Without even blinking, Bob shook his head defiantly. "Correction. *You* made an arse of me. But you're right — I still haven't come to terms with it."

Spiers was about to speak again, but Bob cut him off. "Why did you haul me into this Bertie McGregor case anyway? Did you honestly think I'd been knocked back long enough to turn into the kind of yes-man who'd look in the other direction while you were taking another of your dodgy shortcuts to stardom?"

The rage rose crimson in Jack Spiers' cheeks. "You mummy's boy bastard!" he spat.

"My mother's dead, sir, so I think we should keep her out of it," Bob replied, consciously refraining from rising to the bait of Spiers' favourite insult — a derogatory expression all his own that everyone presumed to be a legacy of his formative years spent in the orphanage.

But those same tough years had also taught Jack Spiers the street psychology of an alley cat. "You're a born loser, Burns," he barked. "A bloody mummy's boy loser. No wonder your wife buggered off with that old lawyer ponce!" The psychology worked. With patent relish he watched Bob's hackles rising, a humourless grin contorting his mouth as he nodded at his subordinate's tightly clenched fists. "Go on, mummy's boy — take a poke at me." He stuck out his jaw. "Make my day!"

Though it was a struggle, Bob somehow managed to suppress his desperate need to land one right on that supercilious, leering mug. "Let me tell you something, Chief," he growled, his voice trembling with bottled-up temper, "I've often wondered what the A in your initials stood for, but now I know."

Still grinning, Spiers motioned him to come out with it.

"To put it politely, sir," Bob responded with a degree of restraint that surprised even himself, "when God put teeth in your mouth, he ruined a perfectly good example of your middle name — arsehole!"

That remark wiped the fake smile off Jack Spiers' face, and it also brought the sham poker game to an abrupt close. Spiers slapped his hand on the desk. "You're not only off the case, Sergeant," he spluttered, "you're bloody well suspended until further notice! There'll be a full enquiry into your disobedience of orders yesterday — a wilful and worthless act, which resulted in a potentially fatal injury to a fellow officer — and your display of gross insubordination to me this morning will be taken fully into account." He took a deep breath and lowered his voice, like a judge about to

144

pronounce the death sentence. "I must remind you that you are required to surrender your police ID and your car forthwith."

He opened a desk drawer and lifted out a cassette recorder which was still running. Switching it off, he continued in menacing tones that had been tuned to perfection over the years in order to put the shits up hapless villains cringing across the table from him in smoky, claustrophobic interrogation rooms. "Your goose is cooked, Burns. And if I have my way, you won't just end up back on the beat as a uniformed constable, you'll be out of the force on your fucking arse!" Exposing the microphone which had been concealed behind the in-tray on his desk, he smirked contentedly, "I've been waiting for the right chance to nail you since you tried to kick the feet from under me after that damned nipper was bumped off behind Powderhall Stadium. And now everything I need is down here on tape."

"Snap!" Bob smiled. He stood up and took a Philips Pocket Memo from his top pocket. Holding it aloft as he walked towards the door, he smugly added, "Except this machine is still recording . . . sir!"

CHAPTER
NINE

It was going to be another warm one. You could tell by the way the the shrouds of mist that still clung to the slopes of Salisbury Crags were already lifting, slowly unveiling the sun.

Bob Burns was in a perfect position to observe, if not entirely appreciate, this promising start to an Edinburgh summer's day. He was standing at a bus stop in St Leonards, after leaving his police Mondeo at the local nick, as Spiers had told him to, for no other apparent reason than because it was on the opposite side of the city from where Bob lived. Naturally, there had been several offers of a lift home from erstwhile colleagues, but Bob had declined them all. Best get accustomed to using public transport, and better sooner than later. That had been his immediate outlook.

Truth to tell, he was still reeling from the indefinite suspension from duties that Spiers had slapped on him, and maybe he wasn't thinking too clearly yet. Sure, he'd been fairly resigned to being taken off the case. He knew that was already on the cards. But the red card . . .?

He checked the details displayed on the bus stop again. It appeared that all routes led to Princes Street, but damned few buses ended up anywhere near Stockbridge. What a bloody system! And those nerds on the Council were hell-bent on barring private cars from the busiest parts of town as well. More city centre car parks and narrower pavements were what was needed — not the other way round. Well, that was Bob's immediate opinion. Hell, he then told himself, he'd only been without his perks of "company" car and taken-for-granted carte blanche to park anywhere in Edinburgh (no matter how much yellow paint had been splattered about) for five minutes, and already he was thinking like a disgruntled civvy. Maybe he should have accepted one of those offers of a lift in a panda car after all.

Bugger it! Bob turned tail and began to hoof it. What he needed to do first and foremost now was think, and a leisurely stroll across town would be more conducive to that than being flung around on the top of some uncomfortable, diesel-spewing double-decker. Besides, although he was loath to admit it, he couldn't for the life of him figure out from that infernal list of routes and numbers how to get by bus from where he was to Stockeree, anyway. And even if he could have cracked the numbers code, he hadn't a clue what the ticket would cost, so all that "Have The Exact Fare Ready" crap would only have ended up in an unholy rammy with the driver. Thus convinced, he set resolutely forth on foot.

He cut through an alley to Nicholson Street and turned right towards the Bridges, savouring sounds and smells that you never experience from the sanitised isolation of a car. The opening-for-the-day bustle of the shops, manifesting itself in a whistling fishmonger slopping out the water from his washed tiled floor onto the pavement here; a yawning, turbaned Asian youth setting out his ranks of jeans and denim shirts there; and everywhere a feeling of near village-like neighbourliness and a buzz of optimistic anticipation at the commencement of a new day's trading. Bob hadn't tasted this atmosphere of the city since the far off days when he used to pad around these very streets on the beat. Even then, he'd been more concerned with keeping alert for the activities of the local shoplifters, pickpockets and miscellaneous other petty criminals than with savouring the warmth of the urban ambience that surrounded him. But now, he found himself smiling readily at the newsagent filling his doorside rack with copies of *The Scotsman* and *Daily Record*, and bidding a cheery good morning to wee women bauchling along, their string shopping bags already dangling low with the essential ingredients for today's mince and tatties. Aye, this was the city life all right.

Twenty sweaty minutes and two excruciating heel blisters later, however, Bob had had enough of the joys of pedestrianism, had retreated limping and cursing from the human scrummage of Princes Street, and was floating down past the topmost branches of a leafy benjamin tree on an escalator bound for the fountain-tinkling sanctuary of the lower level of the

Princes Shopping Mall. He'd heard that there were Continental-style bars and bistros down there, where a body could sit in air-conditioned comfort while sipping a refreshment and enjoy the passing, Muzak-lulled show.

What he really needed to restore his flagging spirits, of course, was a nice creamy pint of his beloved Belhaven Best. But, as Scottish licensing laws still hadn't given the green light to the sale of alcohol quite so early in the day, he parked his weary bones at the table of a "French" pavement café and ordered a mug of sweet tea and a bacon roll instead. He then thumbed a number into his mobile phone. "Good morning, is that the Forth Street Hare Krishna Temple and Kebab House?"

Julie Bryson sounded as if she was still in bed. "Hello . . . Yes . . . My God, it's still the middle of the night!"

"You've either gone blind with the *Strega* you drank last night or else your Wee Willie Winkie night cap has slipped down over your eyes. It's nearly ten o'clock in the morning, and it's shaping up to be a scorcher!"

There was a drowsy moan. "The irrepressible Sergeant Burns, I take it. Don't you gumshoes ever sleep?"

"My crucial early-morning interview with Spiers, remember?"

"Oh, yeah, I remember now," Julie yawned. "You sound too chirpy to have been sent to Siberia, so I presume your fears of being hauled off the case were unfounded after all."

"*Au contraire, mademoiselle! Absolument au con- traire!*"

"Where are you speaking from, for heaven's sake?"

"From a bijou little French bistro. You'd love their bacon sandwiches."

"You're in Paris?"

"Nah — that shopping centre place next to Waverley Station. Listen, have you got a car?" Bob spoke in tones of lively optimism.

Julie replied in tones of intuitive suspicion. "You're thinking through rose-coloured spectacles, Sergeant Burns. Forget it!"

"Just think about painting over those tangerine ceilings, Doc. One good turn deserves another, and two brushes are better than one, right?"

"You drive a hard bargain, Sarge. You're on! What's the deal?"

"The deal is that I'll be at your place a.s.a.p. and explain all. Oh, and by the way, the Sarge handle is u.s. — temporarily, at least. Just call me Joe Public Burns. That's Bob . . . to my friends."

Forth Street is also the home of the Radio Forth local radio station, and it was their ten o' clock news bulletin that the taxi driver was listening to as he swung in off Broughton Street . . .

"*Lothian and Borders Police have just confirmed that the man arrested yesterday evening in connection with the death of seventy-seven-year-old Miss Roberta McGregor outside a geriatric ward at Roodlands Hospital, Haddington, will appear in court this morning, charged with her murder . . .*"

150

"The slammer's too good for radgies like him," the driver called over his shoulder to Bob as he braked the taxi to a squealing halt outside Julie's flat. "Should never huv did away wi' toppin' basturds like that. Three-quid-eighty, mate."

With a keep-the-change shrug, Bob slipped him four, forgetting until a fraction of a second too late that he wasn't on exies any more. Shite! That sort of wild extravagance would have to stop forthwith!

Julie opened the door in her dressing gown, reminding Bob of the old Chick Murray gag, *"That's a strange place to have a door."* He resisted the temptation to repeat it, however.

Julie looked askance at the items which Bob had just handed her. "Beware the polis bearing gifts," she muttered. "It may surprise you to know, Sergeant, that men callers *have* been known to present me with flowers. Sweeties, even. But you — you seek to win my affections with a pair of Wolsey Soft-grip Cotton-rich gents' socks, size six to eleven, and a tin of waterproof Elastoplast." She looked up and dipped her head coquettishly to one side. "Y'aff yer heid?"

"Aye, well, it's been a long time since I pounded the beat," Bob groaned. Gratefully accepting Julie's invitation to step inside, he limped into the living room. "Any Germolene, darlin'?"

"So, you've been relegated to the foot soldiers?" Julie called out amid rummaging noises from the bathroom. She reappeared with a tube of the required ointment in her hand. "Hence your toady horse trading for the use of my wheels, right?"

Bob screwed up his eyes and squinted at the psychedelic decor of the living room. "And I think I got the wrong end of the bargain," he mumbled. "But why paint over these walls when you could charge modern art freaks admission money to look at them during the Festival? Who knows — a bit of long-winded mumbo-jumbo and meaningless ballyhoo in the arts supplement of *The Scotsman* and you could even be on a nice wee earner by stripping the wallpaper and flogging it in signed pieces. I can get picture frames done on the cheap by the lags in the carpentry shop at Saughton Prison, if you're interested."

"Speak up! I can't hear you!" Julie's yell now came from the bedroom, where the sound of drawers and cupboards slamming open and closed and the decisive "*woosh!*" of a zipper being pulled indicated that she was getting dressed — and wasting no time about it. To prove it, she was back in a jiffy. She stopped in the doorway and struck a mannequinish pose. "How's this?" she asked.

Kitted out as she was in navy blue slacks, crisp white blouse and with a floppy Breton cap tilted modishly over one ear, Bob reckoned that she looked like an elfin version of a pre-peroxide Joanna Lumley in one of those early *Avengers* episodes. "I'm fair breath-taken," he gasped. And he was.

Julie patted the cap firmly onto her head. "This was the nearest thing to a chauffeur's bunnet I could find. My open-top, vintage sports car, you see, comes complete with driver."

152

An open-top, vintage sports car! Bob was standing in a daze of approbation, with the tube of Germolene in one hand and his old pair of socks dangling dank and disconsolate from the fingertips of the other.

Julie relieved him of the Germolene. "You'll find a trash can for your socks under the sink in the kitchen. There'll be things in there that'll make them feel at home, I'm sure." Her nostrils twitched at the air. "Uhm, then again, on second thoughts . . ."

Taking the hint, Bob dumped his socks in the communal wheelie bin outside the back door and followed Julie over the little cobbled yard to where her car was parked under a sycamore tree. "Vintage sports car?" he frowned. He squinted first at the car and then at Julie. "I was expecting at least a classic Bentley racer — one of those huge, British-racing-green monsters from the Roaring Twenties. But, well, this is only a wee 1960s Morris Minor."

"Clever boy! Anyway, he's my pride and joy, so no disparaging comments. Now, give me a hand to fold his soft top down." Julie took a deep breath of the morning air — a curious Edinburgh concoction of mown grass, traffic fumes and the malty tang of the city's breweries. "Ah-h-h, magic! Ye cannae whack it, boy!"

"No? Well, after Glasgow, I suppose even the hum of Auld Reekie must seem like a whiff of pure potpourri."

Julie shook her head and tutted. "Last night it was the Masons, now you're having a dig at the Pope. I suppose that's what you call even-handed bigotry through here."

153

Bob willed himself not to smile. He was still feeling a tad punchy, thanks to the combined effects of the late-night liqueur session and the early-morning Spiers show-down. He had no desire to be drawn into a battle of breezy witticisms with Julie just yet. He opened the door of the little roadster for his chauffeuse. "Doon the watter!" he commanded in aped Glesca after belting himself into the passenger seat. "And doan't spare the cuddies!"

Heading eastward out of the city along Seafield, Julie listened intently to Bob's account of the morning's events, the briny smack of the cool air wafting in from the Firth of Forth filling their lungs and buffeting their hair as they bowled along.

"So that's it," Bob rounded off, just as they were passing the Edinburgh Cat and Dog Home. "I can now truly empathise with all those poor, unwanted little fellas in there."

Julie patted him on the head and quipped, "Not quite, Bonzo. Remember, you were cute enough to get yourself re-adopted before you even got the boot from your previous master."

The sea breezes were working curative wonders on Bob's mental fuzziness. "Ah well, every dog has his day, and it's nice to have a new mistress," he wisecracked.

Julie pointedly ignored what could have been construed as a leading statement. "So," she said, "if you've been given the provisional bum's rush out of the police force, what, pray, am I doing driving you in what would appear to be the general direction of the *locus delicti*?"

"That's the scene of the crime, right?"

Julie patted his head again. "Clever boy!"

"I told you before, I want to check out old Bertie's answer to that *Sunday Post* crossword clue, and that means paying a visit to the shrubbery at Roodlands Hospital. *And* I need to question one or two people I haven't managed to get round to yet."

"But you haven't even got a police ID any more! Own up — Jack Spiers has got you well stymied this time. I mean, who, apart from the people you've already interviewed, is going to bare all to some unknown geezer masquerading as the Lone Ranger in a Marks and Spencers blazer, for heaven's sake?"

"Aha, but we have our ways," Bob said with a deliberate hint of intrigue. "And, if all else fails, there's always my main man Mr Candlestein."

"Mr Candlestein?"

"All will be revealed in the fullness of time." He raised his hand above the windscreen and pointed dramatically to the open road ahead. "Hi-ho, Silver! Away-y-y . . ."

Julie sighed in bewildered resignation. "OK, Kemosabe, the A1 high road for Haddington it is."

"Correction, Tonto. The A198 low road for Dirleton it is." Bob checked his watch. "It's still over an hour till lollipop time!"

CHAPTER
TEN

Although he had thought little of it at the time, the near paranoid concern of the old King twins — Jock, the caretaker at Roodlands, and his brother Jimmy, the retired cattleman at Archerfield Estate — for protesting their innocence of being involved in something that had happened in Dirleton during the Second World War had since started to prey on Bob's mind. Could an event that had occurred nearly sixty years earlier somehow have a connection, no matter how tenuous, with the violent death of Bertie McGregor? Could a clue to the motive for her murder, for instance, lie hidden in some ostensibly insignificant detail of that mysterious happening of so long ago? Bob had to find out.

The Fidra General Stores on the outskirts of Dirleton doubled as the village post office, and if anyone could point him in the direction of the most knowledgeable surviving authority on local wartime history, Bob reckoned it would be the postmistress . . .

"I'm preparing an article for *Nostalgia* magazing in the States," he lied, allowing her the briefest glimpse of one of his collection of bogus business cards, "and I'd like to speak with anyone who might remember some interesting anecdotes dating from the war years in these parts. I realise you're much too young to have any personal reminiscences, madam," he flannelled, "but —"

"Wait a minute!" the postmistress cut in, glowering suspiciously. "I remember you. You're the Burns laddie from Halliburton Terrace that went to Tulliallan Police College. What's all that *H. G. Wells, Freelance Journalist* stuff on your card about? Get your jotters off the police, did you?"

Converting a snigger into an unconvincing bout of sneezing, Julie began to clumsily browse through a display of birthday cards by the door.

"Very observant, madam," Bob bluffed, dropping his voice to a stage whisper and closing one eye in a slow wink of confidentiality. "CID cover, you understand. All very hush-hush."

"Mm-hmm, so you say," the postmistress mumbled, still scowling.

"Well?" Bob cajoled through a sheepish smile. "Can you help me at all?"

"I suppose this has to do with that terrible Bertie McGregor business?" the postmistress grumped. Bob's noncommittal shrug was taken as confirmation. "Why couldn't you have said so in the first place, then? Damned Ruth Rendell mysteries!"

Bob shrugged again, but said nothing.

"Angus Forsyth!" the postmistress barked, before stamping the pension book of an old woman who had come in and shuffled her way to the counter, apparently quite oblivious of the somewhat strained conversation already in progress. "Angus was the village bobby here all during the war," the postmistress went on. "Aye, and for many more years and all."

"And where can I find Mr Forsyth these days?" Bob asked.

"Number Fifty-two Amisfield Road in Haddington. Been living there with his sister since his wife passed away fifteen years ago. Don't you dare let on to him I told you, mind!"

Feeling suitably cowed, Bob tugged a forelock and backed away. "Many thanks, madam. You can rely on my discretion."

The old woman lifted her pension money off the counter and turned to grab Bob's wrist. "Save yersel' a lot o' bother, sonny. Go straight tae the Waterside Bar in Haddington." She let out a wheezy cackle. "Angus always liked a good dram afore his grub." Then, digging a boney elbow into Bob's ribs, she added, "Typical fuzz, eh!"

"*H. G. Wells, Freelance Journalist*," Julie gasped in mock wonderment once they were back on the road again. She was attempting to keep a straight face, but making a poor job of it.

"Well, it's worked often enough before," Bob countered, niggled and showing it.

"Yes, I can see how such an original nom de plume would fool just about anyone — provided the fool in question didn't possess that doughty woman's phenomenal gift of speed reading."

"Hmm, eyes like a bloody hawk, that one." Bob was beginning to see the funny side of it now himself. He

158

gave a little laugh. "Yeah, I've got to admit she made me look a real prat, and no mistake."

Julie was giggling freely now, enjoying the unexpected moment of levity and revelling in the rare buzz of hurling her little Morris Minor tourer through the maze of East Lothian's picturesque country lanes, their hawthorn hedgerows showered with a confetti of pinky-white blossom, their drystone dykes overhung with wandering garlands of summer brambles. "Trouble is, you plain-clothes guys never seem to twig that you've got *Polis* written all over you. Doesn't matter how you dress, it's like you've got a blue light blinking on your head."

"Well, we can't all be like Wullie Merryfield, I suppose."

"Who's Wullie Merryfield?"

"Legendary old Edinburgh police chief. Master of bluff — and occasional transvestite. But it's a long story. Some other time, maybe." Bob settled into his seat. "Anyway," he sighed, "at least I won't need to flash old Angus Forsyth any of my bullshit business cards."

"Because it takes one to know one, right?"

"That's it." Bob sighed again and tapped the top of his head. "Unless the battery on my blue light's gone flat, that is."

He needn't have worried.

The setting was a sun-filled patio on the banks of the River Tyne in Haddington's old town. A pair of swans were gliding on the limpid water between the arches of

159

the old stone bridge that spans out from the far end of the Waterside Bistro and Bar.

"Ah, young Burns of the constabulary!" was the cheery salutation from the ruddy-faced old fellow sitting nursing a glass of whisky beneath one of the pub's scattering of Martini parasols. He stood up and beckoned them to join him, offering his hand first to Julie. "I'm Angus Forsyth, ma dear." There was a roguish twinkle in the little dark eyes set deep beneath a canopy of frosty eyebrows that looked as if they'd been transplanted from the forehead of a West Highland terrier. "But if ye don't mind me sayin' so, ye look a wee bit wee for a WPC."

"This is Julie," Bob interjected, holding out his own hand in anticipation of the eventual conclusion of the old boy's lingering hand-shake. "Julie's in, ehm . . . administration."

"Administration, is it?" Angus Forsyth nodded, still looking admiringly at Julie while reluctantly releasing her hand. "Never had much call for any o' that fancy stuff in my day."

Bob grasped the old policeman's hand and pumped it heartily. "Bob Burns. It's a pleasure to meet you, Mr Forsyth."

"Just call me Gus, unless ye're here to ask for money — in which case ye can call me skint." He chortled quietly and lowered himself back into his chair. "Aye, aye, so how're ye gettin' on this weather, Bob?"

"I'm just fine, thanks." Bob was slightly taken aback. "Ehm, I don't want to be rude, but . . . have we met before? To be honest, I can't quite place —"

160

"Oh, I daresay I'll have clipped yer lug a few times for stealin' plums oot o' the big hoose garden at Archerfield, but I cannae rightly mind now. Naw, you Dirleton laddies a' looked the same in them days — the lot o' ye wi' anti-nit haircuts and the erse hangin' oot yer breeks."

Julie faked another sneezing fit.

"Bless ye, pet," said old Angus. "Ye'll need tae wrap up better if ye don't want tae catch a wee chill." He took a surreptitious peep down the front of her blouse. "My, my, no even wearin' a vest, I see."

Bob cleared his throat. "Excuse me asking, Gus, but if you can't recall meeting me before, how did you know who I was when we arrived just then?" He had to consciously restrain his hand from rising to feel if there was anything illuminated sprouting from his cranium.

"Nae bother, lad. The postmistress at Dirleton phoned me at the hoose to tip me off, ye see." He treated himself to another chortle. "They could replace hundreds at Interpol wi' just one o' her. Aye, and that's a fact, right enough."

Julie was gazing out over the broad green haughs on the other side of the river to the imposing outline of St Mary's parish kirk beyond. "What a beautiful setting you've got for your local, Angus," she said. "I mean, all those lovely old mature trees and the flowers and everything. It's really breathtaking."

"Aye, well, it's bonnie enough in its own way, if ye like that sort o' thing," Angus conceded grudgingly. "But it'll never be Dirleton."

"And it's actually Dirleton that I wanted to talk to you about," Bob put in, keen to get on with things. "About the war years, to be exact."

Angus drained his whisky glass just as a young waitress emerged from the bar. "Uh-huh?" he said coyly. "Wanted tae ask me a wee question, did ye, son?"

Bob took the hint. He signalled the waitress. "Another dram of the whisky of his choice for Mr Forsyth, please. And for you, Julie?"

"Just mineral water, thanks. I'm driving, remember."

"Same for me," Bob said. He looked at old Angus and shrugged apologetically. "On duty, you know."

"No drinkin' on the job nowadays? What the hell's the polis force comin' tae!"

"It's about the old King twins," Bob said, getting right down to business.

A frosty brow arched warily.

"No, no, Gus — I'm not suggesting they've done anything wrong. It's just an impression they both gave that something happened at Dirleton during the war that they don't want to be tied in with. I just wondered if you could throw any light on what it might have been, that's all."

Old Angus looked him in the eye. "Nothin' that'll help ye find out who did for Bertie McGregor, anyway."

"OK," Bob said. He paused to pay the waitress. "But tell me all the same, Gus — just to satisfy my curiosity, if you like."

Angus Forsyth contemplated his new dram for a while, then added a modest measure of water to the amber spirit. "This stuff — the whisky, no the water —

162

was like gold during the war. And petrol, too." Pensively, he twirled a whorl of shaggy eyebrow between finger and thumb. "Mind you, the fermers always got more than the basic ration o' petrol. Needed it for startin' the paraffin tractor engines, ye see. Of course, the lads that worked on the ferms had what was called reserved occupations, like. Never needed tae join the armed forces . . . unless they were daft enough tae volunteer." He chuckled quietly to himself. "Never had any bother findin' a buyer for a thieved five-gallon drum o' petrol, yon boys."

Bob held back a moment, then asked, "Did Jock and Jimmy King both work on the farms at that time? Are you saying that they used to knock off their bosses' petrol to flog on the black market?"

The old man's face opened into a broad grin. "Yes, on both counts. And I was their best customer. I had a wee 1934 Ford Eight then, ye see, and . . . well, anyway, least said, soonest mended." He raised his glass. "Your good health! A' the best!"

"Nicking petrol during the war isn't what the King twins are bothered about now, though, is it?"

"No, I daresay it isnae, at that." A coy look traversed old Angus's florid features again. "I'm a proud man, young Burns." He swallowed the dregs of his whisky. "And an honourable one. The King boys were good pals o' mine, ye must understand. Still are, come to that."

Bob gestured to the fortuitously-passing waitress for another dram.

Angus got the message. "Howsoever, seein' as ye're puttin' it that way," he crooned, "maybe there *is* something that's comin' back to me now, right enough . . ." His memory flow was put on temporary hold until the fresh glass of whisky had been delivered and was cradled cosily in his hands. "There was that many servicemen aboot Dirleton durin' the war, ye see — what wi' the aerodrome just up the road at Drem, and that other big yin over at East Fortune — hundreds and hundreds o' airmen — Canadians, Anzacs, English, Welsh, Scottish, Polish. And Waafs as well, of course. But no so many Waafs as airmen. And that was the problem, like."

"The problem, like?"

"Aye." Angus took another gulp of whisky. "There was never enough weemin for men at the weekend NAAFI dances on the 'dromes, see? So, a lot o' the RAF blokes would just descend upon the Saturday night hops at the Dirleton Castle Inn in hopes o' hookin' a bit o' nookie." He smiled benignly at Julie. "Pardon me, pet. Polismen's talk, ye ken?" He turned back to Bob. "Take it from me, son, the nookie was so bloody rampant in them days that the woods on Archerfield Estate at the back o' the Castle Inn were known as the Paris Post Office, 'cos every Sunday mornin' there was that many French Let—"

"Yes, I get the picture," Bob butted in before Julie dissolved into another sneezing spasm, "but what's all this got to do with Jock and Jimmy King's hang-ups?"

"The very item I was just comin' tae!" said Angus. He gave his hands an enthusiastic clap. "Remember

164

how I said that the only ferm boys that joined up was them daft enough tae volunteer? Well, Jock and Jimmy King volunteered." He tapped his temple. "Nice enough lads, mind, but nothin' between the lugs."

Bob smiled. "Yeah, they told me they'd been in the army. Jock in the Royal Scots, and Jimmy in the Tank Corps or something."

Old Angus nodded sagely. "Scots Greys it was for Jimmy." He tapped the side of his head again. "Daft bugger joined the cavalry 'cos he thought he'd get workin' wi' horses!" A wistful chuckle rumbled in his chest. "Aye, any road, by the time 1944 came round, the two King boys just happened to be back in the village at the same time — on a fortnight's leave, like. And that was the start o' it . . ."

His tongue nicely lubricated by Bob's steady supply of complimentary drams, the old policeman spun his yarn with undisguised zeal. He told of how Jock and Jimmy, having learned that those interloping RAF types from the bases were making a habit of plundering the village at every opportunity to snap up what was available in the way of local talent, decided that they would make a stand — literally — for Dirleton's native manhood. The end result was that, nine months later, a certain village lass of known sociable disposition gave birth to a baby boy. Although few of the village folk ever actually saw the infant, he, like numerous other wartime "accidents" in the area, was waggishly dubbed with the surname of Archerfield by the local gossips, the location of conception being irrefutably known, even if the identity of the father was not.

In this particular case, however, the mother was adamant that she knew who the father of her child was. Well . . . almost. It was still a toss-up whether she called the babe Jock or Jimmy.

Old Angus begged Julie's pardon in advance of making his next observation: "It's hard enough for anybody to tell the King twins apart at the best o' times, ye see, pet. So ye can imagine how confusin' it must've been if ye were lyin' on yer back in the middle o' a wood in the blackout wi' nothin' tae help ye identify yer laddie but a wee glimmer o' moonlight glintin' off his bare erse."

Angus Forsyth lapped up the ensuing ripple of awkward laughter with almost as much glee as he was supping up the freebie whisky.

"So, which Christian name did the mother eventually plump for?" Bob quickly asked.

"Ah, well now, it was a long time ago that, and I cannae rightly mind. Aye, and that's the truth o' it."

"Would another dram jog your memory?" Bob blurted out without thinking.

Angus assumed an expression of deep hurt, but didn't commit himself.

By now, Bob was starting to wonder precisely where this load of seemingly irrelevant old tittle-tattle was getting him. "And the kid was adopted, was he?" he urged. "And fifty years later the kid discovers who his true mother is and belts her on the head with a spade for rejecting him at birth. Is *that* what we're supposed to think?" Bob's impatience was showing now. "Or maybe the alleged father is driven to bumping off the mother because she's threatening to sue him for breach of a passion-induced promise of marriage in Archerfield woods more than half a century ago? Come on," he scoffed, "pull the other one, Gus!"

"I'm just tellin' ye a wee story about Dirleton in wartime, like ye asked," Angus shrugged. "And remember, I told ye straight that it wouldnae help ye find Bertie McGregor's murderer."

Bob and Julie looked at each other in bewilderment, a reaction which clearly delighted old Angus Forsyth. "And another thing," he said smugly, "I never even said that Bertie McGregor was the mither o' the bastard bairn."

Bob was making a supreme effort not to lose his temper with this codger, whom he was beginning to regard as nothing more than a freeloading old git. He made to stand up. "Thanks for your time," he said curtly, "but we really must be moving on. We've got a lot more to —"

"The bairn was found dead," Angus declared with dramatic timing, his eyes fixing Bob's in a defiant stare, as if daring him to leave before he had concluded his tale. "Found by one o' the gamekeepers in a shallow grave among some scrub just outside the old walled gardens at Archerfield. Aye, I seen it masel'. Face as blue as a Rangers jersey, lyin' there wi' maggots crawlin' oot its peepers."

Julie shuddered. "The poor wee soul had been murdered?"

Angus patted the back of her hand and shook his head, pausing to sip his dram before revealing:

"Stillborn, the death certificate said." Then, raising his shoulders as if to acknowledge the inevitability of it all, he added, "It was wartime. These things happened where there was a lot o' forces stationed in country places." He began to chuckle again. "Word had it in the village, though, that the faither o' the bairn had crept back and throttled it for fear o' bein' made tae stump up maintainance money."

"Which would explain the we-never-done-nothin' fixations that Jock and Jimmy have got to this day?" Bob muttered rhetorically.

Angus merely tapped the side of his head again and smiled. "Like I said, young Burns, I'm an honourable man."

With a mounting feeling of exasperation and a deep reluctance to spend any more of his own money on liquid inducements, Bob decided to play one last card. "Even if it didn't actually help me find Bertie's killer, would it add anything of interest to your story if I had a chat with, say . . . Pinkie Dalrymple?"

The old chap gave Bob a little congratulatory nod, as if he had just witnessed a grandchild taking his first toddling step. Yet he said nothing.

Bob and Julie rose to leave.

"Afore ye go, Bob," Angus chimed, "— what rank o' polis have ye managed tae reach? Inspector, Chief Inspector now, is it?"

"Nope, only Sergeant," Bob replied matter-of-factly.

"Nothin' wrong wi' that, lad." Angus prodded himself on the chest with his forefinger. "Look at me. I never made it beyond plain Police Constable Gus

Forsyth, but folk still look up to me for who I am, no for *what* I am, or for any stripes or pips on ma jaiket." He stood up a mite unsteadily. Holding onto the edge of the table with one hand and giving Bob a kindly pat on the shoulder with the other, he declared at the top of his voice, "Never forget what yer namesake the bard said . . . *The rank is but the guinea's stamp, The man's the gowd for a' that.*" Then, bravely removing his steadying hand from the table, he put it round Julie's shoulder and gave her a whisky-fumed peck on the cheek. He looked blearily into her eyes and slurred, "And may all yer administrations be wee ones!"

CHAPTER
ELEVEN

Police Constable Andy Green was doing what little he could to assist a harrassed lollipop lady cope with a seemingly endless stream of crisp-scoffing primary school kids bunching up in rowdy packs on the pavement at the busy confluence of Haddington's Court Street, High Street and Market Street when Bob and Julie swept past in Julie's little Morris Minor. Bob indicated to the astounded PC that they would await the pleasure of his company in the nearby Plough Tavern.

"The mysterious Mr Candlestein himself," Bob said to Julie, guiding her to a place by the lounge bar window which afforded them an uninterrupted view of the school crossing patrol in action.

Julie gave him a reproving glare. "Something tells me you're just making use of the poor kid *and* taking the mickey out of him at the same time. Shame on you!"

"No way! It's no worse than a joiner sending his apprentice to the hardware shop for a long stand, or a garage mechanic telling his newest rookie to go to the stores and ask for a bucket of S-H-one-T. All part of the initiation game. Relax!"

Julie's reproachful look darkened into a frown. "What about the young copper who stopped a bullet in the leg for you yesterday? Do you put that down to part of the initiation game too?"

Bob walked over to the bar and returned with two ploughman's lunches that he had ordered on the way in. "Don't worry, my heart was in my mouth when Jack Spiers hit me with that one yesterday, so the first thing I did when I left his office was check up on young DC Bain."

"And?"

"And I spoke to him . . . on his car radio."

"You mean he was back on duty that soon?"

"Yeah, yeah. In fact, he was never *off* duty. The bullet only grazed his thigh — scarcely broke the skin. A splash of TCP and a patch of sticking plaster and he was brand new. The only damage to speak of was to his trouser leg . . . and maybe to the seat of his underpants, but I'm only surmising there."

Julie shook her head in disbelief. "How in heaven's name can Spiers present that to his Super as a credible reason for suspending you?"

Shrugging, Bob took a sip of his mineral water. "He'd say it's the principle that's important, wouldn't he? Anyway, I've been down this road before, remember, so I'm not taking my case upstairs this time until everything's as tight as a crab's bahookie — and that's watertight."

"That poetic turn of phrase again," Julie smirked. "Your much-quoted namesake would turn in his grave."

It was a distinctly breathless and dishevelled Constable Green who joined them some minutes later. Bob motioned towards the lollipop lady, who was now shepherding the last few stragglers across the street. "When are you due back on point duty, Constable?"

Andy Green couldn't hide his joy. "Two weeks on Monday!" He glanced at his watch. "As from three minutes ago, I'm on my annual hols!"

"God almighty!" Bob groaned. "First the Doc here, and now you! Is everybody jacking it in for the summer today?"

"Height o' the local holiday fortnight, intit?" PC Green reminded him. "Yeah, first thing tomorrow morning, me and the mates are offski. So, lock up your daughters, Greek islanders. Andy Green is on the trawl!"

"Corfu?" Julie asked.

"It certainly will be," Andy affirmed, the makings of a worried frown hesitating on his brow. "Mmm, five of us and all our kit in a Mini Cooper. Still, it's only as far as Turnhouse Airport, so we can put up with a wee bit of a squeeze for all the distance it is, eh?"

If Bob hadn't known PC Green better, he might have suspected that the lad had just cracked a joke. But he did know him better. "Listen, Constable," he said, cutting through the stunned silence that had fallen on their little group, "I'm gonna come straight to the point. I need you for a little bit of CID secondment work this afternoon. The word has probably reached the Haddington nick that I'm off the McGregor murder case, right?" He didn't wait for a reply. "That's because

172

I'm now working undercover, so here's the lowdown. That nursing auxiliary who discovered old Bertie's body . . .?"

"Mrs Reynolds? The one with the daughter with the drop-dead particulars?"

"That's the one. I need you to introduce me to her right away."

Constable Green's eyes darted in angst between Bob and Julie.

"I mean the mother," Bob quickly clarified, "not the daughter."

"OK, no probs, if that's what you want." The customary vacant look of boyish innocence returned to Andy Green's face. "But why don't you just go and give her a quick flick of your ID card? I've told her all about you, so —"

"You're thinking too much, lad!" Bob snapped. "It'll stunt your growth . . . and your promotion chances. Just remember, even in undercover work, there are times when the uniformed presence is a distinct advantage. And don't forget, everything I'm asking you to do from now on is strictly C-R-A-P, and the shtum factor has never been more vital."

Julie's expression was mystification personified. "Crap?" she silently mouthed at Bob.

PC Green pulled a silly, lop-sided smile. Then, ogling their empty plates, he rubbed his stomach and asked, "I suppose an undercover ploughman's is out of the question, skipper?"

★ ★ ★

Mrs Reynolds was just finishing her lunch in the hospital canteen. After the usual formalities, Bob apologised for interrupting her break and asked if they might join her for coffee, first having dispatched Andy Green to the women's surgical ward to do some further investigative pumping of probationary nurse "Dolly" Golightly.

"It must have been a very upsetting experience for you, Mrs Reynolds," Bob said, "— I mean, finding old Bertie in such horrific circumstances. And I don't want to put you through any more anguish, if it can possibly be avoided." He noticed that she had begun to wring her hands at the very mention of Bertie's name. "But I'm sure you appreciate that we have to look into every detail, no matter how minor."

Mrs Reynolds clasped her fingers tightly and took a slow, deep breath. "It's all right, Sergeant Burns," she quavered, "I understand."

She was a squarely-built woman in her mid to late forties, Bob estimated — grey hair swept unflatteringly back from her rather homely face, every muscle of which was tense with apprehension. Bob watched her eyes.

"I want you to think back to when you took Bertie her cup of tea in the shrubbery. Did you stay long with her?"

"Only a second or two. I'd forgotten the milk, you see. Bertie always liked to get her milk separately — in a little jug, so she could pour a wee drop into her saucer for Dixie, then add some to her tea with plenty sugar. It was always that way round. Dixie the cat first, then herself."

"So, you returned to the ward kitchen, got the milk and took it out to Bertie. Is that right?"

"No, I didn't go back out to Bertie until . . ." Her voice trailed away and her eyes melted into tears. She began to sniffle into a hankie that she'd pulled from her overall pocket. "I'm sorry. It's just that when I think of . . ."

Julie moved her chair closer to Mrs Reynolds' and took her hand in hers. "It's all right," she murmured. "There's no hurry. Just take your own time."

Bob was glad Julie was around.

There was an uncomfortable interlude of muted sobbing until Mrs Reynolds had pulled herself together sufficiently to continue . . .

"When I went back into the ward kitchen, the staff nurse was there. She was in a bit of a fluster because an old man had had a wee *accident* in his bed at the other end of the ward. She asked me to go and help make him, well, *comfy* again."

"And the staff nurse took Bertie her milk?" Bob prompted.

Mrs Reynolds paused to dab her eyes. She shook her head nervously. "No, I don't think so. But, to be honest, I'm not that sure. There was one of those welfare worker folk there, you see. One of those volunteer visitor women, I mean. It could well be that she took the milk out to Bertie."

Bob and Julie exchanged glances.

"The staff nurse had more than enough on her hands as it was," Mrs Reynolds added. "Ehm, if you know what I mean, Sergeant."

Bob weighed this revelation in silence for a moment or two. "Think about this very carefully before you answer, Mrs Reynolds," he said as placidly as he could, "but that volunteer visitor . . . could she have been Mrs Spiers, the convalescent patient in the side ward in women's surgical?"

"I believe she could have been at that," Mrs Reynolds replied without hesitation, her taut features relaxing a bit at last. "Yes, it could *well* have been her, right enough. She'd been in and out of the ward quite a lot that day, as I remember."

Just then, PC Green re-entered the canteen. He waited by the door until Bob had excused himself temporarily from the two ladies in order to join him. The eager young constable then flipped open his notebook with an officious flourish.

"The answer to question one, boss, is that you can see the door of the operating theatre and the spot where the accused was nicked quite clearly from the window of the side ward in question." He looked at Bob for a sign of approbation, but all he got was an impatient gesture to get on with it. He complied. "The answer to question two is that, yes, the patient in question did leave her room on several occasions during the day of the crime. My informant is of the opinion that this was so that the patient in question could get in a few of her volunteer visiting trips round

176

the crinklies' wards." He paused again in anticipation of a good word from his superior.

"And I suppose you forgot to ask question three," Bob muttered instead.

Constable Green held up a cautionary forefinger. "Incorrect, skipper. The answer to question three is that the patient signed herself out first thing yesterday morning." He slapped his notebook shut and, with a surfeit of policemanly panache, buttoned it inside the top pocket of his tunic. "Bolted the course at precisely 8.30 a.m. on the morning following the felony."

Bob patted him on the shoulder. "Nice one, boy. That's a good job well done."

PC Green visibly grew an extra inch in stature.

Bob hastily scribbled an address on a piece of paper and handed it to him. "Leap into your panda car and zip along to this place. It's a big detached house out on the Gifford road."

"Yeah, I know it."

"OK. Make sure nobody's in, then nip round the back and have a good poke around for signs of a recent bonfire, or one of those garden incinerators, maybe. You're looking for remnants of a pair of cotton gardening gloves, right?" Bob handed him a plastic bag. "If you find anything, stick it in here, and I'll see you back at the hospital gates in about half an hour."

Andy Green didn't look too happy. "What happens if somebody rumbles me when I'm creeping about in the garden, Sarge?"

"*I* don't bloody well know!" Bob bristled. "Tell them you're looking for a runaway tortoise or something. Just use your initiative, for Pete's sake!"

Bob walked back to the table, where Julie appeared to have succeeded in calming down the conspicuously anxious nursing auxiliary, who even managed to greet him with a weak smile.

"I feel so silly, Sergeant Burns. I didn't mean to be such a wimp. It's just that I've never been through anything like this before. I keep seeing Bertie lying there and . . ."

"I know how hard it must be for you, Mrs Reynolds." Bob's tone was sympathetic but firm. "However, Billy Thomson the gardener's chances of ever walking free could depend largely on you." He watched her reaction closely.

She looked up into Bob's eyes, her feelings plainly at sixes and sevens. "Poor Billy. I couldn't believe he had done it at first. But now — all the things people are saying — I just don't know any more."

"Never mind what people say, Mrs Reynolds. Just try to answer my questions as straight as you can. That's all you need bother about right now."

"I'll try my best," she whimpered, wringing her hands again.

"Visitors. Doctor Baird told me that Bertie never had any, except those volunteer people. Is that how it was?"

Mrs Reynolds nodded her assent. "Well, except for that once," she said as an afterthought.

"What once was that?"

"April 4th this year. I remember it exactly because it's our Shona's birthday, and I was rushing to get to the shops to buy a present before they shut for lunch. Then this taxi stops outside the ward and a woman shouts at me through the window and asks if Bertie's ready yet. I says I don't know what she's on about and tells her to get the taxi driver to go and ask the staff nurse."

"What happened then?"

"I just rushed away to the shops, but when I came back on duty, Bertie wasn't in the ward. The taxi dropped her off a while later, and she just said she'd had a nice lunch at the Maitlandfield House Hotel with her friend."

"Did she mention her friend's name?"

Mrs Reynolds shook her head.

"Could you describe her, then?"

She shook her head again. "I didn't get a right look at her, you see. I was in such a hurry and she never got out of the taxi."

"Think hard, Mrs Reynolds. There must have been *something* about her that you noticed. Her age, for instance."

"Oh that? Well, she was quite elderly, I suppose — but all dressed up like a dog's breakfast. Pink hair and bamboo specs, I ask you! At that age, too!"

Bob produced the snapshop of Pinkie Dalrymple and her sister from his inside pocket. "Could this have been the woman, Mrs Reynolds?"

"That's her! That's her exactly!"

"April 4th," Bob said to Julie. "That's the same date that Pinkie checked out of the nursing home."

"Is that helpful?" Mrs Reynolds asked, her eyes flitting apprehensively between them both.

"It may just be the lead I've been looking for," Bob replied. "As I said — every detail, no matter how minor . . ."

Mrs Reynolds looked relieved, if not almost pleased with herself. "As long as I've been of some assistance, Sergeant."

Bob shook her hand. "I'm obliged to you. You've been a great help, believe me. Just one thing before I leave you in peace, though. I'd be grateful if you'd keep the details of this conversation absolutely between ourselves. It could be a life-saver."

"What did you mean by that?" Julie asked him as they left the canteen.

"I meant that, if my hunch is right, Pinkie Dalrymple could well meet with the same fate as her chum Bertie. If she hasn't met with it already, that is."

"You've lost me."

Bob took her by the arm. "Let's have a look at the scene of the crime. Maybe that'll throw up something new today."

The cordon of *POLICE*-emblazoned plastic ribbon was still draped on stakes round the corner of the shrubbery where Bertie had died, and the spot where her body had lain was now marked by a single spray of flowers. Bob knelt down and read out the simple inscription on the card:

180

To Bertie — Until we meet again in a better place, You are ever in our thoughts. From all your friends in Ward 3.

"It suddenly brings it home to you." Julie's voice was hushed and emotional.

"Uh-huh?" Bob replied vaguely, otherwise engrossed in scrutinising the ground in the immediate vicinity of where he was kneeling.

"You know what I mean," Julie went on. "You analyse hundreds of samples of blood and things, swill bits of skin and tissue around in chemicals day after day, and you tend to forget that it all means that someone has died a premature death in terrible circumstances like these." She knelt down beside Bob and tenderly touched the grass. "Bertie," she murmured, "you poor old soul."

"Take your hand away!" Bob growled, the gruffness of his voice startling her.

"I — I'm sorry. I didn't mean to —"

"No, no, it's OK." He gave her hand a reassuring squeeze and smiled. "It's just that you put your finger on precisely what I was looking for." He pointed to the ground, where a small fan shape of dullish grass was just discernible in the lush sward on which they were kneeling.

"Paraquat!" they said in unison.

"Do you get the picture now?" Bob asked as he helped her to her feet. "The culprit spikes the milk with the weedkiller, brings it out here and watches Bertie pour some into her saucer for the cat, then talks away

181

pleasantly to the old dear while she adds a dash of the milk to her own tea and starts to drink it."

Julie was sceptical. "It's a neat idea, but . . ." She pointed at the wedge of withering turf. "I'm not an expert on the effective dilution rates for paraquat, but if that grass is beginning to shrivel like that after less than two days, it suggests to me that, *if* paraquat is responsible, it must have been a fairly strong mixture. Wouldn't Bertie have tasted it?"

"Maybe not. Mrs Reynolds said that Bertie took loads of sugar in her tea, remember? But paraquat does have a pretty distinctive smell, and I'd be surprised if it wasn't a smell that Bertie was familiar with, being a gardener herself. Yeah, and that's where this particular attempt at committing the perfect murder probably went drastically wrong."

"You mean Bertie got a whiff of the weedkiller when she began to drink her tea, then, realising that someone was trying to poison her, threw the contents of her cup onto the grass there?"

"I'm certain she would have done, and maybe that's why she wrote that seemingly daft answer on the crossword."

"*Grass.* She was leaving her own clue to . . . this?"

"That's what's been at the back of my mind all along, anyway. But even so, I doubt if the burnt grass was caused by the paraquat in her tea. The concentration in that would obviously have been a lot more diluted than what was in the milk, OK?"

Pensively, Julie curved a forefinger over her chin and nodded.

182

"So, my guess is that Bertie twigged what was happening, took her walking stick and tipped the saucer over to stop Dixie from drinking any more of the milk." Bob gestured with the toe of his shoe. "That's what's killing off that divot there."

"And your theory is that, when all this happened, the killer panicked, grabbed the spade and battered both Bertie and the cat to death?"

Bob raised his eyebrows. "What else? The choice was between doing that and trying to explain away what was left of a jug of paraquat-laced milk, once Bertie raised the alarm."

Julie was still far from convinced. "Someone would've needed a pretty strong motive to have gone to the trouble of dreaming up a poisoning caper like that."

"And that's where I come up against a brick wall," Bob admitted. "There's still no obvious motive."

"*Plus*, you're only surmising that the discoloured grass there was caused by paraquat. Without a forensic test, there's just no saying what's responsible for it. I mean, it might just be dog pee."

Bob had a little chuckle. "Any dog that lifted his leg and caused a scorch mark like that on the grass has got serious bladder problems — *and* a stainless steel willie!"

Julie gave him a calculating stare. "You've got yourself convinced that Jack Spiers' wife did it, haven't you? But why? Even if your paraquat theory is correct, surely Mrs Reynolds or the duty staff nurse would qualify equally as suspects."

"Except for a couple of things. For a start, I do believe that Bertie's murder was a carefully premeditated act. It needed good timing, and Lauren Spiers — in her side ward in women's surgical — was best placed to effect that. She could see when Bertie left the operating theatre and, knowing Bertie's habits as she probably did, she would've known that, on a pleasant summer's evening, she would most likely have wanted to sit a while in her favourite spot . . . right here. At the same time, she could see that Billy Thomson had started knapsack spraying at the other location, so she knew that Bertie wouldn't be engaged in one of her frequent chinwags with him. It was a reasonable bet that Bertie would be alone and, for once, confined to a wheelchair, because of the operation on her foot. It was probably an opportunity that Lauren Spiers had been waiting for."

"Fair enough. The lack of motive notwithstanding, I'll go along with that so far, just for the sake of it. But then we come back to your poisoning theory. How was anyone — Mrs Spiers included — to know that, on this very occasion, Bertie's jug of milk would be left unattended for a minute or two in the ward kitchen?"

"The most obvious answer is that no one was to know. The fact that Mrs Reynolds did forget the milk was simply an unexpected stroke of good luck for Lauren Spiers. Otherwise, she would have had to find a way of slipping the paraquat into Bertie's tea *and* the cat's milk right here at the scene of the crime. Not so easy."

184

"But surely poisoning the cat would only have drawn attention to the possibility of Bertie having been poisoned too," Julie objected.

"Not at all. Don't forget, the cat wouldn't have dropped down dead on the spot after drinking paraquat. It would just have crept away somewhere quiet to peg out, the way cats do. Chances are nobody would ever have clapped eyes on it again, and chances are that Bertie's death — if she *had* drunk sufficient of the stuff — would have been put down to her serious lung complaint."

"Yes, you went over all that before, but it still doesn't explain why the killer would seriously bother about putting the cat down as well."

"Bertie's will, remember? The cat would have inherited everything, and Lauren Spiers knew that, because she was one of the witnesses to the will."

"But Sister Ramage, or whatever her name is, was the other witness. Why don't you suspect *her* of committing the murder?"

"For the simple reason that she wasn't here the day before yesterday. She was attending her father's funeral in Dundee."

Julie was becoming quite agitated now. "But, heavens above, you can't use that silly will as a legitimate reason for accusing Mrs Spiers or anyone else of murdering Bertie McGregor. She had nothing to leave in her will, and even if she had, the blooming moggy would have been the sole beneficiary. Where's the benefit to the murderer?"

Bob raised his shoulders in acknowledgement. "There's no answer to that at the moment. There *is* a missing link, though, and I suspect that Pinkie Dalrymple is either it, or knows something about it. And, short of finding Pinkie, the only other way I can tie Lauren Spiers in with this is by making a gardening-gloves connection. That's why I've got PC Green snooping about the Spiers place right now."

Julie looked at him as if he had taken leave of his senses. "Talk about wishful thinking. You've about as much chance of winning the National Lottery — or, at this rate, of getting Billy Thomson off the hook."

"Maybe so, but everything's worth a shot in this game." Bob checked his watch. "Come on. Time to go and find out what the intrepid Mr Candlestein has unearthed."

"Nothing! No sign o' the fuckin' tortoise anywhere, Sarge." The knot of vexation that had gathered beneath the peak of PC Green's chequered cap told Bob that he was actually being serious. "I even checked inside the garden incinerator like you told me. Zilch!"

Bob stared at him, unblinking. "Gardening gloves," he snarled through clenched teeth. "What about the bloody gardening gloves?"

The knot between Andy Green's eyebrows untied itself and his dark expression dawned into a sunny smile. "Oh aye — the gloves! I nearly forgot about them for a wee minute there." The knot returned. "Nah, no sign o' them either."

Bob's chest lifted in a shuddering sigh. "That's OK, Constable," he said. "I didn't really think there would be. Thanks anyway." He stood gazing forlornly at his feet, considering his options and trying to remember what the odds of winning the lottery were reckoned to be. After a while, he began to speak to himself in a manner which, to Julie, seemed more desperate than hopeful:

"Pinkie visited Bertie at Roodlands Hospital here on the same day that she checked out of the old folks' home in Scone. We know she didn't book her holiday flights in Perth before she left, so unless she booked them in Edinburgh en route — and she would have had precious little time to do that — there may be just a chance . . ." He raised his head to address the patiently goggling PC Green. "Got any lady friends in the Haddington travel agency, kid?"

In order not to take any unnecessary risks with the possible shtum porosity of his C-R-A-P umbrella, Bob dismissed Constable Green with a few generous words of thanks and encouragement just as soon as the PC had given him the big CID build-up to the predictably top-heavy girl behind the desk.

"The fourth of April," she repeated as she typed the requisite data into her computer. "And the name was Euphemia Dalrymple, you say? Mmm, let's just see." She twirled her ballpoint from finger to finger like the miniature baton of a drum majorette while she waited for the machine to find the relevant file. "Here we are," she said, pointing at the screen with the end of her pen.

"There was actually a flight from Edinburgh on that very date, departing 11p.m. Mmm, it's hardly likely she'd have got on that, but let's look at our list of bookings, just in case . . ."

Julie gripped Bob's arm. The tension was becoming unbearable.

"Bullseye!" the girl suddenly declared. "Miss E. Dalrymple . . . on a Playa Holidays two-week Supersaver!"

A feeling of glorious relief swept over Bob. "So far, so good," he said. "Now, can you tell us which hotel she was booked into?"

"Sorry, I can't do that." The girl was adamant.

"Look, it really could be a matter of life and death," Bob stressed. "I know it's a long shot, but somebody at the hotel — a barman, a waitress or somebody — might just have an idea of where she intended going at the end of her holiday."

The girl hunched her shoulders apologetically. "Honest, I'd tell you if I could. But, on these late-booking bargains, neither we nor the customer know the hotel or even the resort up front. The client's only given that information by the tour rep on arrival at the destination airport."

"OK, but Playa Holidays must have a record of that. Can you check it out for me?"

The girl's expression wasn't too encouraging. "I'll phone their Glasgow office, if you like, but I doubt if they'll know. I shouldn't think their Mallorca branch would even have told them. No real need to." She tapped out the phone number. "Hi! Is that Senga? . . .

Hiya! It's Janet at Haddington Travel here." She told the girl at the other end what she wanted to know, then, after a moment, she put her hand over the mouthpiece and whispered to Bob, "Just as I thought — they don't have that information in Glasgow. But Senga says one of her chums is on the phone to their Palma Mallorca office just now, so she's gonna see if she can find out for you."

The girl proceeded to flip absentmindedly through the pages of *True Romances* with her free hand as she awaited Senga's news.

Bob and Julie swapped nervous glances.

"Hi, Senga! . . . Yeah, I'm still here . . . Oh, magic! . . . Hotel Santa Catalina, eh? . . . Yeah, I know . . . You're joking! . . . Really? . . . Oh, no!" Janet's tone was becoming less promising by the second. "OK, Senga, I'll pass that on . . . Thanks a million anyway . . . 'Bye." She replaced the phone and looked up poker-faced at Bob. "Senga says that the Dalrymple lady was booked into the Hotel Santa Catalina at Palma Nova for those two weeks."

Bob started to breathe again. "Well, it's a start. And many thanks for going to all that bother. Ehm, can you give me a note of the hotel phone number, please? I'll have to —"

Janet wagged her ballpoint at Bob like a slow-motion windscreen wiper. "Senga gave me the good news first."

Bob caught his breath again. "And the bad news is?"

"Senga says that the Dalrymple woman phoned their Palma office a couple of days before the end of her holiday and said she wouldn't be taking the return flight back to Edinburgh. But she did check out of the hotel on the due date."

"Which means?"

"You tell me, Detective Sergeant. That was the end of Playa's involvement with her." Janet re-hunched her shoulders. "She could be anywhere."

"Talk about your one step forward and your two steps back," said Julie, already sharing Bob's sense of dejection. "What now, Kemosabe?"

Bob was thinking hard — and fast. "When, uh, when's the next available flight to Palma Mallorca?" he asked Janet, a trace of panic in his voice.

"You'll be lucky," Janet sniffed. "It's coming up to the crossover of the Edinburgh and Glasgow holiday fortnights. All the flights from these two airports to anywhere in the sun have been fully booked for months."

Bob scratched his head. "Still, there might be a cancellation," he said. "See what your computer says."

Janet punched the buttons of her keyboard, her bottom lip protruding glumly, her head moving from side to side in a slow and ominous arc. "There you go," she eventually said. "Zippo!"

"How about a flight from a bit farther away . . . out of Aberdeen or somewhere?"

Janet shrugged, then fingered the keyboard again. Her face lit up as she scanned the screen. "You've knocked it off! There's a late availability from Newcastle. Ten o'clock tonight. Seven days, self-catering. Any use?"

Bob didn't even ask the price. "Book it!" he said. He turned to Julie with a fatalistic flick of his hands. "It's shit or bust for me now."

Julie nodded her head, then craned her neck to get a better look at the computer screen. "I see the availability's for two."

Janet nodded *her* head.

"OK, book it for me too!" Then, tilting her head impishly to one side, Julie asked the thunderstruck Bob, "Well, what's seven days of solo DIY in Forth Street compared to a dirty week in Mallorca?"

The inscrutable Janet took it all in her stride. "I take it that this will be chargeable to Lothian and Borders Police?" she enquired blandly, while filling in a confirmation-of-booking slip. "Only, the girl who does the accounts is on holiday, so the bill probably won't be sent out until she comes back next week."

Bob's brain was on autopilot. "Sounds perfect," he muttered.

"And who at Police HQ shall we make the bill out to, Sergeant?" Janet asked, still writing.

Bob cleared his throat. "Ehm-uh, Detective Chief Inspector J. A. Spiers will do nicely, darlin'!"

CHAPTER
TWELVE

The night was suffused with the balmy scent of flowers and wild herbs, lingering on the warm air wafting gently in from the sea, and mingling with the resinous breath of the surrounding pinewoods.

Julie's senses were feasting on the heady Mediterranean atmosphere as she gazed from the balcony over the dark expanse of Camp de Mar bay, on which a sprinkling of boat lights twinkled among reflections of the stars. "Isn't it wonderful?" she sighed. "Ah-h-h, it's so . . . romantic!"

"You can say that again," was Bob's pragmatic reposte from inside the apartment. "There's only a double bed in here."

Julie popped her head round the bedroom door. "Settle down, Sergeant," she curtly advised. "When I said a dirty week in Mallorca, I was alluding to your work, not your habits." She shoved Bob through to the lounge and stood him in front of the couch. "I think you'll find that this will make down into an extremely comfortable kip . . . for one!"

She speculated correctly, and she spoke wisely. It had been a long and eventful day, and tomorrow — which was already several hours old — was likely to be another.

Bob awoke to the distant sound of children laughing and to the nearby smell of bacon frying. He blinked at his watch. Dammit! Almost ten o'clock already. He'd better get the hell out of . . . Wait a minute! Stockbridge kids never usually sounded so joyously wound-up as that! And what the blazes was Mrs Jamieson doing cooking breakfast? The thought of that extra tenner must have flipped her lid.

"Good morning, *Sargento*. You're in Spain, remember? So, *tranquilo* — take it easy."

Bob sat bolt upright. That was Julie's voice. Right — so, it hadn't all been a crazy dream? No such luck, his conscience informed him. It was a top-of-the-range, five-star bloody nightmare! For the first time, the full impact of what he was doing hit him like a kick in the proverbial Albert Halls. Not only was he meddling in police business, from which he was expressly barred, but he had also dragged into his meddling a hitherto guiltless young scientist from his own constabulary's forensic laboratory. A young scientist — and a female one to boot — with whom he was now cohabiting in a luxury apartment on a holiday island fifteen hundred miles away, and all courtesy of his as-yet unwitting boss. And for what purpose? Why, to search for an eccentric old biddy who, in all probability, had left the island a couple of months ago and who wasn't guaranteed to be of any significant help to Bob's cause in any case. It was own-up time. Instead of managing to prove Billy Thomson's innocence, Bob was more likely to find himself locked up in the psychiatric wing of Saughton Prison beside the poor bugger!

Julie read the poleaxed expression on his face as she breezed through from the kitchen. "Not having second thoughts, are you?" she asked. She drew the curtains and opened the balcony doors wide. "Shake a leg, laddie. We're eating alfresco!" Then, anticipating Bob's clock-watching objections, she added, "Palma Nova's only about a fifteen minute drive from here, and the staff at the hotel aren't going to forget any vital pieces of information about Pinkie Dalrymple in the time it takes you to down your brekky, so come on out here and get a load of this fabulous view."

Slouched and squinting, Bob shuffled into the sunshine. "I could've *phoned* the Santa Catalina Hotel . . . from Scotland," he mumbled.

"So you *are* having second thoughts. Whatever happened to the *I Did It My Way* policy?"

"It's not me I'm worried about."

"Don't concern yourself on my behalf, sonny boy. I'm on leave, don't forget, and the worst Lothian and Borders Police can do to me is tell me to repay the cost of the trip, which is what I fully intend to do anyway."

Julie squeezed an orange, looked out to the bay and announced with a wide sweep of her arm, "So, you may as well grin and bear it. Whether you draw a blank on Pinkie's whereabouts or not, you're lumbered with all of this *and* me for the next seven days." While Julie squeezed another orange, popped a champagne cork and fixed two generous glasses of buck's fizz, Bob rubbed his eyes and took a good look at the collective objects of her down-to-earth observation. Bearing it, he grinned, might *not* be too much of a problem at that.

The Hotel Santa Catalina stands high, wide and handsome on a small promontory between the twin beaches of the bustling resort of Palma Nova. The forecourt was teeming with holidaymakers spouting multifarious British accents when Bob and Julie drove up in their little Opel Corsa hire car. They parked behind one of the two coaches that were simultaneously disgorging and ingesting their respective cargoes of snowy white and reddish brown humanity.

Bob handed a fake but convincing identity card, complete with mug shot, to the bored and unimpressed desk clerk. "I'm Robert Burns of the Waverley Private Investigation Bureau in Edinburgh, Scotland," Bob said. "My, uh, my partner and I are trying to trace a missing person, and we believe you may be able to help."

"Missing persons are a matter for the Spanish police," the clerk replied flatly, then handed Bob his card back without so much as a glance at it. "I suggest you report your problem to the Guardia Civil in Palma." He gestured with an oblique jerk of his head towards the luggage-toting army of walking milk bottles advancing over the marbled breadth of the foyer. "Now, if you will excuse me, *por favor*."

"Well, we're off to a flying start," Bob grunted as he shepherded Julie out of the path of the surging mob.

"Maybe the guy's got a point, though," Julie suggested. "Why *don't* you ask the local feds to muck in?"

Bob gave her a reproachful scowl. "Because the first thing they'd do is fax their Edinburgh CID counterparts for confirmation of the details of this alleged missing person." He aimed an imaginary pistol at his head and pulled the trigger. "Suicidal I am not . . . yet!"

"OK, but what now, then?"

"Well, it'll just have to be a question of the old C-R-A-P, that's all."

"Crap?"

Bob took Julie's arm and steered her towards the hotel ballroom. "Clandestine Research And Probing. Constable Andy 'Candlestein' Green's CID-secondment speciality, remember?"

The four ballroom barmen were being kept busy dispensing cooling drinks to the assembly of participants in the late morning bingo session, but each found time to look closely at Bob's snapshot of Pinkie Dalrymple and admit that he couldn't recall ever having clapped eyes on her. "Every week too many peoples, *señor. No es posible* for remember them all, *eh!*"

The photograph elicited the same reaction from the head waiter and his team of waitresses, who were already putting the finishing touches to the dining room for the first lunch sitting. Similarly negative shrugs were proffered by the head porter, the souvenir shop assistant, the in-house hairdresser and assorted passing chambermaids.

Bob returned to the bar, ordered two coffees and led Julie out to the terrace, where they made themselves comfortable beneath a straw parasol by the side of the swimming pool. "May as well panic in style," he shrugged.

The day's organised entertainment was already in full swing out here as well, a tall girl of unmistakably Nordic appearance stoically conducting competitions and supervising games for a squawking gaggle of temporarily-dumped kids over by the pool's shallow end.

Julie adjusted her sunglasses and remarked, "It says something for the accepted image of the Brit senior citizen abroad when an extrovert old raver like this Pinkie doesn't even stand out enough from the crowd to stick in anyone's memory — pink hair, bamboo specs and heaven knows what else besides." She weighed that remark for a second, then added, "Mind you, when you take a gander at the get-ups of some of those old bingo grannies in there . . ."

Bob was rapt in thought. "There can only be two possibilities — either the girl at Haddington Travel was given a bum steer by the tour company and Pinkie was never booked into this hotel at all, or —"

"Or she altered her image for her stay here?"

"I can cover the first alternative as soon as I figure out a way to get beyond that desk clerk and have a gander at the guest list. Yeah, but if the other alternative turns out to be the case, this snap of Pinkie is gonna be as much use to us as a torch to a blind man down a coal mine."

"What then, Kemosabe?"

Bob scratched his head. "Then we launch into the serious Research And Probing aspect of the game. We set about hoofing it round every airline office in Palma to find out if one of them had Pinkie's name on a manifest of passengers flying out of the island about that time."

"But even if you do come up with something from the flight companies, and that could take the rest of the week, it would only move your current problem to another destination."

Bob's gloomy look expressed his acceptance of this hypothesis.

"Hi, there! Just arrived, have you?" It was the professionally-cheery greeting of the Nordic girl, who was springing lightly over to them with a smile which matched her voice. "I'm Astrid — entertainments manager here. Welcome to the Hotel Santa Catalina!"

"I bet I know what's coming next," Bob muttered to Julie out of the corner of his mouth. "I'm gonna be press-ganged into entering the daddies' knobbly knees contest." He shook his head in despair. "That's all I bloody well need!"

"Go for it, boy!" Julie muttered. "From what I've seen of your equipment, you've gotta be in with one helluva great chance of lifting the silverware."

Smiling wearily, Bob stood up, made the required introductions yet again, then offered Astrid a seat.

She was the very embodiment of bronzed good health, the definitive fit-as-a-butcher's-dog blonde Scando. Lacking even one gram of superfluous meat on her graceful bones, she was a living endorsement of a wholesome lifestyle fuelled by an Omega-3-rich diet of rollmop herring and smoked-salmon smorgasbord. Bob instinctively pulled in his stomach. Julie discreetly covered her exposed pallid parts. They envied her in unison.

"I wonder if you recognise this woman?" Bob routinely asked, half-heartedly indicating Pinkie in the photograph.

Astrid took a moment to answer, but when she did, a glimmer of recognition was shining in her ice-blue eyes. "Lady Euphemia!" she beamed. "And wearing the same novelty wig and glasses that she wore on the Psychedelic Night in our Bow Bells Lounge when she was here. How could I forget her?"

Bob was momentarily stuck for words. "So, ehm — so, what was her appearance like the rest of the time?" he eventually stammered.

Astrid raised a golden shoulder. "Just what you'd expect of an elderly, aristocratic lady, I guess. You know, silver-grey hair softly waved, designer spectacles, elegant clothes of classic style. Of course, everything about her oozed expense, but in an understated way. I mean, we do pride ourselves in attracting a very nice type of client here anyway, but her ladyship was, well, a cut above the rest, really. Yet she always carried it off very modestly." Astrid puckered her lips and gathered her brows into a discerning little frown of approval. "A sure sign of her breeding, no?"

"No — I mean, yes . . . of course." Bob's head was reeling. Surely this Astrid bird had got her Nordic wires crossed. "But are you *quite* certain we're talking about the same woman here? I mean, can you remember her surname, for instance?"

Astrid didn't hesitate. "Dalrymple. Lady Euphemia Dalrymple. Such a noble name. It simply rolls off the tongue, doesn't it? Such a name is so, well, so British upper class, I guess, no?"

Dumbfounded, Bob nodded his head in silence. Sure enough, old Jimmy King at Archerfield had said that Pinkie had more patter than Al Jolson, but her performance as depicted by Astrid seemed in the Oscar-winning class. And her only an old country dearie who seemed hard pushed even to write a grammatical postcard. Bob flashed Astrid a thin smile. "She, ehm, she didn't answer to the name of . . . Pinkie, by any chance, did she?"

Astrid didn't reply. She didn't need to. Her disdainful snort spoke louder than words.

Bob's reply was a suit-yourself shrug. "And I don't suppose you know where this, uhm, this *Lady* Euphemia went at the end of her holiday, do you?"

Astrid raised the other golden shoulder. "Home, I guess. Doesn't everyone?"

"What did she do with her time while she was here?" Julie put in, trying another tack. "I mean, did she make many friends?"

200

"Oh, yes! They all wanted to speak to her ladyship. And she was just so, well, *natural* with everyone. Yes, even with the more — how do you say? — *common* element." Astrid smiled reflectively for a moment, then added, "Mind you, we really didn't see much of her during the daytime. She nearly always left the hotel after breakfast."

"Do you know where she went on those occasions?" Bob pressed.

"No, but I can tell you that she spent every single evening in the Bow Bells Lounge here, sitting listening to Juan, our resident keyboard player. She would always sit alone at a table right by him. They used to talk a lot during his break periods. There was some connection, I guess — like they knew each other before, maybe." Astrid raised both golden shoulders. "Who knows?"

"Presumably this Juan guy does," Julie reasoned.

"That's right," Bob concurred, hope springing detectably. "Where can we find him?"

Juan was already seated on his podium in the far corner of the lounge, surreptitiously slipping floppy disks into his Korg keyboard and slickly superimposing his own vocals over some very plausible backing-track replications of Frank Sinatra's Greatest Hits. His performance, as usual, was for the delectation of groups of Littlewoods Summer Catalogue-outfitted hotel residents, drifting in for after-dinner drinks and, perhaps, the prospect of a digestion-promoting sing-along session.

Having deposited Julie at what he considered a suitably discreet table, Bob made his way over to the bar, where he found himself standing beside a panatella-puffing Mancunian behemoth with volume-coordinated shirt and voice. Between spontaneously-combusted guffaws, this walking advert for gluttony seemed determined to let everyone within the room know that he was on first name terms with the barman and that "me and the missus" had been coming to this hotel at the same time every year for the past fifteen years without fail, like.

"Spain? Magic! Nowhere like it, Meegwell. Wouldn't miss it, *amigo*. Yeah, that's right, Meegwell. Two pints o' Boddington's, lad." He guffawed again, slapped Bob's shoulder, then bellowed tunelessly, "*EE, VEE-VER ESPANYER!*"

God, how Bob loathed all this. He felt totally out of place, conspicuous in his staid navy blazer and charcoal grey slacks. Worse than that, he was starting to feel neurotic about the thought of the blue nick-nick-nick lamp winking away relentlessly through his ample thatch of hair. He glanced across at Julie. To his dismay, she looked perfectly at home. She was thoroughly enjoying herself, in fact, her head rocking rhythmically from side to side, one leg crossed over the other, and a high-heeled peep-toe tapping out the beat of *Somethin' Stupid*. An afternoon of gently basting herself on the apartment balcony had already bestowed upon her skin the makings of an attractive tan, which she had skilfully set off with a jazzy little navy-and-white polka-dot frock. Suddenly, Bob felt the eight-year differential in their ages expand into decades.

202

"Lighten up, Methuselah," she chirped at him when he arrived back with their drinks. "Get with it! It's holiday time!"

"I stick out like a thistle in a barley field in places like this," he grumped. "I really do."

"Nonsense!" Julie studied Bob's glum expression for a moment, then flashed him an impish smile. "People been coming up and asking you for directions, have they?"

Bob slumped down into his seat and attempted to appear invisible. "Like I said, we can't all be like Wullie bloody Merryfield!"

Juan finished his Sinatra medley, milked the pitter-patter of applause which stuttered round the lounge, then announced over the PA in a curiously clipped and glottal Hispano-American accent: "You're a wunnerful audience and Ah *adore* ya all. Hey! And thank you for the clap, as the actress she said to the bishop!"

The Mancunian mammoth let rip with a guffaw in chorus with a cackle of mirror-shattering decibels from his missus.

Juan gave them a nod and trumpeted out a fanfare on his keyboard. "*Muchas* grassy arse, Alf and Ena. Always nice to welcome old friends . . . which is why it's too bad you two decided to come back again."

The bellows and shrieks of approval which exploded from the twin victims of his gibe served as a guarantee of at least one steady supply of free drinks for Juan during the next fortnight.

Another fanfare.

"And it's always nice to welcome new friends, as well," Juan boomed. "*Señoras y señores*, let's hear it for a man who's got more nick-nick-ability in his little finger than Taggart, Columbo, Inspector Morse and the whole of The Bill put together. My old *compadre* . . ." He paused to stand up and point theatrically at Bob, then thundered, "BOB-BEE BURNS! YEAH! TAKE A BOW, BOBBY! *OLÉ!*"

Bob tried to burrow a way through the seat of his chair with his backside. He was mortified. "How the hell did that bugger know who I was?" he growled into his chest, covering his forehead with his hand.

Julie was already joining in the applause. "You may as well relax and enjoy yourself now," she giggled. "No point in blowing your cool . . . as *well* as your cover."

Bob was still smarting half an hour later, his embarrassment level kept well topped up by many a passing wag pausing at his table to salute, genuflect akimbo and hail him with a warm, "Evenin', all!" He was on the verge of throwing in the towel for the night when Juan announced that he was about to take a short break. The barman pressed a button, and piped piano music began to tinkle away beneath the hum and babble of animated conversation, punctuated with regular bursts of uninhibited holiday laughter. The Bow Bells Lounge was buzzing.

Grinning from ear to ear, Juan elbowed his way through the throng to Bob and Julie's table. "Ye cannae remember me, can ye, Bobby?" he enquired in a broad Scots accent.

Bob answered his question with a frown of bafflement. He surveyed the roly-poly physique and the chubby features fixed in a cordial smile that the eyes revealed as genuine.

"It's me. Ian ... Ian Scrabster," Juan laughed. "Remember? I was in the first year at North Berwick High when you were in the fifth. You were a prefect, always giving me lines for being late. Remember now?"

"Wee Crabbie Scrabster!" Bob smiled, as a glimmer of recognition finally sparked. "Your excuse was always that you'd been out half the night playing your accordion in your old man's band." He poked his erstwhile minor's midriff and joked, "You could get three or four of the wee laddie I remember in *there*, though!"

Ian grinned proudly and stroked his Zapata moustache. "I didn't have this in those days either, of course."

"Aye, well, it goes with the Juan handle, I suppose. But what's all that phoney gringo stuff about, anyway?"

"Listen, when I first came over here ten years ago, I soon wised up that the punters don't want to come all the way to Spain to be entertained by some muso with a Jock name like Ian Scrabster." He patted his belly. "For a kickoff, I couldn't have afforded this if I hadn't turned myself into Juan the organ man."

Bob chuckled softly and shook his head. "Wee Crabbie Scrabster, eh? Well, well, well, who'd have credited it!" He was jolted out of his reminiscing by Julie clearing her throat loudly and giving his ankle a sharp kick under the table. Bob apologised and did the belated honours. "Julie's a colleague of mine. Over here helping me out on a missing person case."

Ian's jovial expression darkened slightly. "Yeah, Astrid mentioned that a Mr Robert Burns and his partner had been here earlier, wanting to talk to me about something like that. But it wasn't until I noticed you walking over to your table from the bar tonight that I tied the name in with Bobby Burns from good old North Berwick High." He grinned again and gave Bob a hearty slap on the back. "Hey, I hope you didn't mind me giving you a plug over the mike, Bobby. It's all just ballyhoo. You know, for the punters. They love all that visiting celebrity bullshit."

Bob raised his shoulders into an insouciant shrug and drawled, "Yeah, no sweat, mate." He swatted the air limply. "No worries — I'm hip to all that jive."

Julie almost choked on her drink, but covered up quickly by asking, "So, Ian, you know this, ehm, *Lady* Dalrymple, do you?"

"You mean Pinkie? Sure, I've known her since I was a kid. Me and some of the boys used to nip along to Dirleton for a bit of under-age drinking in the public bar at the Castle Inn, if we had a few bob between us." The memory of it made him laugh. "Yeah, Pinkie and her old buddy Bertie McGregor used to lie to the barman for us when he asked our ages. Bringing the younger generation up in the faith, was what they used to tell us. What a pair of cases!"

Bob decided it was time to adopt a more professional demeanour with his old school acquaintance. "How come the Lady Euphemia bit?" he probed. "What was she trying to hide? And where did all the expensive threads come from? The word I got in Scotland was that she was supposed to be near enough completely skint."

Ian, hands aloft, adopted the surrender position. "Ease up, Bobby. You're asking me a load of questions I can't answer, man."

"Can't, or won't?" said Julie, emulating Bob's deadpan delivery.

"Come on, back off, you guys," Ian balked. "Don't give me the heavy treatment all of a sudden! I'm all for helping you, if I can. But hey, so far you haven't even told me what this is all about!"

"I take it you haven't heard any news from back home over the past couple of days, then," Bob stated dryly.

"News?" Ian scoffed. "*Hombre!* The only news I listen to these days is the Spanish lottery results!"

"OK, so I won't burden you with the details right now," Bob went on. "It's enough to say that someone of Pinkie's acquaintance has died in somewhat suspicious circumstances, and I believe that Pinkie may know of something that happened a long time ago which *may* have a bearing on the case." He eyeballed Ian in a stare that would have paralysed a rabbit. "And if we don't locate her soon, I wouldn't rule out the possibility of Pinkie being harmed herself."

Ian was clearly shaken.

Julie grabbed the moment to administer some psychological soft soap. "Look, Ian," she murmured, "if you're as fond of Pinkie as I think you are, it's essential that you tell us *anything* you know about her current whereabouts . . . without delay."

Ian's brows were now bunched into creases of real concern. But concern tempered with caution. He took a beer mat and drew a little map on the reverse. Passing it to Bob, he said, "I'll be doing a gig at that place the day after tomorrow. I'm not promising anything, you understand, but if I *can* come up with something, I'll have it for you then. Be there at seven sharp." He darted glances at them both in turn. "But just one thing," he cautioned, "— press the pause button on your enquiries in the meantime. For a start, you won't get anywhere. And secondly, you could do more harm than good by even trying."

Without another word being exchanged, Ian then swaggered back, larger than life, to his dais, while Bob and Julie walked away in pensive silence into the darkness of the car park.

Unknown to them, however, their every move was being watched closely from the cover of a grove of small palm trees by the shady figure of a woman. An elderly woman, dressed incongruously in tweeds.

CHAPTER
THIRTEEN

Port d'Andratx was bursting at the seams. The narrow back streets and alleyways of the one-time unspoiled fishing village, which was rapidly developing (or degenerating, depending on your point of view) into Mallorca's answer to St Tropez, were heaving with excited families, all thronging towards the little church on the hillside looking out to the sweeping crescent of the port. It was the the Fiesta of La Virgen del Carmen, and with the late afternoon sun already brushing the pine-topped ridges of the western mountains, the moment for the graven Madonna's annual outing was rapidly approaching.

Albeit at odds with his nature, the only investigative work Bob had done during the past couple of days had been to grudgingly rake, at Julie's insistence, through rack after rack of summery clothes in a succession of gents' outfitters, until he came across the way-out (for him) ensemble of pastel-hued paisley shirt, duck-egg-blue chinos and white espadrilles, which he was now self-consciously sporting. As much as he was resigned to the fact that the road to Pinkie Dalrymple was now controlled, for better or worse, by Ian Scrabster, Bob's earnest attempts, at Julie's behest, to be optimistically fatalistic about the situation weren't really working. The likely consequences of Ian *not* coming up with a positive lead today were just too dire to banish completely from his thoughts.

Julie grabbed him by the elbow and wheeled him left, against the flow of the human stream. "It's down this way," she said, brandishing the beer mat map. "And cheer up!" she goaded. "You can't complain about feeling out of place now. You look just like all the other merry pilgrims."

Bob scanned his flamboyant clobber with suspicion, then replied, "Yeah, and if I was still a bona fide policeman, I'd likely arrest myself!"

To loud cheers from a couple of blocks away, the village children's passionately-discordant bugle and drum band struck up with a series of variations on a three-note theme, which had obviously been composed by a deaf sadist with a grudge against those not so fortunately impaired. Happily, Bob and Julie were headed in the opposite direction, away from the church and down towards the sea — to the vicinity of *La Lonja*, the old fish market, outside which Ian's map told them he'd be performing.

If anything, the crush of people intensified as they approached the waterfront, everyone milling around and jostling for the best vantage points from which to view the impending pageant. The harbour was ablaze with colour, the air charged with anticipation. It seemed that the entire local fishing fleet was tied up cheek by jowl along the quay, every boat bedecked by its crew from gunwhale to mast top with balloons, streamers and bunting in celebration of the day of their patron saint.

The oddly-Latinised strains of *Somethin' Stupid* drew Bob and Julie along the palm-lined length of the wharf. They nudged a path through the crowds until they eventually reached a roped-off area in the square fronting the fishermen's market, where a raised wooden dance floor had been erected. There, on a canopied rostrum, sat Ian, doing his amplified utmost to compete with the distant but relentlessly approaching clamour of bugles and drums. In front of him, a troupe of traditionally-costumed couples of mature vintage keenly twirled, stomped, dipped and swooned their way through a dance that had its roots in the *paso doble*, but its feet in the grape-treading pit.

"Did you hear that?" Bob shouted, turning round sharply and straining to see over the heads of the crowd.

Julie looked blankly up at him.

"There it goes again." Bob was standing on tiptoe now, a steadying hand on Julie's shoulder as he peered back along the quayside. "It sounded like somebody calling out to me."

Julie shook her head in disbelief. "I told you, you should've bought that straw hat when you got the rest of your gear yesterday. The sun's addled your brains!"

The jarring blare of miscellaneous brass instruments blasting out an unruly flourish from aboard one of the larger fishing boats put paid to Bob's deliberations and hailed the emergence of La Virgen del Carmen into the broad esplanade overlooking the harbour. A great roar went up from the crowd as the sacred manikin came into view, her painted, coronalled head jerking about perkily above the cheering melee, as her team of litter bearers staggered gamely onwards in the bugle and drum band's wake.

Pandemonium reigned with adoration. Ian jacked it in with alacrity.

"The golden rule of Spanish musicians," he shouted from the bandstand while preparing to pack his keyboard into its case, "— never pit your organ against a wooden Virgin. And I'm not talking about getting splinters!" He beckoned Bob and Julie to join him. "Anyway, that's the end of this gig for me. Back to the heathen sanctuary of the Bow Bells Lounge tonight, thank Christ!"

Bob decided to forsake polite formalities in the interest of exigency. "What's the word on Pinkie Dalrymple?" he said.

Ian opened his arms and made a calming motion with his hands. "This is Spain, Bobby man. The land of mañana, right?"

"OK, but I haven't got too many mañanas left, so have you got anything to tell me or not?"

Ian wasn't going to be hurried, though. He held out a hand to Julie. "Come up on the platform, petal. You'll get a better view of the goings-on from here." He lobbed Bob a set of keys. "Do me a favour, pal. Nip round the back of the fish market there and fetch my car while I'm packing up the rest of my stuff."

Bob was beside himself with frustration. Under the circumstances, however, his choices were strictly limited. He had to admit that he was hardly in a position to threaten Ian with a charge of impeding the police in the course of their duties. He looked at the keys. "OK," he sighed. "What kind of motor is it?"

"A Merc. A grey one. The number's on the fob there."

Another cheer rose from the crowd. The bugles and drums fell silent at last, only to be replaced by the marginally more tuneful outpourings of the brass band. This, it now became clear, was ensconced aboard the large fishing boat onto which the Madonna, swaying about atop her regalia-swathed palanquin, was now being ceremoniously loaded.

"That's boat *numero uno* for this year's celebrations," Ian explained to Julie. "A great honour. It'll lead the fleet out into the middle of the port, then they'll all sail off in single file into the sunset — out of the bay and way out into the Med there. Quite a sight."

"But look at all those kids clambering on to the boats!" she gasped. "The little hooligans! The fishermen'll do their nuts!"

No, that was all part of the tradition, Ian pointed out. The boats were chock-a-block with goodies for the youngsters to eat and drink, and they were all encouraged to come aboard and join in the fun and spectacle of the procession. Then, when the last boat had disappeared round the far headland and the flotilla had reached a hallowed place revered by the sailors for generations, the high jinks would be interrupted for the solemn ceremony of La Virgen blessing the sea. This, according to seafaring belief, would ensure another year of safety and good fishing for the Port d'Andratx boats.

"Yeah," Ian laughed, "they say they even used to dip the old Madonna there right into the water. Going for maximum insurance cover, sort of thing. But maybe it was beginning to shrink her frock, never mind rot her wooden legs, 'cos nowadays they let her do her thing on deck, without even getting her big toe wet."

"A sign of the times, maybe. Improved conditions for working Virgins, and all that?" Julie quipped.

"Could be, but it's all taken very seriously by the fisher folk in these parts. And who can blame them? When things get rough in that job, you need all the help you can get." He looked directly into Julie's eyes, his expression suddenly stern. "But it'll take more than a carved saint to save my hide if I do the wrong thing by Pinkie."

Julie raised her eyebrows. "You know where she is, then?"

Ian continued to stare intently at her. "Ask the lassie, Pinkie told me. Don't trust the polisman until ye've looked the lassie in the eye and asked her to tell you the truth about him."

Julie was totally nonplussed. "What do you want me to tell you, for heaven's sake? That he's a general in the Salvation Army, a fully paid-up member of the Cliff Richard Fan Club or something?"

Ian wasn't about to be so flippantly brushed aside. "That old woman went to a lot of bother to cover her tracks — all that Lady Euphemia bit and everything — and she didn't do it for nothing. I don't know what it's all about, but she's trying to keep out of *somebody's* way. She's told me that much. And the last thing I want to do is —"

"Look," Julie butted in, a note of irritation in her voice, "that *polisman* hasn't just gone to a lot of bother to *uncover* her tracks, he's put his job and his whole damned future on the line. And it's for *her* good, not his own. I mean, I'm not even sure that he really knows why, but as he told you himself, he honestly believes that Pinkie's in some kind of danger. There's already been one murder, and he's convinced that Pinkie could be next in line." Seeing Ian's jaw drop, she added testily, "So you'd better stop farting about with all that look-the-lassie-in-the-eyes bollocks and tell us where she is!"

Her words stung him like a crisply-delivered slap on the face. "Murder?" he gulped. "Did you say *murder*? Jesus, that's heavy-duty stuff, so why the hell haven't you brought the Spanish cops in on the act?"

"That's a long story. But never fear, they'll be in on the act soon enough if somebody wastes old Pinkie." Julie inclined her head towards the approaching grey Mercedes and stated bluntly, "So, Ian, if you really care about her welfare, it's about time you started coughing up to your Dirleton *compadre* there. You're just gonna have to take my word for it — we're the good guys all right, but if *we've* managed to get this near to finding Pinkie Dalrymple, there's nothing to stop the baddies from doing likewise. *Comprende?*"

Ian swallowed hard. "Gimme a hand to pack my gear into the car, Bobby," he shouted. "Your lady friend's

215

eyes have just convinced me that it's time to pay Pinkie a visit."

Bob's heart skipped a beat. Trying hard to maintain an air of calm, he walked round slowly to the back of the car and unlocked the boot. "You mean she's still on the island?"

Ian nodded. "Unless she was spirited away by the baddies while I was playing for the fandango team, that is." He dropped his voice. "But I think I would have noticed, don't you?"

Julie gaped at him. "You — you mean to say that Pinkie Dalrymple was one of the *dancers?*"

"Only the leader of the pack, that's all," Ian chuckled. "Yeah, as she says, she may not be a native Spaniard, but she can still pass a doble with the best of them."

Julie was quick to latch onto Ian's line of thought. "Uh-huh, and I suppose that's why you asked us to meet you here today. You wanted to give Pinkie a chance to check us out, right?"

Ian nodded again. "And if she hadn't fancied the look of what she saw, she'd have given me the ticktack before she shot the crow."

Bob was only half listening to all of this. He was more immediately intrigued by something he had noticed in the boot of Ian's car. Holding up a can of Castrol R racing oil, he said, "Excuse me asking, but what do you keyboard players use this for? Good finger lubrication for getting round the fast numbers, is it?"

216

Ian forced a smile, clearly unimpressed. "Oh, very droll, Bobby. Yeah, nothing quite like a copper's sense of humour, I always say."

"Don't piss me about, mate," Bob snarled. "What *do* you use this for?"

"Hey! What's with all the third degree stuff all of a sudden? I'm on the side of the good guys, remember?"

"OK, OK, so I shouldn't have snapped at you. But this is the second time this stuff has cropped up recently, and in this game you never take *any* coincidences at face value." Bob tapped the tin with his fingers. "What's the story?"

"No big deal, man." Ian raised his shoulders. "I race karts, that's all. The real go-like-shit Grand Prix ones. Hey, and talking about coincidences, it was an Edinburgh copper who got me hooked on karts in the first place. Well, the *wife* of an Edinburgh copper would be nearer the mark."

Bob was fascinated. "Tell me more."

"Yeah, Lauren Order, the lads called her." Ian grimaced. "What a pain in the neck she was!"

"Lauren *Order*?"

"That's right. Lauren Order. She was a copper's wife, get it?"

"Yeah, yeah, yeah, I'm not *that* bloody thick. But what was her real name? That's what I want to know — her *real* surname!"

Ian stared vaguely into space. "Now you're asking. I mean, it was a long time ago. Twelve years at least."

"Think! It's important!"

"She was one of those do-gooders," said Ian, thinking aloud. "One of those voluntary social workers or suchlike. Yeah, she used to organise days out to the motor racing circuit at Knockhill in Fife for underprivileged teenagers. Underprivileged teenagers?" he scoffed. "Under-civilized young thugs was what I called them. I was attempting to teach music at a school for those low-lives in Edinburgh at the time, see, and Lauren Order and her hubby would turn up every so often in a police van to pick a few of them up. I was dragged along as their keeper, sort of thing, and that's how I got hooked on karts."

"Or speared?" Bob suggested, dangling the carrot.

Ian snapped his fingers. "Right on! That was it — Lauren Spiers!"

Bob and Julie exchanged knowing glances.

"A right pain in the arse," Ian rambled on, "and her old man wasn't any better. Ex-orphanage kid, he boasted he was. Said he could relate to the young reptiles masquerading as members of the human race that they took on those trips. Yeah, right, and welcome to them. Should've drowned the little bastards at birth, that's what I say!"

"I don't suppose you know if this Lauren Spiers still gets involved in the karting thing, do you?" Bob pressed.

"I know for a fact she does," Ian replied. "Yeah, a couple of the Knockhill track staff were here on holiday at the Santa Catalina Hotel just a month or so back, and we had a few chats in the bar about the old days. Naturally, Lauren Order's name came up, and the lads said she was still doing her good deeds for society, arriving with the occasional Black Maria full of budding car thieves and apprentice joy riders keen to brush up their driving techniques."

Smiling contentedly, Bob placed the oil can back in the boot of Ian's Mercedes. "Well, well, well," he said. "Like I say, you can never afford to take coincidences at face value in this game . . ."

The Villa Vista Dragonera stood proud and pink in the glow of the setting sun, its site, high on the mountainside above the mouth of Port d'Andratx bay, commanding a priceless view over pine trees to the open sea and westward to the island of Dragonera, from which it took its name.

Ian led the way through the ornate wrought iron gates and along the palm-fringed terrace by the swimming pool. "Some pad, huh?"

Bob looked up at the graceful conformation of the classic Spanish villa and voiced his agreement without hesitation. He let his eyes wander over the cascades of scarlet geraniums overflowing the balustraded balcony that spanned the width of the house. He whistled through his teeth. "Jeez! No shortage of pesetas here!"

How in heaven's name had Pinkie managed to land a job in a place like this, a rubber-necked Julie wanted to know. And at her age, too! "Housekeeper, cook, is she?" she asked Ian.

Ian said nothing, but instead tweaked the left nipple of the life-size bronze statue of a naked Aphrodite standing by the heavy oak door. Instantly, the melodic chime of the first two bars of *Stop Yer Ticklin'*, Jock echoed from within. A few moments later, a Filipina maid in tartan-trimmed white uniform appeared and, recognising Ian, cheerily welcomed the visitors inside.

Bob cast his eyes round the sumptuously-comfortable interior and let his thoughts drift back to what he had seen of two of Pinkie's previous residences — the lowly cottage built into the garden wall at Archerfield Estate, and the depressing bleakness of the old folks' home in Perthshire. "Wow," he exclaimed, "even if she only cleans the karzies, she's got it made here!"

"You better believe it, boy," said Ian, as he gestured with a sweep of his arm towards the archway at the far end of the spacious drawing room into which the maid had guided them. "Bobby Burns, Julie Bryson, I present your hostess — fandangoist supreme, ace raver and prima donna of the Mallorcan karzie-cleaners. Her Disgrace, the Lady Euphemia Dalrymple!"

The presence now posing before them was a monument to over-the-top eccentricity. Pink hair, bamboo specs, crimson-and-gold silk kimono, harpoon-length cigarette holder, gold lamé Frankenstein boots, the works!

"Welcome to my humble abode, one and all," she articulated in an accent of most regal Windsor, champagne flute to the fore, little finger elegantly elevated. "Nice of youse to drop by."

220

CHAPTER
FOURTEEN

Bob hadn't seen the fist until the split second before it smashed into the side of his jaw. And the last thing his eyes noticed en route to oblivion was the upwardly-passing hem of a tweed skirt as his face sped towards a rendezvous with the polished marble floor.

He saw only red, tasted only blood. He blinked, shook his aching head, spluttered, spat and blinked again. The room was swimming in a fiery light. It was the unmistakable blaze of sundown. Befuddled though he was, Bob reasoned that he couldn't have been out cold for long.

"Get your hands up! UP! Look lively, and don't move a fuckin' muscle, or you're dead meat!"

The yelled order came from behind him. The contradictory nature of the command and the high-pitched warble of the voice indicated that the owner was in the grip of sphincter-loosening panic. Bob knew from experience that this was no time for heroics. He struggled to his feet and turned carefully, hands raised.

"Hi, Sarge!" The voice was suddenly calmer, relieved to the brink of exuberance, as the switch of recognition clicked. "Seems like my timing was a wee bit off, eh?"

Bob struggled to screw one of his eyes into focus. "Christ!" he mumbled incredulously through a thickening lip. "It can't be . . ."

"It *is*!" The voice was positively ecstatic.

"But you're in . . . *Greece*!"

"I'll take your word for it, skipper." The voice was genuinely nonchalant.

"But — but this is Mallorca. And Mallorca's . . . *Spanish*!"

"Spanish, Portuguese, Italian, French — it's all bloody Greek to me!" The voice was blissfully ignorant.

Bob opened the other eye, closed it again, then rubbed it, his expression contorting into one of deep confusion. Slowly, he looked PC Green up and down. "But you're not wearing a . . . skirt," he said, mistily.

"Sorry to disappoint, Sarge," Green grinned, his cheerful shrug provoking a curious slopping noise to emanate from the revolver that he held in his right hand. "I mean, I'm as open-minded as they come, but skirts — I'm not into them. Well, when I say I'm not into them, I don't actually mean I'm not *into* them, like. Up them, yeah, but —"

"Shut your face, Green," Bob grunted. He was now concentrating all his mental energies into sorting out the jumble of thoughts that were having bumper car rides round the inside of his throbbing skull.

A three-part harmony of whimpering caused him to glance sideways. Over by the dining alcove, Julie and Ian were sitting back-to-back on two chairs. They were gagged and trussed up with brown parcel tape like a pair of Siamese chickens. The Filipina maid was sitting

222

slumped and cross-eyed on the floor against Ian's knees, an angry contusion beaming out purple vibrations from her forehead.

"What the blazes happened here?" Bob rasped.

He looked back at Andy Green, but the only response he got was a stumped stare from a face as blank as a flush-panelled door.

"Quick!" Bob barked at him. "Help me untie them!" For a second, his eyes zeroed in on Constable Green's nervously palpitating right hand. "And for God's sake get rid of that stupid pistol! You're squirting water all over the woman's bloody floor! Which reminds me . . ." He darted feverish glances round the room. "Where the hell's Pinkie?"

It was Julie who was given first opportunity to reply, by PC Green ripping (a mite over-zealously) the sticky tape from her face. She screamed briefly, swore, then blurted out, "She's been kidnapped. It was a woman. She had a gun. She just stormed in through the French doors and clobbered you when you were about to shake Pinkie's hand. She grabbed Pinkie, held the gun to her head, made the maid tie us up like this, then walloped her on the brow with the butt of the gun for her trouble!"

"Right, what does she look like?" Bob's voice was quivering with urgency, his fingers trembling as he struggled with the muddle of tape that bound their ankles and wrists together. "Come on, for Pete's sake — somebody describe her to me!"

This time, PC Green did respond, and he was quick to do so. "Just over five feet, I'd say. About nineteen, long hair — dark like her eyes — nice legs, neat figure, thrup'nies small but perfectly-formed, attractive Oriental bone structure. Pity about the welt on the forehead, right enough, but that'll soon —"

"I'm not talking about the bloody maid!" Bob exploded. "I'm talking about the bloody woman who melted her. And me!"

"Real ugly bitch," Ian wheezed in a tortured treble, as Andy Green enthusiastically tore off his adhesive gag along with a fortnight's worth of top-lip Zapata. "Real butch-looking Amazon type. Reminded me of one or two career-spinster schoolmarms I've worked with in my time. You know the sort — about as much feminine allure as a wart hog in Harris tweed!"

"With grey, permed hair, National Health specs and hairy legs?" Bob asked, with Julie simultaneously speaking the same words as a statement of fact. "Aye, and a right hook that Mike Tyson wouldn't be ashamed of," Bob added, tenderly kneading his chin.

Andy Green waited until he was sure Bob had finished, then said, "See, that's why I was trying to catch your attention down at the harbour, Sarge."

Bob flashed Julie a who's-brains-are-addled-now? look.

"Me and my mates were trying to get on to one of the boats, like," PC Green continued. "The one with the local beauty queen and her maids of honour on board. The birds were nothing too brilliant, mind. *Well* rough. But, you know, any port in a storm — especially on yer hols, eh? The one I fancied best — I saw her giving me the glad eye, like — was the one in the mermaid kit with the phenomenal pair of —"

"Green!"

"Sorry, Sarge. Went off at a tandem there. Yeah, what was I saying again?" He started to nibble his thumb nail, frowning. "Shit, you've made me lose my drift now . . ."

"Harris tweed and hairy legs," Bob prompted, sighing.

"Oh, yeah! Yeah, that's right! It was well busy down by the boats there, OK. Everybody barging about and lifting their nippers up to see better and that. Then I feels this thump in the back, and this dragon in drag elbows past and she's muttering to herself about that bastard Burns. Freaky! So, I looks where she's looking. And right enough, there's you and the Doc away over by the bandstand listening to Fats Domino here. I'm tellin' you, Sarge, I thought I was seeing things. You know what it's like — me and the boys was well bevvied up on the *San Miguels* down on the beach until about seven o' clock this morning. Fifteen bottles, me, before I flaked, like. Magic! I mean, I've heard about yer pink elephants and that, but —"

"GREEN!"

"Sorry, Sarge. Yeah, so then I sees the dragon woman fumbling in her handbag, and I sees she's got a rod stashed."

"She had a concealed handgun?" Bob questioned rhetorically, wearying fast.

"Jackpot! So, I puts two and two together . . . bastard Burns, gun . . . bastard Burns, gun. Trouble, I says to myself, just like that. Keep the heid, I thinks. Don't panic! So, I shouts 'Sarge!' at the top of my voice. Nothin'! Too much noise. Trumpets and drums and that. OK, kid, you're in the polis, I says to maself. So, think bent. Right away, I sees this local gadgie next to me with his sprog on his shoulders, and the sprog's got a water pistol, right? OK, so I whips out my Lothian and Borders Constabulary ID card and says to the gadgie, 'Interpol! C-R-A-P!' Just like Kojak. Then I snatches the pistol off the sprog. The sprog yells blue murder, and I yells 'Sarge!' again. Still nothin'!" PC Green yanked the last length of sticky tape from Ian and Julie's wrists and panted, "I seen you looking round, like, but you couldn't see nothin'! Too many people trying to get near that wooden statue babe in the pantomime gear that they were loadin' onto that big boat on a fancy stretcher thing."

"The Madonna," Bob grunted, exasperated.

"Looked more like Alice Cooper than Madonna to me," Green came back.

"What about your mates?" said Julie, bending forward to help Bob peel the tape from her ankles.

"Search me. Maybe they made it onto the beauty queen's boat. Maybe not. I just started following the dragon, and the next time I looks back, the lads have disappeared. No kiddin', Doc, I was shittin' bricks! Just me and a water pistol against the world!"

"A frightening prospect," Bob opined under his breath.

"So, I just follows the dragon followin' you. But as soon as she sees you getting into the Merc, she nicks a moped from outside one of the bars and zaps off in hot pursuit." Andy Green held out his trembling hands. "No wonder I'm knackered. I had to run all the bleedin' way up here!"

"You did well, lad," said Bob, then helped the Filipina maid off the floor and onto the chair just vacated by Julie. "But if you'd scoffed ten less bottles of beer last night, you might've got here in time to save me getting a belt in the chops."

"More important," countered Ian, visibly vexed, "you might've got here in time to save old Pinkie from being snatched." He rounded on Bob. "And come to that, I thought you smart-arsed CID guys were trained to suss when you're being tailed!"

Bob knew well enough that he'd been a wee bit less vigilant than he normally would have been in somewhat less exotic surroundings. But he wasn't about to admit it. Not in front of a rookie beat constable, and *certainly* not in front of Julie Bryson. "Yeah, well, my arse may be smart," he retorted, "but it hasn't got an eyeball peeping out of it!"

Andy Green roared with jittery laughter. "Aw, nice one, skipper! Straight Kojak, that one!"

Bob pretended to pay no heed. He knelt down in front of the glassy-eyed maid and held up five fingers. "How many?"

There was a brief arithmetic hush. "Ereven!" the maid hazarded hopefully.

Bob patted her knee. "That's near enough. You're still alive, darlin'."

Julie tutted reproachfully and gave the girl's hair a sympathetic stroke.

Bob got to his feet. "Right, let's get the hell out of here. The dragon lady's got a big enough head start on us as it is."

From outside came the full-throated roar of a car engine revving up.

The blood drained from Ian's cheeks. "Bugger me," he spluttered, "that's my Merc! The bitch must've hot-wired it!"

He led the charge for the door, past the swimming pool and out into the road. Away to the west, the outline of Dragonera Island was already plunged into silhouette against the rosy-mauve of the twilight sky, while the lights of the returning fishing boats moved slowly homeward across the linking expanse of sea.

But this was no time to pause and admire the view.

"Where does Pinkie keep her car?" Bob shouted at Ian, just as the Mercedes' brake lights disappeared round the first hairpin down the mountain road.

Ian leaned his elbow against the trunk of a handy pine tree and struggled for breath. "Hasn't got one . . . Uses taxis . . . Only thing in her garage is my kart . . . She let's me keep it here . . . Safer than —"

Bob was already at the garage door, frantically wiggling back the bolt. "Let's get the bloody thing mobile, then. Come on! You drive. I'll stand on the back!"

"Hey! Look what I've found, Sarge!" Andy Green was semi-submerged in the nether regions of a giant rubber plant by the gate. "It's the dragon's moped!" He hauled it out, mounted it, and pumped away furiously at the kick-start until the little two-stroke motor coughed itself into a rattle of blue-smoked life.

Julie hitched up her skirt to a point between pelmet height and indecency, swung her leg over the pillion, clutched PC Green's waist firmly with both hands and yelled, "OK, Stavros! Follow that kart!"

Such a crazy chase down the tortuous mountain road would have been fraught enough at the best of times. But tonight of all nights, with so many village people scaling the heights by car and on foot to watch the spectacle of La Virgen del Carmen's homecoming armada, the odds against reaching the bottom without serious incident were reduced to the low side of short. The blaring of its horn as it screeched round switchback after switchback at least warned the ascending column of the Merc's oncoming menace, but the hapless sightseers were ill-prepared for the twin hazards hurtling down on them in its smoking tyre tracks. Many were the stunned pedestrian groups who found themselves plucking the spikes of roadside blackthorn from their buttocks, only to be forced into the prickly undergrowth a second time and a third.

Irate Spanish cries, describing all Englishmen as *louts del lager*, and proclaiming every German's mother to be a member of womankind's oldest profession, drifted off over the still sea to meld with the joyful songs of praise floating out from the approaching convoy of fairy-lit fishing boats. Despite such malevolent curses, however, the Mercedes made it safely to the coast. The kart and moped, too.

As one seriously-pricked villager put it whilst gathering blackberries from his wife's hair, "The devil, being a foreigner, looks after his own!" He might also have cited that there is no devil like a she-devil, especially one driving a high-powered Mercedes without its owner's permission.

The half mile of narrow shore road back into Port d'Andratx is bounded on both sides by smart villas, many with equally smart cars outside, and it was through this slalom of parked status symbols that the Merc-kart-moped train was obliged to weave. All other road users prudently committed their vehicles to the pavement at first glimpse of the approaching stampede. But the nearer the chase got to the centre of the village, the greater the congestion of traffic, and the denser the throngs of people awaiting the return to port of La Virgen and her fleet.

Although the night was already quite dark, Port d'Andratx was a riot of light. Garlands of coloured bulbs were strung from lamppost to palm tree along the entire length of the harbour, their reflections shimmering over the inky waters of the bay. And the local revellers occupying the tables of the waterfront bars weren't particularly surprised to see a Grand Prix go-kart carrying two waving and shouting men into town. *Hombre!* it was Fiesta, and such things were to be expected — even more so since the men were shouting in English and could be reasonably assumed, therefore, to be drunk. Similarly, the windswept youth on a little motorbike, with a pretty, show-a-leg girl clamped to his back didn't even warrant a second glance. The streets, after all, were full of such carefree young bikers.

What *was* creating shock waves, though, was the irascible hag in the big grey Mercedes, who, judging by the petrified look on the face of her elderly passenger, seemed hell-bent on driving them both to sudden destruction, along with countless innocent merrymakers. Merely to attempt to negotiate such a bulky machine along the crowded waterfront on this particular night of the year was well nigh unheard of, but to do so at such alarming speed was surely verging on the homicidal.

Without warning, Ian made a right turn, tilting the little kart onto two wheels, and all but tipping Bob over the side. "There'll be less punters up these side streets, Bobby," he called over his shoulder. "I'll take a couple of short cuts and head the thieving bastard off further along!"

Meanwhile, PC Andy Green, being well-versed in the subtleties of TV-movie police chases, noted his leader's diversionary tactic and bombed straight ahead.

There was only one exit route at the far end of the village, and Ian got there just ahead of the horn-blaring Merc. He skidded his kart to a halt in the narrow street between two ranks of illegally-parked cars.

Bob wiped the perspiration from his brow with the back of his arm. "Nice driving, son," he puffed. "We've got the bugger now!" Waving frantically with both hands, Ian began to run towards the rapidly advancing headlights, deaf to Bob's yelled reminders that the dragon woman had a gun.

"CAR!" Ian hollered at her. "YOU'RE GONNA HIT THAT GODDAM CAR!"

But the Merc thief had been too busy looking for a way out of this dead end to see the little Renault 4, its driver oblivious to the imminent danger, reversing out of a side street. The metallic thump of the collision merged with the sound of shattering glass and the clatter of wheel trims to mask Ian's howls. They also covered Julie's screams, as PC Green dropped the moped into a sideways slide that ended with the little bike and its two unseated jockeys sprawled in an undignified scatter across the street.

"Get out of the way!" Bob roared at them. "The crazy bitch is gonna reverse the Merc over you!"

He could see the driver clearly now, her contorted features illuminated in the amber glow of a street light, whorls of her tightly-curled grey hair falling over her eyes as she fumbled frantically with the gearshift.

The zinging grind of gear cogs being forced to mesh rang out in concert with the swish and whoop of rockets being released into the night sky to signal that the lights of La Virgen del Carmen's leading boat had been sighted rounding the headland of the bay.

Ian was struggling to free himself from Bob's grip. "Let me at the bastard!" he growled. "She'll rip the bloody gearbox out of my motor!"

"Better a buggered gearbox than a head full of bullet holes, mate!" Bob nodded towards the terrified face staring out at them from the Merc's passenger seat. "And that goes for your old pal Pinkie as well as you. Now, get a grip of yourself and listen to me!"

232

"My car and Pinkie wouldn't be in this fuckin' mess now if I hadn't been daft enough to listen to you in the first place," Ian spluttered, wrenching himself loose. "So, you can go stuff yourself, officer! I'm going after my —"

At that, the Mercedes crunched into gear. Julie and PC Green swiftly picked themselves up from the ground and flattened their bodies against a shop window as the car sped backwards past them, its engine screaming, its dangling front bumper and attached bits of mangled Renault 4 bodywork leaving a trail of sparks to rival those of the fireworks now exploding high above.

"Take it easy!" Bob shouted to his little team. "The bitch isn't going anywhere fast. Look!"

An impenetrable mass of people now blocked the avenue along which the Mercedes was reversing. Many eyes were turned towards the spectacle slowly unfolding out at sea, but others were more intent on watching the drama being played out at high speed right there in the street beside them. A few cynical cries of "*OLÉ!*" rang out every time the Merc's flanks ricocheted off a lamp standard or yet another stationary car.

Ian buried his face in his hands. "Tell me this is only a bad dream," he groaned.

Just as the Mercedes' rear end was about to ram into the frantically scattering crowd, the driver appeared to catch a glimpse of a possible escape route. In one tyre-screeching manoeuvre, the car was suddenly hurtling headlong down a dimly-lit alley, its wings and doors scraping the rough stone walls on either side.

233

Ian was on the point of throwing up. "It's taken me ten years to save up for that motor," he moaned, "and the bloody thing's only insured third party!"

"Don't worry, Fats," PC Green piped up. "Lothian and Borders Police'll stump up for it, won't they, Sarge? Damage incurred in the course of CID secondment work and that, right?"

The sickening sound of the car hitting something solid spared Bob the acute embarrassment of having to own up that there was about as much chance of Lothian and Borders Police coming good for Ian's potentially written-off Mercedes as there was of Andy Green passing a geography test for five year-olds. Then a male voice was heard shouting excitedly in Spanish from the general direction of the smash.

"What was that gibberish all about?" Bob asked Ian as they started to leg it down the alley.

Ian's reply came in a breathless, self-pitying wheeze: "The guy just said that the crazy whore has gone and totalled her indestructable German automobile against an old wooden bollard — Spanish wood, of course!"

"Still, might've been worse," Bob panted, emerging from the alley onto the quayside and catching his first glimpse of Ian's car sitting rammed against a stout hawser post, steam belching from its mangled bonnet. "If it hadn't hit that thing, it would've ended up at the bottom of the harbour. And just think what that would've done for your keyboard and PA gear in the boot!"

"Oh, thanks a million, *mate*. That makes me feel a *lot* better!" Ian's voice was breaking in sympathy with

234

his heart. He stopped in his tracks, took one long, disbelieving look at his beloved Merc, and sank to his knees. Devastated, he pressed his forehead to the cold paving of the wharf, his fists beating the cobblestones. "Why me?" he wailed. "Why bloody well me?"

With the morbid fascination that invariably attracts onlookers to the scene of an accident, a group of young people, who had been dancing to the music of a rock band on the platform over by the old fishmarket, were already milling round the stricken car — albeit from a suitably circumspect distance — in hopes of seeing what carnage might lurk within.

Bob strode towards them, gesticulating vigorously. "Get back!" he yelled. "Get out of the way! She's got a gun!"

A dozen youthful faces turned towards him, eyes wide with puzzlement. "*Qué?*" they queried.

"*Cuidado! La mujer tiene una PISTOLA!*" It was Julie's voice, shouting a translation from a prudently-taken position behind Bob's back.

Their appetite for the gruesome abruptly blunted, the youths dispersed with some urgency. Bob, meanwhile, gave Julie a nod of appreciation. The sudden revelation of her ability to communicate with the natives in their own tongue somehow came as no real surprise.

She gripped Bob's arm. "Don't go any nearer the car. It's up to the Guardia Civil now. They're bound to be here any second."

"I wouldn't bet on it," Ian mumbled into the cobbles.

Bob rounded on him. "Well, where the hell *are* the local fuzz? This place should be swarming with them by now!"

Ian raised his head, muttering, "For *them*, read *him*." He struggled back onto his feet with a helping hand from PC Green. "And *him*, like the sensible Mallorcan he is, will be along the front there in the Bar Central, minding his own business and enjoying the Fiesta with a glass of *coñac* in his hand." Ian took another look at his car and cast Bob a disdainful glance. "Yeah, and it's a pity a certain Jock polis I know hadn't taken a leaf out of his Mallorcan counterpart's book a couple of hours ago."

"Stop whingeing about your bloody motor for a minute," Bob growled back, "and spare a thought for the poor old soul who's inside it at the the mercy of that bampot with the gun." Deep down, though, Bob was burning with guilt and gripped by foreboding at the thought of the trail of damage that his unauthorised villain-hunt had already caused. But showing such feelings right now would only be taken as a sign of weakness. And that was one trait that a policeman displayed at his peril. "So, Ian," he barked, "do me *and* Pinkie a favour. Get your arse along to that Bar Central quick-smart and tell Constable Coñac or whatever his name is to bugle up the cavalry . . . *pronto!*"

If Ian had had any doubts about the wisdom of such a course of action, the gun shot that cracked out from the kicked-open door of his stricken Mercedes quickly changed his mind. He was off and barging through the crush of spectators in an ill-humoured stream of curses.

236

"*Cuidado!*" Julie repeated at the top of her voice, while gesturing to the crowd to keep their distance from the armed woman in the car. "*Cuidado con la pistola!*"

She could have saved herself the trouble. The sharp report of a second shot from the vicinity of the Mercedes had even the most recklessly curious diving for cover.

PC Green threw himself to the ground and shielded his head with his hands.

"Keep 'em all well back," Bob shouted to Julie, "and for God's sake take cover yourself! Come on, Green — we'll rush the car before that crazy bitch can —"

His call to action was cut short by the crazy bitch in question staggering out of the Mercedes and firing off another round. It hit the cobbles at the side of Bob's right foot and whined off to thud into the wooden hull of a small boat lying at the top of the nearby slipway.

A grating, falsetto shout rang out from behind the Mercedes. "Stand back! That's your last warning!"

Pinkie Dalrymple was then hauled crudely out of the car, the muzzle of the revolver pressed hard against the back of her head. Bob could see her captor angrily mouthing something to her, but the words were drowned by a cheer for the returning Madonna rising up from away at the seaward end of the harbour. It was immediately evident, however, that whatever had been said to Pinkie was not to her liking. Her response was to turn round, ignoring the gun barrel now pointing between her eyes, and spit squarely into her abductor's face. This only exacerbated the rough handling to which she was already being subjected.

The dragon woman looked frantically about her, pulling Pinkie backwards along the quay, her eyes searching desperately for a way out. In front of her, the centre of the village was now a solid mass of people, pressing forward to regain vantage points surrendered after La Virgen's exodus. Behind her lay only the square beside the fishmarket. A dead end.

Another starburst of fireworks exploded in the sky above the port, painting the bay with a rainbow of light, and illuminating the way ashore for a motorised rubber dinghy. It was laden with chattering yachties, heading into town from one of the many luxury craft moored out in the bay. The little inflatable purred to a halt alongside the slipway, and its passengers clambered ashore just as another rocket popped and spluttered a brilliant fusillade into the still night air.

By the time Bob's eyesight had grown accustomed once more to the comparative dimness of the street lighting at this end of the wharf, the mysterious woman in tweeds had siezed the opportunity. She was little more than a dark shape disappearing with her prisoner into the watery blackness, while the wash from the dinghy's outboard sent ripples splashing up the slope of the deserted slipway.

CHAPTER
FIFTEEN

"What now, Kemosabe?"

Bob returned Julie's question with another. "Do you know the Spanish for 'This is police business, pal — we're nicking your boat'?"

She raised a shoulder. "I'm sure I'll think of something."

He pointed along the quay. "The guy tying up that water ski launch at the side of the fishmarket there. He's got an obliging sort of face, wouldn't you say?"

"Mm-hmm, and that little tub of his'll go like a greased dolphin with a Roman candle up its bahookie!"

Bob was already heaving the still-prostrate PC Green off the ground by the scruff of his neck. "Get that Lothian and Borders Police ID card of yours handy, Kojak. You're about to graduate from water pistol snatching to speedboat commandeering!"

"I've handled one of these babies before," said Julie as she slid behind the wheel and fired up the powerful aquajet motor. Then, as if throwing away a handful of coins at a wedding, she added, "We used to have a wee summer place down the Clyde at Millport, you know. Yeah . . . used to put the wind right up the dinghy-dabblers and terrorise the wet suits off the windsurfers in a ski tug just like this one. Wow! What a buzz!"

"Well, you know what they say," Bob shouted over the rumble of the idling engine. "The things you pick up during a misspent youth have a way of coming in handy some day." He extended a hand seaward. "Catch *that* dinghy-dabbler, and you're up for a major prize!"

"Oo-ooh, promises, promises," Julie coyly cooed. "But," she firmly added, "we'll have to find her first." Turning to Andy Green, she yelled, "There's a spotlight at the side of the windscreen there. Better switch it on. Can't see a blind thing out there between firework bursts."

She eased the throttle back and surged away into the night, leaving the dumbstruck Spanish owner of the boat standing on the shore to ponder the meaning of the obscure verb *nicko* and to contemplate the significance of the letters C-R-A-P.

"Keep your eyes peeled for all those flash cabin cruisers and yachts parked in the bay here," Julie called to her two white-knuckled companions as she steadily built up speed. "Wouldn't want the owners to spill their champers or anything, would we?"

"Where do you reckon the she-dragon's headed with the old bint?" PC Green shouted in Bob's ear.

"Just far enough out to be certain that the old bint has no chance of swimming ashore. That would be my guess. A nice drowning accident, with no witnesses. Know what I mean?" He inclined his head towards Julie's. "See that lighthouse up ahead? That's the end of

240

the breakwater. Let's get round the other side of that and see what there is to see, OK?"

"Aye, aye, cap'n! Hold onto your breakfast!" With that, Julie dragged the throttle fully open, and the boat was was sent scudding over the water, its prow thudding into the crests of the swell that met them as they cleared the breakwater and headed for the open sea.

Andy Green let out a blood-curdling whoop.

Bob Burns swallowed hard and tightened his grip on the dashboard grab rail. He was silently praying, meanwhile, that La Virgen del Carmen's newly recharged powers of maritime guardianship might be extended to cover three well-intentioned perpetrators of speedboat theft. The lights of the returning fishing fleet now came into full view, the leading vessel only some fifty metres ahead of them as it made its leisurely way back to port with a deck party in full swing. Bob motioned Julie to steer across its bows and circle round behind, a manoeuvre which provoked a fanfare of good-natured honks on the boat's foghorn.

"Have you seen a rubber dinghy . . . with two ladies?" Bob bawled at the mob of on-deck ravers, who had now forsaken hymn-singing for hip-swinging to the music of a scratch combo comprising a handful of well-lubricated brass band musicians and a couple of similarly-inspired flamenco guitarists. All this jollity was taking place under the benign gaze of the Madonna herself, perched aloof and angelic on her saintly throne on the wheelhouse roof, her bobbing head discreetly supported and kept in time by the reverent hand of the parish priest. "Rubber dinghy?" Bob reiterated. "Two ladies? One pink hair? One grey hair?"

"*Ay! Gracias, señor!,*" the skipper called back from his bridge, waving cordially, his face aglow with bonhomie and a bellyful of Communion wine. "*Feliz fiesta a ustedes, eh! Viva la Virgen!*"

"He thinks you're wishing him the compliments of the occasion," Julie shouted at Bob while sweeping round the fishing boat's stern. She nudged the throttle forward to synchronise her speed with that of the slower craft as they drew alongside. She then yelled Bob's question in Spanish to a grinning fisherman, who nodded his head in vague affirmation and pointed the neck of his wine bottle in the general direction of the breakwater. There wasn't just one rubber dinghy there, however, but a flotilla of a dozen or more, bouncing out from the inner harbour to meet the fleet and, presumably, to escort it back to the quayside and the waiting crowds.

"Dammit," Bob muttered, "if the bitch has been crafty enough to get mixed up amongst that lot, we're sunk . . . for want of a better expression."

"Nah! Just do what Starsky and Hutch would've done," PC Green piped up. "Just get tucked in behind this big fishing boat here. Out of sight, like. Then, when them rubber jobs come whizzin' by, we zap out like a bat outa hell whenever we spy the dragon woman. She's taken by surprise, OK? You jump out, Sarge, and grapple with the dragon in the dinghy, and I lean over, grab the old Pinkie bird and haul her in here."

"You conveniently forget to mention that I get to grapple with the dragon *and* her gun. I like the way you delegate, boy. As I've said before, you'll go far in the force."

"But we don't even know that one of those dinghies is actually hers," Julie reminded them. "I mean, for all we know, she could just as easily be half a mile out into the Med by now."

"Maybe so, but I've a hunch we've nothing to lose by giving Green's Starsky stunt a whirl." Bob jerked his thumb over his shoulder. "Line astern, bosun!"

Once they had gained the haven of their home waters, the fishing fleet began to fan out over the broad crescent of the bay that forms the inner harbour of Port d'Andratx, each boat slowing down to allow those farther back in the procession to take up position for the final return to the rejoicing multitudes crowding the waterfront. The welcoming squadron of dinghies had now grown into a great, buzzing swarm of small craft of all descriptions, circling the fishing boats like hyperactive moons, and churning the surface of the bay into a choppy turmoil on which the moored ranks of luxury yachts now bucked and tossed as if caught in a storm.

As instructed, Julie had steered the launch directly behind the lead boat all the way in, and PC Green had deployed the spotlight on every rubber dinghy that swept past. But to no avail.

"Looks like she's given us the slip, Sarge," he concluded at last. "What's next in the master plan?"

"Whatever, it'll be like looking for a wasp in a hornets' nest now," said Julie. "Look at them all! It's like a floating Dodgem derby out here!"

Bob was thinking fast. "And in among this lot is exactly where our tweedy friend will *not* want to be, if I know the devious git's way of working."

"You sound as if you've twigged who she is," Julie said, a look of surprise on her face.

"The Merryfield factor," Bob said, as if to himself. "It has to be."

He looked back towards the breakwater. Out of the gloom, the hindmost fishing boat was now approaching the lighthouse, from which a spoke of silver wheeled slowly over the black water, picking out the shape of a gaggle of little tenders arriving late on the scene from somewhere amidst the forest of masts that surrounded the jetty of the Andratx Yacht Club at the far side of the harbour. He watched them swerving in loose formation past the streamlined hull of a large schooner that was swaying at its solitary mooring in the middle of the bay. A barrage of pyrotechnics lit up the sky, announcing the safe homecoming of the last of the fleet, and marking the start of the celebrations proper. Just then, Bob noticed the grey outline of a rubber dinghy slipping out furtively from behind the moored schooner and tagging on behind the cluster of little boats racing to meet the rearguard of La Virgen's convoy.

"There they are!" he shouted. He gave Julie a sharp nudge on the elbow with the back of his hand. "Do a one-eighty and try to head them off before they reach the breakwater. Yeah, and give it all the welly you've got!"

Julie wrenched the steering wheel to her left and applied maximum throttle. With a gurgling roar from its motor, the ski launch stood on its tail and burst out from the lee of the leading fishing boat, leaving a semi-circle of seething white water in its wake, and propelling the off-guard Constable Green backwards over the open deck and into the foam.

Julie instinctively decelerated.

"Don't bloody well slow down!" Bob barked at her. He grabbed a coil of tow rope and hurled it towards Andy Green's upheld hand. "If we let them out of our sight now, the chances are we'll never see Pinkie Dalrymple alive again!"

"But PC Green . . . we can't just stern-haul him. He hasn't even got water skis!"

"No, but he's got the next best thing — a fine pair of policeman's big, flat feet. Now *boot* it!"

With a shrug, Julie duly coaxed the throttle lever back. The rope played out and went taut, as the prow of the ski boat and PC Green's head and shoulders rose simultaneously from the waves.

"Lean back and tuck your knees up!" Julie screamed at him over her shoulder. "And hold on for dear life!"

Only then did she boot it, glancing round constantly as the released power propelled the boat onwards. Suddenly, Andy Green was transformed into a laid-back foetal ball skimming over the surface of the water. Bob smirked at the sight of a spectacular bow wave arrowing out from the curve of his sidekick's backside.

"Now straighten your legs!" Julie hollered. "And keep your toes up!"

Bob noticed a look of panic contorting Andy's face. "Go on, Green!" he shouted. "There's a lot of flotsam about, so if you don't want a driftwood enema, just do as she says! *Do* it!"

Andy Green did it. And it worked. Even without the additional sole area of his Doc Martens, his size thirteen, flip-flopped feet rose to the task in hand and elevated him bodily from the water like a sodden phoenix.

Bob angled the spotlight on him, so that at least he'd be noticed by the occupants of the rash of dinghies now scooting about in all directions. They already constituted a serious enough danger to themselves without an unseen, ski-less water skier introducing the additional hazard of decapitation by tow cable.

"The kid's a natural!" Julie shouted, looking back in awe.

"Just watch where you're going!" Bob snapped. "And steer a wide berth round that tail-end fishing boat. We might just manage to head the dragon's dinghy off before she reaches open water." He gestured ahead. "Careful you don't whip Green into the lighthouse, though. We need all the illumination we can get!"

A solo yell of, "Yeah! Go for it, Andy boy!" bellowed out from the fishing boat as PC Green hurtled past, a gruesome grin of terror fixed on his floodlit face.

Further cries of encouragement followed as the rest of his four mates cottoned on to what was happening.

Soon the beauty queen and her motley maids were at it, as well . . .

"*Adelante, Andee-ee! Arriba-a-a!*"

Julie banked the ski boat to the right, going for the gap between the back of the fishing boat and the end of the breakwater. She made it.

PC Green made it, too — though, for a few heart-stopping moments, it looked as if his one-legged cornering technique was destined to end in disaster. But he somehow stayed upright, his speed increasing as the tow boat circled sharply back towards the inner harbour. He was launched into a wide slingshot that looked certain to put him on a collision course with the target dinghy.

Bob now directed the spotlight away from the out-of-control constable, the idea being that it would be less nauseating only to *hear* his ultimate demise, and aimed its beam directly into the eyes of Pinkie Dalrymple's captor.

Blinded, she released a shot from her revolver, which ricocheted off the gunwhale of the ski boat and hummed away into the darkness. She held her forearm over her eyes, desperately jerking the wheel of the dinghy round. But it was already too late.

Out of the murk, a spine-chilling howl cut through the night air, and a flailing blur of arms and lanky legs came somersaulting into the searchlight's glare. The dragon woman was caught squarely on the temple by a flying elbow, dispatching her over the side of her dinghy.

Cries of, "*Viva, Andee-ee-ee!*" chimed out from the girls on the fishing boat.

The whimpering PC Green and a somewhat stunned Pinkie Dalrymple were now lying in a tangle of thrashing limbs, wet Bermuda shorts and pink bloomers in the bottom of the dinghy. Its helm was jammed hard over, throttle fully open, the little boat circling round and round in a wide loop.

Julie broadsided the ski boat to a stop just beyond the periphery of the dinghy's circuit. "Look there!" she called to Bob. "There's something floating on the surface. Shine the spotlight on it!" Seeing Bob's blank expression, she pointed furiously. "There! In the dinghy's wash. It's like bits of paper and stuff. It must have spilled out of the she-dragon's handbag or something. Come on! I'll try to ease in a little closer. Scoop them up before the dinghy comes round again."

Suddenly, there was a squelching thump from the direction of the runaway dinghy. The screaming of its outboard motor dropped a couple of octaves, faltered, then steadily rose in pitch again as its propeller regained maximum revs.

"Here it comes again!" Julie yelled, while inching the boat forward in the pitching swell. "Quick! Grab the papers!"

Bob leaned out and snatched up as many of the bobbing items as he could. He cupped his wet hands to his mouth as the dinghy came scudding by yet again.

"Stop floundering about in there like a capsized sheep, Green, and get that bloody machine under control!"

A second pulpy thud. The dinghy's outboard complained once more, then whirred violently as it bucked clear of the water, the sudden jolt of re-entry jerking the helm free and propelling the little craft in a beeline out to sea. In the enveloping darkness, PC Green could just be seen, hopelessly clawing his way, like a rubber-legged infant on a bouncy castle, over the still sprawling Pinkie in a desperate attempt to reach the tiller.

Bob shook his head in despair. "Say a prayer for them," he droned. "Africa's out there somewhere."

"I shouldn't worry too much," said Julie with deliberate calm. "Look — his pals on the fishing boat have got the message. They're getting the skipper to turn about and go after them. Yeah, they'll soon reel 'em in, never fear."

A battery of rockets streaked into the night sky and a great roar rose up from the shore as the first of the fleet berthed at the quayside. La Virgen was safely home, with her adoring gallery blissfully unaware of the high drama still unfolding away out at the mouth of the port.

Bob angled the spotlight onto the soggy scatter of papers that he'd thrown onto the seat beside him. The first thing that caught his eye was a British passport. He picked it up and peeled it open.

"What the hell?"

"What's up?" Julie was all eyes. "You look as if you've seen a ghost."

"That's just what I have seen. Look . . . this passport . . . it's Bertie McGregor's!"

Bob began to dredge through the other papers. Scribbled notes, numbers, the writing all smudged and running. He found a notepad. He tried to separate its clinging pages, his pulse racing. More indecipherable scrawls, page after page. Then he came upon something that took his breath away. There, printed clearly in large letters, were exact details of his and Julie's flight arrangements *and* the address of their apartment at Camp de Mar.

The hairs stood on the back of his neck. "God almighty," he muttered, "the crafty bugger's been on to us all along."

His fingers trembling, he lifted a dripping envelope and fished out the contents. "Well, I'll be damned," he gulped. "An airline ticket. Made out in the name of Roberta McGregor, and departing Gatwick Airport just three hours after we flew out here from —"

Julie let out a scream.

A hand, blood oozing from a deep gash above the wrist, had risen out of the water and was attempting to grasp the boat's side rail immediately behind Bob's back.

Bob spun round. He instinctively took hold of the arm, its gory shape caught now in the searchlight beam of a motor launch that was speeding towards them from the harbour. He heaved the arm upwards, only for the wet skin to slip through his fingers as the desperately-clutching hand disappeared back beneath the surface. All that remained above the water was a hank of soggy, grey hair. Bob lunged over the gunwhale and grabbed it with both hands.

"Hold onto my legs, Julie," he yelled. "This is gonna take some doing!"

Bob braced himself and, with all his strength, yanked at the matted mane. But there was no resistance. The hair simply flew upwards and landed with a loud splosh on the deck between Julie's feet.

She screamed again.

A nervy voice, which Bob instantly recognised as Ian Scrabster's, called out from the motor launch, now heaving to alongside. "Got here as soon as I could, mate! What's the score?"

Bob looked up to see the words GUARDIA CIVIL emblazoned along the launch's hull. "Tell the Spanish cavalry there that they'd never have made the grade in a John Wayne movie," he snarled.

Ian was leaning over the rail of the police launch now, peering down into the well of the ski boat. "Where the hell's Pinkie?" he cried out.

Bob inclined his head in the direction of the dark void of sea beyond the breakwater. "You might try Algiers," he retorted dryly. "But in the meantime, the nasty person who re-designed your Merc for you is busy drowning down here, so if you want somebody to claim damages from, you'd better tell Constable Coñac and his amigos to belay their grappling irons and fish the bugger out kinda smartish!"

Ian promptly rallied the four green-uniformed officers and rattled out a barrage of Spanish. There was a sudden flurry of activity, and a powerful floodlight was aimed over the side. Amid much highly-strung Latin shouting, a spreadeagled, tweed-skirted shape was duly spotted, floating face down in a spreading, crimson slick.

Julie turned her head away as the body was hauled out of the water, its few remaining clothes ripped to shreds. Ragged lacerations and deep, weeping cuts exposed flesh and bone in an ugly criss-cross of wounds that had been carved into chest and abdomen by the slashing blades of the dinghy's propeller. One arm hung semi-severed at the shoulder.

Bob Burns felt physically sick. He forced himself to look at the ghastly, blood-drained face as the mutilated body spun slowly round on the end of the grapnel.

A chill shiver ran down his spine. "Jack Spiers," he said in a hoarse whisper.

He sat motionless, transfixed, while the Civil Guards pulled the limp shape on deck.

"OK, Ian," he finally shouted, "just tell me one thing. Is the lousy bastard still alive?"

CHAPTER
SIXTEEN

Bob had been in many a prison cell in his time, but never in one quite so basic as this, and never in the company of a fellow officer who didn't have a key to the door.

Not that the breeze-block outhouse of the humble headquarters of the local Guardia Civil could be fairly described as a jail in the strictest sense of the word. But what good was nit-picking? The shack had bars on its one tiny window, a stout, bolted door, and Bob and PC Andy Green were locked inside it.

Considering they were in *Mañanaland*, things had happened surprisingly swiftly after Jack Spiers' cross-dressed hulk had been fished bleeding from the sea. And Jack Spiers had lifted the prize in the VIP-treatment stakes once the Guardia Civil motor launch had returned to harbour. An ambulance had been waiting on the wharf to rush *him* to hospital in Palma, preceeded by an escort of two motorcycle outriders. Bob and his little team, meanwhile, had been summarily bundled into the back of a police van and had been subjected to a lengthy interrogation session by the *Capitán* of the local Civil Guard himself, a gruff man by the name of Lopez.

The upshot was that Pinkie and Ian, once established as victims of the night's several crimes, had been duly dismissed, under oath to remain on the island as material witnesses until legal proceedings against the felons had been completed.

Bob, being one of said felons, had been charged with stealing a speedboat and causing same to be driven in a manner and at a velocity likely to endanger others — particular account being taken of the fact that the criminal act had been perpetrated during the busiest and most venerated night of the year in Port d'Andratx. Bob's protestations that he was only doing his duty as a police officer in pursuit of a kidnapper seemed only to exacerbate his already dubious position in the eyes of the Guardia Civil. This, after all, was a Spanish institution not known for its sympathy towards foreigners presuming to take the law into their own hands — certainly not without the required documentation and permissions, and probably not even then.

Julie, perversely, had been released on bail, payment suspended, passport surrendered. The important detail that she had been an equal accomplice in the theft of the speedboat *and* had actually been its driver had been, apparently, of little significance to *El Capitán* Lopez. He had clearly been influenced by the fact that Julie was a woman, and one who was able to put her case in his own language. That, at least, had been Bob's impression during the interrogation.

Lady Luck, conversely, hadn't presented such a smiling face to Police Constable Andy Green. He had been charged, not only with water skiing in the inner harbour — a totally forbidden activity at the best of times — but also with doing so after sundown, without water skis, and in a reckless fashion which had resulted in the serious and potentially fatal injury of a transvestite foreigner. Further charges of assisting in the theft of a speedboat, stealing a stolen rubber dinghy, stealing a stolen moped, and robbing a child of a water pistol were pending.

PC Green was right in the deep stuff.

"But what about this?" he'd objected with quivering lip, when presenting his Scottish police identity card to the interrogating *Capitán*, with Ian Scrabster acting as translator. "Have ye never heard of C-R-A-P!"

The inscrutable *Capitán* Lopez hadn't answered. Instead, he'd bluntly asked PC Green why he'd come all the way to Mallorca to chase an ageing bisexual up and down a mountain, through the village and round and round the harbour during the Fiesta of La Virgen del Carmen. To this, of course, the hapless young constable had no plausible answer. He'd been condemned, therefore, to incarceration in the outhouse with his boss . . .

Bob sighed and looked at his watch. Almost two o'clock in the afternoon. Nearly ten hours since they had been dumped into this hell-hole, and there had been neither sight nor sound of another living soul since the mugs of creosote coffee and two dried-up pastries had been poked through the hatch in the door at breakfast time. God, it was hot! And those damned flies! And that smell! The hotter the day grew, the stronger the stench became.

Bob held his nose. "Hell's bells, what a bloody pong!"

PC Green gave an embarrassed shrug. "Sorry about that, Sarge. Yeah, I think it happened when I fell out of the ski boat. I'll change 'em just as soon as —"

A key rattled in the door.

"At last!" Bob gasped. "Maybe they're finally gonna transfer us to a proper nick."

"For favour, come you," a stern-looking Guardia Civil corporal said in broken English. He beckoned the two prisoners doorwards with his revolver. "You are for food, *sí*?"

"What's he on about, Sarge?" warbled Green.

"They're either gonna feed us or eat us," Bob muttered. "Either way, it's got to be better than suffocating to death in here." He took PC Green firmly by the elbow and urged, "Now, do as the nice man says. Come you, and come you fuckin' smartly!"

They were soon back in the interview room of the little police building where they had spent several tense and sweaty hours at the mercy of *El Capitán* the night before. But now, the inquisition table was set for lunch. In the centre was a bowl of pickled olives and a small plate of crusty bread, flanked by two glasses and a plastic-stoppered bottle, half full of purplish wine. At opposite sides of the table sat two earthenware dishes, brimming with what looked like a thin chickpea stew, on which floated some slivers of rabbit and a few black sausages.

The corporal motioned them to sit. "For favour," he repeated, "you are for food. Good profit, *hombres*."

Andy Green sat where instructed. "What's all this 'good profit' business, Sarge?" he muttered. "I mean, are we supposed to eat this stuff or sell it, like?"

"I'm told it's the local expression for 'enjoy your meal'," Bob replied. "And I think you should do just that," he further advised, smiling rather warily at the muzzle of the corporal's revolver, "no matter what it tastes like."

In fact, it tasted much better than it looked. It was a hearty meal more suited to a cold winter's day in Scotland, perhaps, but a tasty and thoroughly enjoyable bit of nosh, nonetheless. Bob indicated as much to the overseeing corporal by raising his wine glass in appreciation.

The corporal merely frowned, checked the safety catch on his revolver and puffed lazily on a stubby cigar thrusting upwards from the corner of his mouth.

Andy Green was patently impressed. "Heh, Sarge, just like Clint Eastwood in one o' them spaghetti westerns," he observed, before aping the corporal's cigar-posturing with a chunk of black sausage. "Some cool dude, eh!"

"I'd scoff that banger before the guy uses it for target practice, if I were you, boy. He thinks you're taking the piss."

PC Green squinted furtively at the guard's menacing scowl, then promptly choked on his sausage.

El Capitán entered the room to the spectacle of what, at first glance, must have appeared like Prisoner

Burns trying to wallop the living daylights out of Prisoner Green, battering, as he was, a resounding tattoo on his cowering subordinate's back.

"*Basta ya!*" barked *Capitán* Lopez, dishes and glasses rattling and bouncing as his fist smashed down on the table. "*Prohibido pelear!*"

"He wants you to know that brawling won't be tolerated." It was Julie, following Lopez into the room. She looked at PC Green's florid, tear-stained face, then held up a silencing hand to Bob. "And I shouldn't bother attempting to explain that you were only trying to save your colleague from choking to death. Our captain here's the sort of bloke who'd regard such humane action as a complete waste of energy."

While Andy Green wheezed and coughed his way back from the brink, *Capitán* Lopez rattled out a command to the corporal, who threw him a sloppy salute and swaggered out. Lopez then said a few words in Spanish to Julie, flashed her an exaggerated smile, then left the room himself, closing the door behind him.

Bob raised his eyebrows. "How the hell did you manage to persuade him to let you in here for a private chinwag with us?" he asked Julie.

"I just walked into his office and insisted on it. No probs." She batted her eyelashes, then added in the broad twang of her native city, "Oh aye, pal, it's surprisin' what effect the exotic allure o' a wee Glesca Hairy Mary has on these Spanish guys."

"No, but seriously, how *did* you wangle your way in here?"

Julie wagged a finger at him. "Patience, patience, Kemosabe. All will be revealed in the fullness of time."

"Yeah, well, time is something I don't have enough of right now, so better tell me what news you've got before your Hairy Mary spell wears off and the *Capitán* gives you the bum's rush."

Dismissing that slight with a shrug, Julie revealed that, while Ian Scrabster and Pinkie Dalrymple had been assisting a traffic policeman to identify and catalogue the various vehicles and other stationary objects that had been bashed by Ian's hijacked Mercedes the previous evening, she had spent much of the morning on the phone from Pinkie's house to Police HQ in Edinburgh.

She had decided to make contact first with Bob's one-time buddy (and Jack Spiers' doting sidekick), Detective Inspector Bill Blackie. On hearing her account of his boss's bizarre exploits and violent defrocking, his initial reaction had been to sneer, "Yeah, pull the other one, hen!" But his attitude had rapidly changed once Julie's story had been authenticated via a series of phone calls and faxes between his office and its counterpart in Palma. He would personally take the matter to the highest level in the constabulary, he'd ultimately promised, ever ready to save his own bacon, and all necessary wheels would be set immediately in motion.

They'd better be, Julie had curtly informed him. And while he was at it, he'd better make a mental note to address her by her proper handle in future — no female member of the domestic poultry genus having attained, to the best of her knowledge, a PhD in any of the recognised academic disciplines.

Bob smiled a touché-tinged smile. "So, where do we go from here, *Doctor* Julie darlin'?"

"That's still anybody's guess. But what I *can* tell you is that the toady Bill Blackie and none other than your very own Chief Constable George Drinkall MBE will be winging their way on a scheduled Iberia flight from Heathrow to Mallorca first thing tomorrow morning."

"Big Chief Drinkall himself, eh? How the blazes did you swing that one?"

"Oh, easily enough. I mean, *anyone* could have done it," Julie said with feigned modesty. "You know, just a quick phone call about DCI Spiers' weirdo activities to the editor of the *Majorca Daily Bulletin*, who speedily tipped off the relevant news agencies in London, who in turn checked out the story with the public relations officer at Lothian and Borders Police HQ in Edinburgh. And, hey presto!"

Bob's quiet chuckle of approbation was drowned out by a guffaw of unrestrained glee from PC Green. "Aw, nice one, Doc!" he laughed. "Yeah, sharp move! I'd never have thought of that one in a month o' Sundays!"

"Hmm, anyway," Julie continued, "the final bit of news is that, after he finished with the traffic police this morning, Ian Scrabster took me to see the British Consul in Palma. And guess what. He's an ex-student — failed — of my father's. 'Specky' Drysdale. I haven't seen him since I was about twelve, when he used to come round to our house to get some extra tuition

260

from my old man. Monster crush he had on me. Gave me the heebie-jeebies. A real wimpy slob!"

"Very interesting," Bob mumbled, "but just cut to the chase, eh!"

"OK, OK, keep your kilt on." Julie couldn't resist a self-congratulatory smirk. "But just guess who Specky's number one chess-playing chum is these days. Give up?"

Bob and Andy nodded in unison.

"Well, it just happens to be the actual head honcho of the Guardia Civil for the entire Balearic Islands. Yep, and my old admirer promised to get him on your case double pronto."

"Hey, magic, Doc," Andy Green beamed. "We're as good as outa here!"

Bob's reaction was more tempered, however. "Sounds promising," he said. "But, ehm, what about Pinkie? Did you tell her about old Bertie McGregor's murder?"

Julie shook her head. "No way, Sergeant. I hadn't the heart. No, I'm afraid you're on your own when it comes to that little chore."

"And Jack Spiers . . . what did Pinkie say about him?"

"Only that she honestly believed he was going to kill her. I couldn't bring myself to push her for any more info just yet — not after what she's just been through."

At that, the door opened and the corporal ushered two distinguished-looking gentlemen into the room. One was dressed in a white linen suit of the type once favoured by British Imperial administrators, the other in the uniform of a high-ranking officer of the Guardia Civil.

The linen suit smiled shyly at Julie, who introduced him to Bob and Andy as Hugh Drysdale, the British Consul. She added with an impish wink that Hugh was his "Sunday name". The Consul blushed.

Then the high-ranking uniform stepped up to Julie and said in flawless English, "Permit me to present myself, *señorita*." He gave a stiff little bow and clicked his heels. "I am Bartomeu Monserrat Barceló, officer commanding His Spanish Majesty's Civil Guard in these islands."

Once the remaining formalities were over, the Guardia Civil CO promptly took control of matters. He turned immediately to Bob.

"You must appreciate, Sergeant Burns, that I can in no way condone your unauthorised and highly dangerous activities in the Port of Andratx last night. You and your colleagues broke the laws of Spain, and you must answer for that. However, in the light of those mitigating circumstances, as related by Miss, uhm, *Doctor* Bryson to my good friend the British Consul here, I am confident that a more lenient than usual line may ultimately be taken by our judiciary in this case. The investigation of a murder is, after all, a most serious affair, and it would appear that your decision to take the law into your own hands was one that was forced upon you. Your superior officer, this Detective Chief Inspector Spiers, has a lot to answer for . . . *if* he lives."

Bob was quick to convey his appreciation to the Guardia Civil chief for his sympathetic attitude. "But, if you'll forgive me, sir," he pressed, "what exactly did you mean when you said, *if* DCI Spiers lives?"

"Simply that he has undergone extensive surgery during the night, and the last information I have is that he is now on a life-support machine."

"And his chances of survival?"

"Ah, as we say in Spain, *solo Dios sabe*. Only God knows."

Bob couldn't disguise his frustration. "It's just that he could be the key to the solution of the murder enquiry which brought us here, sir. It really is essential that I interview him as soon as he regains consciousness. And Miss Dalrymple — the victim of last night's abduction by Spiers — I have to talk to her urgently as well. It's absolutely vital that —"

"Ah, but you forget one important detail, Sergeant," *El Supremo* cut in. "You are still under arrest." He cast his eyes round the sparsely-furnished room. "I admit that these conditions are more spartan than those in which we would normally wish to accommodate fellow police officers from another country, but the circumstances *are* of your own making. Consequently, you must remain in custody here until such time as I have had an opportunity to consider the case carefully and, what's more, to discuss it thoroughly with your own Chief Constable when he arrives."

Bob took a moment to control his rising temper, then asked flatly, "Can you please explain to me, sir, why I'm being held on remand, while my professional colleague, Doctor Bryson here, has been allowed bail — payment suspended?" He allowed a few seconds to pass in awkward silence before pointing out, "After all, my crime was no more serious than hers."

Clearly rattled, *El Supremo* huffed and puffed, then exchanged a few whispered words in Spanish with the Consul. "It would appear, Sergeant Burns," he said at length, "that our *Capitán* Lopez may have acted precipitately in his handling of last night's unfortunate incident. Uhm, excessive pressure of work, due to the Fiesta and so on." He cleared his throat. "Yes, quite, but in any event, I think it would now be in everyone's best interests if we were to make a fresh start. After all, a satisfactory solution to the whole affair will depend upon the *full*est cooperation — in every sense of the word — between our two forces." He summoned up a starchy smile. "Would you not agree, Sergeant Burns?"

Bob tried hard to suppress a self-satisfied smirk. "My sentiments entirely, sir."

"Excellent! In that case, I am pleased to inform you that my good friend, the British Consul here, has offered to stand guarantor for your good conduct if you and your constable are, like Doctor Bryson, put under an informal type of house arrest, just as soon as the corporal has completed the necessary paper work."

"You mean we'll be free to go?"

El Supremo nodded his head. "Your passports will, however, be retained by the Guardia Civil . . . as a matter of course, you understand."

"Of course," Bob readily agreed.

The Consul then spoke up. "I've given my word, Sergeant Burns, that you will all remain on the island until the Spanish authorities give you permission to leave — which could, of course, take quite some time. And I've also pledged that you'll report to the Guardia Civil every day. Do I have your agreement to all of this, Sergeant?"

"You do indeed."

Julie sidled up and planted a deliberately lingering kiss on the Consul's cheek. "Mm-mm, thanks, Specky," she cooed into his ear, before adding, "Wait a minute, though. I almost forgot. This is Spain, isn't it? Well now, that means I'll have to give you one on the side, doesn't it, Specky? Oh!" she exclaimed, as if only just being struck by the double-entendre element of what she'd just said. "I meant one on the *other* side, of course!" She then planted a kiss on his opposite cheek. "Mm-mm-wah!"

The Consul was beside himself with embarrassment, but a boyish giggle revealed his underlying delight at having at last experienced a fleeting moment of affection from the long-standing object of his fantasies.

El Supremo decided it was time to take control of things again. He flashed Bob and PC Green a professional smile. "Gentlemen," he gushed, "I'm afraid that we must now take our leave of you, but I trust that the corporal will have your release papers in order within the hour. In the meantime, is there anything in particular that you require?"

Bob signified the negative with a courteous dip of his head. But Andy Green, whose position at the table had been given an increasingly wide berth by everyone during the course of the meeting, eventually mustered up sufficient courage to enquire:

"Ehm, I suppose a clean pair of underpants is out of the question, General?"

CHAPTER
SEVENTEEN

"Bertie McGregor is dead."

Bob watched the expression on Pinkie Dalrymple's face change from its normal jovial through shocked to grief-stricken. The weight of his words seemed to age her before his eyes.

She turned her head away and, dabbing the corners of her eyes with her hankie, stood up and walked slowly and in silence to the French doors, where she stopped and gazed disconsolately out towards Dragonera Island. She rested the side of her head against the door frame, her usually-erect back stooped, her shoulders heaving as she struggled with her emotions.

Bob had intended to break the news gently, but Pinkie's seemingly uncontrollable urge to keep chattering excitably about anything and everything had ultimately put paid to that.

She had invited Bob and Julie, Ian Scrabster and Andy Green to her villa for drinks to celebrate Bob and Andy's release from jail, and to treat all of them to a slap-up dinner as a token of her thanks for almost certainly having saved her life. After a seemly period of light-hearted conversation over continuously-replenished glasses of Pinkie's Scotch-based version of *sangría*, Bob had given Julie a pre-arranged signal for her to coax Andy and Ian out of the room, on the pretext of helping the Filipina maid with the meal preparations. Bob, in the meantime, would make use of the resultant period of privacy with Pinkie to gradually guide the conversation round to the painful subject of her old friend's tragic death.

But it hadn't worked out that way.

"I had a feelin' somethin' was up. That's why I've been chatterin' on like a cluckin' hen," Pinkie eventually said, her back to Bob, her eyes still staring sadly out to sea. "I could see it in the Julie lassie's face. Somethin' to do wi' women's intuition, ye ken."

The fragile veneer of refinement which Pinkie liked to put on in public was now discarded. She blew her nose loudly, removed her bamboo spectacles, then wiped her eyes on the sleeve of her kimono.

"Daft auld bugger that I am . . . bubblin' like a bairn an' everything."

Her shoulders began to shake more noticeably now, the involuntary spasms intensifying little by little, until she was standing slumped there in the open doorway, sobbing her heart out.

"Aw, Bertie, Bertie lass . . . ye should've came wi' me . . . I telt ye — ye should've came wi' me . . . ye stubborn auld hoor . . ."

Her tears splashed like warm raindrops onto the cool marble floor.

Bob stood for a moment, looking at the sad silhouette of this outlandish but lovable old character. Until only a few minutes ago, she'd seemed almost indestructable, so apparently complete had been her recovery from her horrendous ordeal of the previous night, so infectious her sense of humour, so inextinguishable her spark of life. But now, she was only a frail old soul, all dolled up to the nines, standing alone, her feelings in tatters, in an exotic place and in opulent surroundings that had all so suddenly become alien to her.

He walked quietly forward and put an arm around her, gently patting her back as he would a little lost child's.

Pinkie buried her head in his shoulder. "I'm sorry, son," she whimpered. "It's just that, well, seein' yon island there in the evenin' like this, it makes me mind o' the times when me and Bertie were lassies, like. Aye, when we used to go down to Yellowcraig beach at Dirleton on summer nights, carryin' on wi' the village laddies in the sand dunes . . . and lookin' out to the sun settin' behind the Isle o' Fidra." She sighed and gave a plaintive little laugh. "My, my, what carry-ons we used to have, right enough . . ."

Bob chuckled softly. "Yeah, old Angus Forsyth, the ex-village bobby, told me about some of the things that went on around Dirleton in the old days."

Pinkie stiffened. "Eh . . . what exactly *did* old Gus tell ye?"

"Well, he said quite a lot, but without actually telling me very much, if you know what I mean."

Pinkie cast Bob a quizzical look, and a wary note crept into her voice as she remarked, "Oh, aye? Is that right, then?"

"Uh-huh, that's right." Bob was playing it cool. "And that reminds me, Pinkie — there *is* actually something about the wartime in Dirleton that I wanted to ask you about. When you feel up to talking, that is."

Pinkie pulled herself away and wandered out onto the terrace. She sat down on a bench beneath the drooping branches of a gnarled old pine tree, then turned to face Bob. Her look was sombre. "Before anything else," she said, "I think ye'd better tell me just exactly what happened to Bertie."

For all the times his job had called upon him to break the news and explain the circumstances of the sudden death of a loved one to the victim's distraught family or friends, the experience was always a distressing one for Bob, and never more so than now. Pinkie's expression grew ever more stunned as she listened to the grim details.

"I can only try to guess how hard all this must be for you, Pinkie," Bob said finally, his voice hushed and understanding, "and I don't want to upset you any more, believe me. But I've got to know — just what *is* your connection with Jack Spiers? Why did he threaten to kill you last night? And why would his wife have wanted to murder Bertie McGregor?"

Pinkie looked down at her tightly-clasped hands. A little shudder ran through her body, and she shook her head despairingly, fighting to hold back the tears.

Bob laid a hand on hers. "I'm sorry, Pinkie, but I really do have to know. You see, you're the only one who can point me towards the missing pieces in this mess of a puzzle."

Pinkie lifted her head and took a deep breath. She looked at Bob through moist, reddened eyes. "I promised I'd never tell anybody, ye understand." Her voice was clear and steady now. "But then again, I never thought things would ever turn out like this, did I?" After a thoughtful pause, during which her gaze returned to the shadowy profile of Dragonera Island, its sprawling bulk back-lit now by the fiery halo of the setting sun, Pinkie began to tell her story . . .

She told of how her first real contact with Jack Spiers had been some thirty-five years earlier, when he, a moody and belligerent fifteen-year-old, had gone to live with her sister Molly Mathieson — the same sister with whom Pinkie had eventually gone to live in Perth, and who had died only this year in the Gowrie Nursing Home shortly before Pinkie checked out of the place for Mallorca.

Having spent the first ten years of his life in an orphanage, Jack had then been fostered out to an Edinburgh couple called Spiers. They had ultimately adopted him, and he took their name. But then Mr and Mrs Spiers were tragically killed in a road accident. At the most crucial stage in his young life, Jack was suddenly faced with the prospect of being taken back into care at the orphanage, or, perhaps worse, of being fostered out once more to total strangers. It had been then that Pinkie's sister Molly and her husband Charlie had decided to step in and take the youngster to live with them in Perth.

"But how did that come about?" Bob asked. "I mean, how did your sister even get to know about Jack Spiers and his problems?"

Molly had made a point of being kept informed, albeit at a distance, of the boy's welfare ever since the day he was born, Pinkie went on. "Seeing as how the bairn's natural mother was related to her, in some way or other, like."

Surprised, Bob raised an eyebrow. "Did you say . . . related?"

"Aye, aye," Pinkie retorted, brushing that question aside. "But that's no important." Jack, she promptly continued, had turned out to be a right bloody handful, much of his sullen stubbornness a legacy, more than likely, of his unsettled childhood. For all that, it was a trait that turned Molly's and her husband's previously uneventful life into a nightmare. Most notably, there had been the all-too-frequent complaints from the school about his disruptive and rebellious behaviour in class, about his incessant bullying of younger pupils, and about his dogged determination not to take any of his studies seriously. This latter outlook led inevitably to his being made to repeat his fourth year in high school. The ego-denting experience of being grouped with a class of pupils who were all at least one year his junior only served to exacerbate the situation, however. Before long, Jack had started to skip school, sometimes for days on end, and had taken up with a bunch of young layabouts and petty criminals. He adopted their lifestyle with a vengeance, hanging about outside seedy cafés until all hours of the night, skulking up unlit alleys or, in the darkness of public parks, drinking rough wine or any other quick-buzz booze that their misbegotten cash could buy.

Pinkie's sister and brother-in-law were at their wits end. They tried every approach from pleading to threatening in their never-ending effort to steer young Jack back on to the rails. But all to no avail. It was only after they found him sprawled semi-comatose in his room one night, an empty beer can in his hand and an assortment of what turned out to be amphetamine tablets scattered on the floor, that they'd finally decided that influences more able than theirs would have to be called upon to save the boy from this drift towards self-destruction.

Molly's husband had never been the most robust of men, and his health eventully started to deteriorate noticeably because of the worries heaped on him by their uncontrollable young charge. He appealed for help to the Perth Social Work Department, who in turn requested background reports from their opposite numbers in Edinburgh, and in particular from the orphanage where young Spiers had spent his early years. It was then that fate had taken a hand.

Pinkie recounted how Wullie Merryfield, the then Chief Constable of Edinburgh City Police, while on one of his regular visits to such homes for disadvantaged children, had chanced to hear of this particular case. At his behest, the errant Jack Spiers spent most of his next school holidays on an informal work-experience stint at Police HQ in the capital, even living as a surrogate member of the Merryfield family in their spacious Victorian house in Edinburgh's prestigious Trinity area. It turned out to be an experience that was to affect young Spiers profoundly.

Until then, he'd harboured a deep mistrust of the police. This outlook may have been understandable, given his early life. But, thanks to Wullie Merryfield's shrewd judgement of human nature, the down-to-earth, risen-from-the-bottom-of-the-heap police officers, with whom he ensured that the lad spent those few important weeks, succeeded in teaching him (almost without his realising it) that, if you must be a streetwise hard man, it's a lot smarter to be one on the *right* side of the law.

Yet, it was Wullie Merryfield himself who had made the biggest and most reforming impact on the budding young tearaway. For here was a man who had also suffered the emotional privations of being brought up in an orphanage, and who had not only survived, but had risen from the bottom of his own particular heap to scale the heights of his chosen profession. And, possibly even more significantly, Jack Spiers had seen in the well-to-do Merryfield household just what having a worthwhile goal in life could produce materially. Moreover, the youngest of the four Merryfield children, a lad of similar age to himself, had taught him — by way of a sound thumping on his very first antagonistic night in the house — that, contrary to the indoctrination of his wayward peers, not all kids from secure and happy families were necessarily pansified mummy's boys.

274

Young Jack Spiers was impressed, to the extent that Wullie Merryfield became the idol of his life. When, perhaps inevitably, Jack eventually became a rookie policeman himself, it surprised nobody that he adopted Chief Constable Merryfield as his role model. Even the smallest details of the many legends of bravery, single-mindedness and uncanny ingenuity which surrounded the man were diligently absorbed into young Spiers' psyche.

While Pinkie paused to draw breath, Bob remarked, "Like the famous story that's still told in the force, about how Merryfield infiltrated and busted a Leith vice ring back in the 'forties by dressing up as a hooker and strutting his stuff round the dock area at night with the real tarts, right?"

It was obvious, though, that Pinkie wasn't particularly interested in such minute detail. "I suppose," she replied blandly.

Bob was lost in his own thoughts now. "And yet," he said, more to himself than to Pinkie, "I never connected the photo of Merryfield in Spiers' office and that hooker story with the tweedy old bird who was raking about Perth looking for you the day after Bertie's murder." He stroked his chin reflectively — and gently. "Yeah, it was only the force of that belt on the jaw I got here last night that started me wondering if there just might've been a connection." He shook his head. "But no, it all seemed too far-fetched, even then."

Pinkie pulled a slow shrug and pushed her bamboo specs up over the bridge of her nose. "Aye, well, when ye get to my age, laddie, *nothing* surprises ye any more."

"Unfortunately, one thing that arsehole Spiers didn't manage to copy from Wullie Merryfield was how to be successful without being a devious, self-centred bastard," Bob muttered. "*If*," he added with an apologetic dip of his head, "you'll pardon the French."

"Listen, I couldnae care less about a couple o' wee swearie words like that," Pinkie replied, unashamedly unfazed. "Nah, I've heard a lot worse during a lifetime o' workin' in the gardens at Archerfield and bumpin' into the likes o' Jimmy King every day." Then, as if suddenly realising that she might have inadvertently steered the conversation in the wrong direction, she promptly reverted to the subject of Jack Spiers. "Anyway, one o' the things he *did* pick up from Merryfield was this thing about lendin' yer own time to helpin' them that's worse off than yersel' — to them that's slidin' down the slippery slope, like. For Jack Spiers, it was tryin' to help junkies kick the dope habit, havin' once been teeterin' at the top o' that slippery slope himsel', of course." She put two fingers in her mouth and faked a retch. "Tellin' ye, son — there's nothin' as fuckin' puke-makin' as a born-again paraglide o' virtue!"

Fortunately for him, Pinkie didn't notice Bob's involuntary smirk of amusement at her poetic turn of phrase. She was getting more wrapped up in her story by the second.

"And," she went on, with a pseudo-confidential air, "as if *that* wasnae bad enough, it was through all his there-but-for-the-grace-o'-God fartin' about that he met and married that bitch Lauren!"

"She was a drug counsellor, then, was she?"

"No chance," Pinkie said, then paused dramatically with a wait-for-it twinkle in her eye. "Na, na, na, son," she announced at length, "she was a drug *addict!*"

Leaving a stunned Bob to ponder the significance of that little bombshell, Pinkie went back inside the house and returned a few minutes later with two large whiskies. She handed one to Bob. "Here," she said, "ye look as if ye need this. *Slange!*"

Deep in thought, Bob was staring ahead at nothing in particular. "Yeah, aye, cheers," he replied vaguely. "Hmm, so *that* was why everybody at Roodlands Hospital was so damned tight-lipped about why Spiers' wife was tucked away in that side ward."

"Aha, but that's no the half o' it!" Pinkie proclaimed. She settled down on the bench again, warming to her theme. "Don't forget, I never even finished tellin' ye about the juvenile Jack Spiers yet, did I now?"

As the long twilight shadows merged into darkness, Pinkie continued her tale to the accompaniment of a chorus of crickets hidden in the nearby pines . . .

Spiers, she remembered her sister telling her, had returned from his spell with the Merryfields a reformed character in many respects, but an even bigger burden in others. He had seen how the other half lived, he wanted his slice of that enticing cake, and he wanted it now! A new bike, a record player, fancy sports gear. He expected, and was given, comparatively little things like that at first. Then, after he'd left police college, endless pleas for money to supplement his modest cadet's wages were hurled at the Mathiesons from his digs in Edinburgh. Before long, he'd developed a taste for fashionable clothes, he wanted a smart little car to compliment his carefully-developed, young-buck-about-town image, he demanded assistance with the rent of a "suitable" flat of his own. Then there came the frequent demands for Molly and Charlie to clear debts resulting from Jack's new penchant for running up slates at any trendy pub or restaurant that fell for his glib flannel.

"And were your sister and her husband well enough off to cope?" Bob asked.

"That's the trouble, see. All they had was Charlie's pay as a railway clerk. That and the wee bit o' savings Molly had put aside for a rainy day during her years workin' as a school dinner lady."

"So, in other words, Jack Spiers took them for all they had, right?"

Grim-faced, Pinkie nodded her head. "For all they had *and* more. Charlie even took a job in a bar at nights and at weekends to help make ends meet." She swallowed hard before adding, "Aye, it sent the poor soul to an early grave."

"But *why*?" Bob was astounded. "I mean, didn't they realise they weren't doing the bloodsucking bugger any good by giving in to him?"

The colour rose in Pinkie's cheeks. She lowered her eyes. "Like I said," she replied, almost inaudibly, "they kind o' felt responsible, like — and them never havin' had a family o' their own and that."

278

"Let's face it, they were a soft touch, and Spiers knew it," Bob instinctively opined, then immediately wished he hadn't.

Pinkie's chin was quivering. "What does it matter now?" she said, the words catching in her throat. "Molly and Charlie were only doin' what they thought was for the best. They were that pleased to see the laddie doin' well, ye see — keepin' on the straight and narrow and everything."

"Yeah, well, I just hope the rat gets what he deserves now," Bob muttered through clenched teeth.

To Bob's surprise, Pinkie let out a mischievous little titter. Then, a smile suddenly glinting in her tear-filled eyes, she said, "Jack Spiers, ye'll get yer fairin', in hell they'll roast ye like a herrin' — as yer immortal namesake might have put it, Bob, eh?"

Bob laughed quietly along with her. "Aye, I suppose Rabbie Burns had a rhyme to cover just about every occasion, at that." After a judicious pause, he suggested, "Except a yuppie policeman marrying a junkie, maybe?"

"Mm-hmm, now there's a thing, right enough," Pinkie reflected. "And that was just the start o' Molly's problems, so to speak. Ye know, wi' Charlie bein' dead an' all, like."

"How do you mean?"

"Charlie's life insurance. Jack Spiers knew about it, and over the years he wheedled every last penny o' it away from Molly."

"And it amounted to quite a lot, did it?"

"I cannae rightly tell ye how much. I was still livin' at Archerfield wi' Bertie, see. But it would've been enough to see Molly through nice and comfy for the rest o' her days. Charlie would've seen to that, I can assure ye."

"But what did Jack Spiers need all this money for, anyway? Hell's teeth, by that time, he must have been on a good enough earner from the police to keep Lauren and him in reasonable comfort. They never had any kids, so . . ."

"Aye, but it would have been cheaper to bring up a few bairns than feed the monkey on Lauren's back, d'ye no think? And as if that wasnae enough, there was always the flash sports car for her nibs, social climbin' at the Masons and the golf club for him. And the houses — every one bigger and swankier than the last. I'm damned if I know how they afforded it, even wi' all the money they sponged off Molly!"

Bob mulled that over for a moment or two before revealing, "True enough, it was always a talking point in the force — how Spiers always managed to live way beyond his means." He hunched his shoulders. "Everybody just assumed he must've married into money when he got hitched to Lauren."

Pinkie almost choked on her whisky. "*Money! Lauren?* Ye must be jokin'! That toffee-nosed trollop never had a pot tae piss in before she fell in wi' Jack Spiers. Nah, fur coat and nae knickers was always her style. And it's the same to this day, I'll bet ye anything!"

Bob was beginning to get a bit confused by certain aspects of all this. "OK," he said, holding up his hands, "so far, so good. But something doesn't add up."

280

Pinkie cocked her head inquisitively.

"If Spiers rooked your sister Molly so dry, how come she could afford to sell her house in Perth to that young Thorn couple for just over a hundred-and-forty grand? I'm no real estate expert, but I reckon that wee house could have fetched twenty or thirty thousand more, and no problem."

Pinkie said nothing, but gave a coy, maybe-so nod of her head.

Bob looked up at the impressive facade of the villa. "And what about all this?" he said, spreading his arms. "You didn't buy all this with the peanuts that Mrs Boyd at the old folks' home said you had left out of the proceeds of your sister's house sale." He made an apologetic gesture with his hands. "Pardon me for being so blunt, Pinkie, but I think an explanation's in order, no?"

Pinkie threw her head back and let rip with a good-going cackle of a laugh. "See you polismen? Ye're a' the same. Bloody suspicious o' the day ye never saw. Pathetic! Did ye suspect that I robbed a bank or somethin', ye daft bugger that ye are?" She cut straight through Bob's stuttering stab at a reply with a delighted exclamation of: "Littlewoods! Have ye never heard o' the football pools?"

Bob was stuck for words. "You mean you . . .? What you're saying is . . .?"

"That's right," Pinkie beamed. "Scooped the jackpot on the treble chance, me and Molly did! Nearly two million quid, and all for our usual wee 60p stake — any eight frae ten, ye ken. Trouble was, though, the shock nearly killed Molly, what wi' her illness and that. So, I just says tae her, 'Bugger it, hen, we'll flog the house as quick as we can — stuff valuations! — and we'll get ye intae a nice nursin' home where there's folk that can look after ye right'. And that's exactly what we done. Mark you, for masel', I would've shot the crow out o' Perth to a place like this there and then. But it was Molly." Pinkie lowered her eyes again and shook her head. "I couldnae leave her — no in the state she was in. She was failin' fast, like. Aye, wi' the Auld Timers' Disease, it was." Pinkie dropped the corners of her mouth and added dolefully, "No nice tae see yer own flesh and blood driftin' away tatas like that. Hmm, awfy sad . . ."

"And you never let dab to the matron at the old folks' home that you had that kind of money, I suppose?"

Pinkie's pencil-drawn eyebrows scaled her forehead in astonishment. "D'ye think I'm stone glaikit or somethin'? No fuckin' way, José, as we say in Spanish! Nah, nah, I got Littlewoods to stash the lot in the Bank o' Scotland in Jersey for us bloody fast. Oh aye, too damned right I did, and never a cheep tae anybody — least o' all tae them money-grabbin' granny farmers!"

Bob was trying his best not to appear too gobsmacked by all of this. "Fair enough," he said, "but in the light of recent events, it would appear that Jack Spiers still managed to get wind of your big lift. Correct?"

Pinkie grimaced. "Molly again. Away wi' the fairies half the time. Went and let the cat oot the bag to Jack

282

on the phone just before we moved into the nursing home, the silly auld besum that she was." She folded her arms resolutely, before adding the qualification: "No her fault, mind. Nah, didnae even know what planet she was on whiles."

"She told Spiers how much you'd won, then?"

"No — thank God. I just managed to grab the phone off her before she blew the gaff. It was touch and go, though. Any road, Jack Spiers started phonin' me at the nursin' home after a while. He told the lassie in the office he was a distant nephew or suchlike. Kept pesterin' me for Molly's share o' the money. Said his need was greater than hers, and she was goin' to kick the bucket soon, anyway." Pinkie looked askance at Bob, one eybrow raised. "Bloody charmin', eh?"

Bob was intrigued. "But why didn't he speak to Molly herself?"

"Oh, he wanted to, right enough, but she was too far gone to speak to anybody most o' the time. Put it this way, she wouldnae have known his voice on the phone from Santa Claus's. So, I just tells him that he's sucked enough out o' Molly and Charlie over the years, *and* ruined their lives into the bargain. Aye, and I just tells him to away and raffle himsel', if he's that desperate for money, like. And then I hangs up."

"Good for you," Bob smiled, well relieved that he seemed to be getting somewhere near the nitty-gritty at last. "And I'm told you had the final showdown with him on the day of Molly's funeral . . ."

"Aye, he come on the phone again. Really doin' his nut, rantin' and ravin' like a bloody eejit. Tells me he's entitled to Molly's money now that she's deid, and says he'll get mine when I croak — him bein' the next o' kin and that. And unless I cough up Molly's money fast, he's goin' to see to it that I'm no goin' to be around to enjoy my share for long. Bloody impidence!" Pinkie set her jaw and knotted her brows into a scowl of defiance. "Know what I says to him?"

Wide-eyed, Bob bit his lip in anticipation.

"I says to him, 'Hard cheese, sonny boy! You can damn well whistle for it, 'cos I've already willed the whole jing-bang to my old friend Bertie McGregor!' And then I listens to him buildin' himsel' up for a nuclear explosion at the other end o' the phone. But before he can come out wi' anything, I just takes a great, big, deep breath and shouts at him, 'So, you can take a runnin' jump at yersel' and FUCK OFF!'." Pinkie smiled demurely and concluded, "Then that nosey parasite Mrs Boyd comes back into the room right on cue, so I just puts the phone down nice and gentle, and makes one o' ma graceful exits."

She sat back against the tree trunk and allowed herself a smug little grin. But her smile quickly slid into a gape of horror as the terrible consequences of her careless disclosure to Jack Spiers began to dawn on her.

"Oh, my God almighty!" she wailed, clasping a hand to her heart. "What have I did! I've went an' handed poor Bertie a cemetery ticket!" She started to wring her hands. "Aw, buggeration, I as good as murdered her masel'!"

Bob winced, painfully aware that placating hysterical women had never been one of his more notable talents.

284

"Come on, now," he said, then gingerly touched her hand as she began to bawl uncontrollably, "don't you go upsetting yourself. You weren't to know that what you said to Spiers would result in the . . . ehm, would end with Bertie being . . . well, would lead to —"

"There, there, there, Pinkie," Julie crooned, coming out of the house just in time to get the floundering Bob off the hook, "just you get it all out of your system." She folded her arms round the old woman and gave her a comforting hug. "That's right, have a good old cry on my shoulder." She gently stroked the lacquered pink tresses. "I know, I know," she murmured, "it's bad enough losing your best friend, but losing her in that way . . . and then the shock of finding out about it after all you've just been through . . ."

Pinkie raised her streaming eyes to meet Julie's. "But it's all my fault," she warbled. "And — and it's no as if Bertie even knew what it was all about. See, I never told her how much I was worth, otherwise she would never have agreed to ma will. Too proud, like. Aye, so I just told her I was leavin' her all my worldly possessions. *Sniff*. That's why she made her own will out tae the bloody cat. Likely thought she was only in line for fifty quid! *Sniff, bubble*. Oh, dearie me! Poor Bertie . . ."

Pinkie's heart-rending sobs lent a melancholy note to the soothing sounds of the Mediterranean night — the lazy chirp of the crickets, the warm breeze sighing through the pines, the cascading trill of a distant nightingale.

"I see the old dear never took the bad news too good, Sarge," PC Green whispered as he shuffled self-consciously onto the terrace.

Bob cast him an incredulous look. "I'd call that a masterpiece of understatement, lad."

Andy Green smirked proudly. "Aw, thanks, skipper. Yeah, the Doc was just givin' me and Fats the full gen on this case in the kitchen there. Talk about yer twisted webs, eh!"

Ian Scrabster joined them, his face drained of colour. "Hey, heavy-duty scene, Bobby man," he mumbled. "Old Bertie stiffed with a spade. Shit, I never realised what I was getting myself into when I bumped into Pinkie at the hotel back in the spring."

"Maybe you'd better tell me all about it," Bob suggested, then prudently directed him back inside the house.

It had all happened quite spontaneously, as Ian recalled. He had been halfway through his nightly after-dinner session in the Bow Bells Lounge, when he was approached at the end of a song by this demurely-dressed woman. He hadn't noticed her in the hotel before, although she looked totally out of place among the rest of the garishly-attired holidaymakers. She'd introduced herself as Lady Euphemia Dalrymple, and had asked Ian to join her at her table for a drink during his next interval. This he had done with pleasure.

"Hob-nobbin' with the customers is all part of the gig," he paused to point out. "And, of course, there's

286

always the chance of a few free bevvies in it, *if* you lay the right line in bullshit on them."

In fact, he went on, he had just been getting into his sugary Juan-the-Latin-Entertainer spiel, when Lady Euphemia stopped him in his tracks with a quietly growled:

"Drop the dago crap, son! It's me ye're talkin' tae!"

With that, she had dipped into her handbag and had discreetly pulled out a pair of bamboo specs, with which she replaced her more conservative pair for just a moment. But it had been amply long enough for Ian to make the connection.

"Christ!" Ian had spouted. "It's Pinkie Dalrymple! But hey, what's the score with the highfalutin name and the town-and-country threads?" Then, pointing to her soberly-styled hair, he had queried, "And what's with the grey Fred Astaire? Shocking pink gone outa style all of a sudden, has it?"

"No that it's any o' your business, Crabbie," Pinkie had snarled out of the corner of her mouth, "but the grey hair's a bloody Irish jig, ye dingly bugger, and the Ladyship handle and frumpy togs is just part o' the same guise." She'd then leaned forward and gripped Ian firmly by the wrist. "And if *you* as much as whisper any o' this tae anybody, I'll have yer nuts for marbles. I'm warnin' ye!"

She had then proceeded to divulge to Ian that, for reasons that he didn't need to know, she had decided to settle incognito in Mallorca. She had come into "a wee drop money" and wanted to buy a wee place — "fairly secluded, like, but no too far off the beaten track." If

Ian could help her find such a property and guide her through the Spanish legalities, there would be "a nice wee somethin' in it for yersel', never fear."

"And that's why she disappeared out of the hotel after breakfast every day," Bob surmised.

"Right on, Bobby. I'd meet her in a café along the street, and off we'd go around the Palma estate agents." Ian's lips curved into a wry smile. "I remember the first morning. I asked her what price range she had in mind. About fifty K, top whack, for a titchy studio flat up some back street was my guess. Hey! imagine how it hit me when she pipes up dead cool-like, 'A million, son — pounds, no pesetas. Aye, about a million. Even a wee bit more. But it's got tae have *class*, mind. Oh, and a nice sea view.' No kiddin', man, you could've felled me wi' a swizzle stick!"

Bob allowed his eyes to wander round the handsome trappings of the lounge. "Yeah, it's a far cry from that miserable wee cottage in Archerfield Estate where she used to live with Bertie, and that's for sure."

"That was just it, you see," Ian said. "Pinkie always hoped that Bertie would come over and move in with her here. Said she visited Bertie before she came on holiday. Tried to persuade her to come along. Even took her to Tesco's to get a photo taken in the booth for a passport." Ian pulled a disconsolate shrug. "But, it wasn't to be . . ."

"Rabbie Burns' best-laid schemes o' mice an' men," Bob pensively concurred. He thought for a few seconds, then asked, "Did Pinkie never give you a hint about who she was hiding from? Did Spiers' name never crop up at all?"

"She never said, and I knew better than to ask. She gave me a really good backhander when the paperwork for buying this house was completed. Enough to make it possible for me to go and buy that Merc, as it happens. However, when she handed over the cash, she made me promise on my mother's life that I'd never let slip a clue about her whereabouts to anyone without her say-so." A perplexed frown wrinkled Ian's brow. "It started to worry me after a while, though. I mean, Pinkie seemed happy enough around the villa here, I suppose, but when she was out and about — down there in Port d'Andratx, even — she never seemed totally at ease. OK, she wasn't exactly looking over her shoulder all the time, but there *was* something — something edgy about her, something not just right."

"And you never asked her what was wrong?"

"Oh yeah, I tried a couple of times. You know, coming at the subject around the lighthouse, sort of thing." Ian shrugged again. "But Pinkie wasn't for coming clean. No, she would just crack a joke and start prattling on about something else entirely." He looked Bob in the eye. "So, when you arrived on the scene and asked about her, I was well relieved, believe me. At last, somebody I could talk to, who seemed to have Pinkie's best interests at heart." He chuckled to himself. "I was still shit scared to let too much outa the bag until her Ladyship had given the all clear, mind you."

Bob was deep in thought again. "Even then, my coming here almost cost Pinkie her life. Hmm, I wonder how that bastard Spiers got on to our trail . . ."

"Could be the Chief Con and DCI Whatsisface'll have some gen on that when they arrive tomorrow, Sarge," Andy Green chipped in. "Doc Julie says she spilled all the beans on the blower to them yesterday, so . . ."

"Uh-huh, *if* they've come clean and put the proper CID crack troops on the job, instead of trying to cover their own arses," Bob muttered with more than a trace of scepticism. "But, we'll find out soon enough . . . *mañana*."

CHAPTER
EIGHTEEN

As Bob entered the small office assigned for the use of the Lothian and Borders Police *delegación* at the Guardia Civil Headquarters in Palma, Bill Blackie strode forward and shook his hand enthusiastically, his demeanour oozing self-assurance.

"Well done, old mate!" he smarmed, while slapping Bob on the back — a mite *too* heartily for Bob's liking. "Well, well, trust you to pull a trick like this out of the bag, eh! Yes, bloody good show, mate!" he grinned.

Stone-faced, Bob waited until Bill had finished pumping his hand, then commented dryly in a voice that was loud enough to fill the room, "You're putting on a surprisingly happy face . . . considering it's got egg all over it!"

Bill let go of Bob's hand as if it had suddenly caught fire. The fixed grin faded from his face, which rapidly turned a violent shade of scarlet.

"Ah, do please come in, Sergeant Burns," Chief Constable George Drinkall called diplomatically from behind a large desk by the window. "Uhm-ah, I'm sure we've met before . . . haven't we?"

Bob conceded the possibility with a slight dip of his head, followed by a polite: "Good afternoon, sir. Good of you to come in person."

With a grunt, Chief Constable Drinkall directed him to take a seat. He then proceeded to drone in theatrical tones, "It is indeed regrettable that I find myself having to apologise to our Spanish colleagues for their having been dragged into this unfortunate affair, which — not to put too fine a point on it — has the potential of becoming extremely embarrassing for our constabulary, unless we —"

"And so it should be embarrassing," Bob butted in.

His interruption left the Chief Constable gawping at him with the look of a stunned goldfish. Bill Blackie gave Bob a couple of nervous digs with his elbow.

Ignoring both responses, Bob went on, "Embarrassing, because this whole mess should never have been allowed to spread outside our own turf. And the person initially responsible is sitting right here beside me." He cast DI Blackie a belittling glance. "What price your precious bacon-saving policy now, Bill? If it hadn't been for the chip on my shoulder, as you called it, there would have been one more corpse for Lothian and Borders Police *and* the Guardia Civil to be embarrased about by now!"

"Now, look here, Burns," Drinkall spluttered, "kindly remember your place, and do *not* slight our Spanish colleagues by —"

"Excuse me, sir, but I'm very aware of my place. And permit me to remind you that three of your staff, myself included, are still officially under arrest by our Spanish colleagues. And, in case you don't know, if it hadn't been for Doctor Julie Bryson's family connections with the local British Consul, young Constable Green and I would still be sharing a breeze-block sweatbox at the back of Andratx police station!"

"How dare —"

"We are under arrest, sir, for certain spur-of-the-moment actions taken in the pursuit of a highly dangerous individual, who turned out to be none other than your own Detective Chief Inspector Jack Spiers. A bent copper, if ever I saw one, who should have been bombed out of the force years ago!"

The Chief Constable was livid. "Really, Sergeant," he fumed, "I think this has gone far enough! I've no doubt that your experiences during the past few days have been a touch traumatic at times, but I have to remind you that, until this instance of uncharacteristic behaviour by DCI Spiers, there was nothing in his record to suggest that he has ever been anything other than a totally trustworthy police officer of the highest calibre."

"I won't trouble you with the details right now, sir, but there was at least one occasion that I know of — admittedly some years before you joined us — when Jack Spiers' rampant self-interest, coupled with his immediate superiors' knack of burying their heads in the sand, resulted in the preventable murder of a young child. Spiers got promotion for that bungle, by the way." He turned to Bill Blackie. "I'm sure you remember the occasion, *sir*?"

DI Blackie opened and closed his mouth a few times, but no words emerged.

"No, probably not," Bob muttered. "You'd be too busy at the time, climbing career ladders with the other movers and shakers, to notice what was going on under your own arse-sniffing nose."

Chief Constable Drinkall cleared his throat. "Because of the stress that you've been under, I'm prepared to regard what you just said as off the record, Sergeant. But I warn you, any more such talk will be taken as gross insubordination and will certainly do your prospects of advancement in the police force no good. You have my personal guarantee of that!"

"With due respect, any influence that *you* may have on my future will depend entirely on whether *I* decide to remain in the police force or not. And at this moment in time there's every chance that I won't!"

Before the Chief Constable could react, Bill Blackie chipped in with an ingratiating, "Excuse me, sir, but Sergeant Burns and I go back a long way. I think I know him better than most." He simulated a smile. "May I . . .?"

With an irritated flick of his head, Drinkall invited him to carry on.

Bill laid a hand on Bob's shoulder. "Hey, come on, mate," he fawned, "don't be like this to your old —"

"And how the hell else do you expect me to be, for Christ's sake? The last I heard of you was when I was being treated like a pariah by Jack Spiers in the Granada service station at Kinross, and you were doing a nice job of creeping up his jacksy down the phone!

Yeah, a little stunt that helped me get kicked off the McGregor case, as it happens, and we all now know what that resulted in, don't we?"

"Now, be fair, Bob. Let's face it, I was only —"

"You were only obeying orders? Yeah, that's what most of those dutiful sidekicks of Hitler's said at Nuremberg, wasn't it? The fact, Bill, is that if you'd backed my hunch when I was in your office earlier that day, instead of falling over yourself to help Jack Spiers do a quick stitch-up on that poor gardener guy, things would have turned out *very* differently, right?" Bob neither expected nor waited for a reply. "For a start," he went on, "if you'd given me a little bit of support, Jack wouldn't have been able to get on with his rotten shenanigans quite so unhindered, would he? *And* good old Lothian and Borders Police wouldn't have had to rely yet again on yours truly, Sergeant Muggins here, being daft enough to spend his own time, risking life and limb doing dirty work that ends up making a few more-senior officers look a lot less bloody incompetent than they really are!"

Chief Constable Drinkall was about to explode now. "I won't hear any more of this!" he shouted. "I'm warning you, Sergeant, unless you retract these outrageous comments immediately, I'll —"

"You'll what? Suspend me? Threaten me with demotion, or the sack, even?" From his pocket, Bob produced the mini-cassette-recording of the final showdown he'd had with Spiers in his office at Edinburgh Police HQ. Lobbing it to the Chief Constable, he said, "Have a listen to that sometime.

You'll find that DCI Spiers beat you to it on all counts by eight days. So, at this moment in time, I've got nothing to lose by speaking my mind, and I'm telling you that something about this whole business stinks. I sniffed it from the word go." He glanced again at Bill Blackie. "But this time I'm gonna make sure there's no cover-up to save anyone's bacon." He turned back to the Chief Constable. "And I don't give a damn how many high-ranking toes I have to step on in the process. Like I say, I've got bugger all to lose, have I?"

"All right, all right, you've made your point," Drinkall blustered, clearly rattled, "and if you have any evidence of impropriety in the constabulary before my appointment as Chief Constable, you can take it that the appropriate action will be taken against those responsible. I do not accept, however, your assertion that any of my officers are guilty of collusion with DCI Spiers in this current series of events. Since Doctor Bryson's extremely detailed account of the whole affair was relayed to me yesterday, every available resource of manpower has been channelled into making a thorough re-investigation of the McGregor murder, and there has been absolutely nothing to suggest that any other member of the force was in any way implicated."

"Except through mindless obedience to orders, brought about by a terminal dose of careerism, maybe? And it's a damned poor reflection on our outfit when the only thing that saved a second old woman from being murdered was the do-it-yourself gumshoe work of a wrongly-suspended sergeant, helped — through sheer good fortune — by an on-leave forensic scientist and a holidaymaking rookie bobby, both of whom also put their own lives at risk without a second thought, by the way."

Patently crestfallen, Chief Constable Drinkall now adopted a more conciliatory tone, albeit reluctantly. "Naturally, Sergeant Burns, we are extremely grateful to you and your two colleagues for your actions, which were undertaken, it has to be said, above and beyond the call of duty."

Bob resisted the temptation to tell him that, as neither he nor his two colleagues had even been on duty, his begrudged vote of thanks could be regarded as something of a contradiction in terms.

"Yes, above and beyond the call of duty, sir," Bill Blackie truckled. "I couldn't agree more." He feigned a laugh. "But hey, Bob, you'd have been in trouble if you'd charged this trip to the firm the way you did and hadn't found this Dalrymple woman before Jack, eh?"

"Not as much trouble as you'd have been in, pal!" Bob retorted tartly. "And while we're on the subject, how come Jack Spiers was so quick on my trail, anyway?"

Bill Blackie was compliance personified. "It was the girl at the travel agency in Haddington," he eagerly revealed. "As soon as you left the shop, her boss made her phone Jack Spiers' secretary for confirmation that the police would pick up the tab. That was all. Nothing sinister there, I can assure you, mate."

"But, instead of having me stopped at the airport, Spiers decided to follow on in hopes of me leading him to Pinkie Dalrymple, right?" Bob smiled coldly. "The crafty bastard. And Bertie McGregor's passport," he went on, "how did Spiers get a hold of that?"

"Your guess is as good as mine," Bill shrugged. "Probably took it out of her locker when he was doing his preliminary investigations after the murder."

"And he assumed her identity to travel out here, I take it?"

"That's right. That way there'd be no clue that Jack Spiers had ever been in Mallorca at this time. Apparently, he just told his secretary that he was going to London for a few days on an urgent family matter."

Bob shook his head in astonishment. "Flying around Europe dressed up as an old woman, and one that his wife had just bumped off, at that! Hell's teeth, his great hero Wullie Merryfield must be turning somersaults in his bloody grave!"

Drinkall and Blackie looked blankly at each other, then at Bob. It was the Chief Constable who spoke first, his tone bordering on the apologetic . . .

"Whilst your single-handed investigative efforts following the McGregor killing deserve nothing but admiration, Sergeant Burns, I'm afraid that your deductions — as communicated to us by Doctor Bryson — are entirely incorrect in one vital respect."

Bob frowned, his curiosity tinged with mistrust.

"You see," Drinkall continued, "Mrs Spiers did *not* commit the murder. She couldn't have. And even the accused, Billy Thomson the gardener, has vouched for that."

Bob's frown deepened. "Oh yeah? So what are you trying to tell me?"

Chief Constable Drinkall's manner was becoming more conciliatory by the moment. "To obviate the slightest risk of our being suspected of a whitewash in a case in which one of our own officers is embroiled, I personally arranged for your work on the enquiry to be replicated by Detective Chief Superintendent Shannon of Strathclyde Police and a hand-picked team which includes DCIs Grant and MacKay from that same constabulary. Three officers who command the highest respect throughout the CID." He paused briefly to watch Bob's reaction. Seeing that it was one of eyebrow-raising approval, he went on:

"Because of the manpower resources at their disposal, DCS Shannon and his team were able to establish relatively quickly that Mrs Spiers was in her own side ward undergoing counselling at the time of the murder. This has been confirmed by the drugs counsellor who had travelled down specially from Edinburgh to see her that day. His statement has been corroborated by Doctor Baird, the head man at Roodlands Hospital, and by the gardener, who, from where he was working with his sprayer, was able to see Mrs Spiers sitting in the window of her room throughout the period in question."

"I don't get it," said Bob, scratching his head. "Mrs Reynolds, the nursing auxiliary, told me that Lauren Spiers was in the kitchen of Bertie McGregor's ward at the time. She even said that Lauren took a jug of milk out to Bertie in the shrubbery." Bob raised his shoulders. "I mean, that's what I based my whole case against Lauren Spiers on."

"And a reasonable enough hypothesis it was, Sergeant Burns, in the limited time you had at your disposal." Chief Constable Drinkall flashed him a weak smile. "But the fact of the matter is that what Mrs Reynolds said to you has since been proved to be wrong."

Bob hesitated. "You — you mean it was Mrs Reynolds *herself* who did the dirty with the milk?"

"Another understandable enough supposition, I agree. But, no. DCI Shannon's men left no stone unturned, and they established that the highly excitable Mrs Reynolds was merely a victim of her own confusion, compounded by a desperate wish to cooperate with the law, I expect." He smiled thinly again. "I'm sure you're familiar with the sort of thing, Sergeant. You ask a traumatised witness a specific question about a specific person and, quite inadvertently, your question plants a seed of suggestion in the witness's mind."

Bob pursed his lips reflectively. "Yeah, well, that could have fitted the bill in the Mrs Reynolds scenario, I must admit."

He noticed that Bill Blackie was unable to conceal a smirk of gratification — a reaction which didn't go unobserved by Chief Constable Drinkall, either.

"Something amusing you, Inspector?" he asked straight-faced.

The colour rose in Bill Blackie's cheeks again. He shifted uncomfortably in his chair. "Ehm, no . . . no, sir. Just a passing thought, that was all."

300

Drinkall glared at him. "While you're entertaining these amusing little thoughts, it may benefit you to bear in mind that, if it hadn't been for Sergeant Burns' intuition and initiative, you would be sitting on an even more uncomfortable seat than you are right now."

"Nice one, boss," Bob said to himself. He was beginning to take a bit of a shine to this bloke.

"To let you into the picture, Sergeant," said Drinkall, coming straight back to the point, "it transpires that Mrs Spiers had indeed been helping out in Miss McGregor's ward on the day of the crime. Mrs Reynolds was absolutely correct about that. But the voluntary helper who was in the ward at the crucial time was someone else entirely. She was a member of the WRVS, whose name escapes me, but who, I'm told, is not unlike Mrs Spiers in appearance."

"Poor bugger," Bob muttered to himself, before asking. "And where was she when I was questioning the rest of the ward staff?"

"She'd gone off duty before the body was discovered, it seems, and had left almost immediately for a week's fishing in the Highlands with her husband. She hadn't even realised that she was a key figure in a murder enquiry until she returned to duty at the hospital yesterday."

Bob was in a quandary, his mind spinning. "So *she* was the one who'd taken the jug of milk out to Bertie, then?"

"That's right. She readily volunteered that information as soon as DCI McKay spoke to her."

"Yes, but the thing is, Bob," Bill Blackie piped up, desperate to get his nose in, "she never actually got as far as delivering the milk to the victim, and that's where that little *theory* of yours went a bit off course, if you'll pardon —"

"Ah-ehm! If you don't mind, Inspector," Drinkall interrupted, "*I* am conducting this briefing!" He turned again to Bob. "Now, as I was saying, Sergeant, the WRVS lady left the ward kitchen to take the milk to Miss McGregor, but before she reached the shrubbery, she was hailed from the nearby car park by someone she recognised from his regular visits to the hospital. It was a particularly hectic time of day for the WRVS tea trolley ladies, so when this person offered to save her time by taking the milk to Miss McGregor himself, the lady gladly accepted and returned to the kitchen."

Bob felt his flesh start to creep. "I'm beginning to get the picture," he grunted.

Sombrely, Chief Constable Drinkall nodded his head. "And from then on, events — as far as we've been able to ascertain — may well have happened pretty much as Doctor Bryson said you had envisaged." He paused to sigh, then admitted. "No clear motive has yet come to light, however . . ."

Bob glanced at Bill Blackie, who was still looking distinctly sheepish after the Chief Constable's put-down. "No little *theories* of your own on the motive front, Inspector Blackie?" he prodded.

Bill Blackie said nothing.

"No?" Bob goaded. "Ah well, not to worry. I've got that all sorted out for you, as well."

He then proceeded to recount Pinkie's story in detail. The story of Jack Spiers' ill-starred origins, of his eventual involvement with and selfish exploitation of Pinkie's sister and brother-in-law, of his wife's drug problem, and of their over-extravagant material appetites, culminating in Jack's last desperate attempt to extort money from Pinkie under threat of death.

An interlude of pensive quiet followed, while the Chief Constable digested these latest disclosures. It was he who ultimately broke the silence by revealing that Doctor Baird at Roodlands Hospital had actually divulged certain details of Lauren Spiers' history of drug abuse to DCS Shannon the day before.

"It's a damned sight more than I managed to wheedle out of him," Bob owned up. "Yeah, Doc Baird was as tight-lipped as a lobster's bahookie about the mysterious Lauren!"

With a slightly supercilious smile, Chief Constable Drinkall indicated the pip-adorned epaulettes of his white shirt. "Aha," he declared, "but it's amazing what the blatant throwing-about of rank can achieve in such circumstances."

"Not to mention a funny handshake or two," was the immediate thought that ran through Bob's mind.

"In any case, Sergeant Burns, the upshot of all this was that two of our people visited Mrs Spiers in the detoxification unit which she had booked herself into on the morning after the murder."

Bob was puzzled. "She went of her own free will from rehab straight back into detox? But why?"

"In an attempt, perhaps, to avoid police questioning? I don't know, and it's not really important." Drinkall folded his arms on the desk and leaned forward. "What is significant, though, is the link between Mrs Spiers' personal drug problems and her involvement with kart racing."

Bob cocked an intrigued ear. "Tell me more," he urged.

"On chancing to overhear the information you passed on to us — via Doctor Bryson's phone calls — regarding Mrs Spiers' organising of karting day-trips for underprivileged youngsters, Sergeant Steven of our drugs squad was prompted to take a fresh look at a problem he'd been struggling with for some years — namely the infiltration of drugs into certain young offenders' institutions in and around Edinburgh."

Bob had already started to knead his temples. "Jesus wept," he groaned. "I don't think I want to hear what's coming next."

Chief Constable Drinkall's face was expressionless. "Sergeant Steven paid a visit to Saughton Prison, where an ex-inmate of one of those same young offenders' institutions is currently on remand, awaiting trial for dope peddling at rave venues and the like. Ecstasy, that sort of poisonous muck. What that young hoodlum divulged, in exchange for our promising to appeal for leniency at his trial, resulted in Sergeant Steven and DCI Grant popping by for a quiet little chat with Mrs Spiers."

Bob was shaking his head incredulously now. "So, Steven fed her the line that the young pusher had grassed on her, quickly followed by Grant breaking the news that her hubby had been fished half-dead out of a Mallorcan harbour after a muffed attempt at extortion-with-intent while wearing a tweed skirt."

"Or words to that effect, yes."

"And after a spell of exposure to some *gentle* interrogation, Mrs Spiers broke down and sang like a canary, right?"

Chief Constable Drinkall stood up slowly and turned to look out over the ochre-tiled rooftops of Palma. "Not only had she been feeding her own habit for years with the money made from supplying those kids," he said, his voice filled with a mix of contempt and revulsion, "but she and Jack Spiers had been pocketing a tidy profit for themselves into the bargain. It was the perfect cover. A highly respected CID officer and his wife doing their selfless bit for society's young rejects."

Bill Blackie shattered the stunned hush that followed with a badly-timed assurance that, of course, no-one in DCI Spiers' unit had had the slightest inkling of any of this business — least of all himself. There was a discernible edge of anxiety in his delivery as he added, "I'm sure you'd back me up on that, Bob, wouldn't you?"

Bob didn't even bother to look at him. "I can only speak for myself, but everybody in the outfit knows that, if I had twigged something was going on, I'd have done something about it. And bloody fast, at that!"

Without shifting his gaze from the window, the Chief Constable stated firmly, "And hell mend any officer of lesser principles who's exposed in the course of the inquiry that I intend to set in motion."

"Hear! hear!" Bill Blackie replied. "My sentiments entirely, sir!"

Pointedly ignoring that, George Drinkall moved away from the window and sat on the corner of the desk with his back to Bill Blackie, his attention directed solely at Bob now. "From a professional standpoint, Sergeant, I'm sure you'll be interested to know that DCI Grant promptly followed up Mrs Spiers' drugs-racket confession by confronting her with your theory of how *she* had murdered Bertie McGregor."

"Obviously, she hadn't a clue that he already knew of her rock-solid alibi."

"Obviously. All Grant wanted to ascertain was how, if at all, Mrs Spiers might have been implicated in the killing. Needless to say, he played her weaknesses like a fiddle, stressing that her cooperation with the police in the murder enquiry might be given favourable consideration during her separate trial for drug trafficking."

A knowing smile traversed Bob's lips. "And the payoff?"

"She immediately spouted that all she'd done was to call her husband on her mobile phone when she saw the McGregor woman leaving the operating theatre. When asked why, she merely said that this was what her husband had instructed her to do."

"The Nuremberg syndrome again, eh? Yeah, and as soon as the heat's on, the dutiful Lauren promptly fingers her beloved Jack. Nice people." Bob gathered his thoughts for a while. "OK," he eventually said, "so we now know who killed Bertie McGregor, and we also know why, but we've still got to make the rap stick. I mean, we've got the WRVS lady's testimony that Jack Spiers was there at or about the time of the murder. But, that said, Spiers himself made it known from the outset that he was the first person on the scene *after* the event, remember?"

"True, and that's why every effort was put into finding the gardening glove that you were convinced would turn out to be the crucial item of evidence." George Drinkall returned to his seat behind the desk. "How often, Sergeant Burns, have you found that the old adage that familiarity breeds contempt can be applied to the hardened criminal, often leading to his downfall? Many times, I'm sure." There was an almost impish glint in his eye as he added, "And I think we can also say that over-confidence breeds carelessness, certainly in the case of bent coppers."

He went on to reveal that a pair of cotton gardening gloves and an empty cough cure bottle had been found tucked into the side pouch of Jack Spiers' golf bag in the boot of his car. It had already been confirmed that the bottle contained paraquat weedkiller. Also, the provisional results of forensic tests so far undertaken left little doubt that the traces of blood, oil and herbicide on the gloves would match Doctor Julie Bryson's analysis of the shred of cloth found beside the body.

Drinkall gave Bob a few seconds to take all of that in, then said with a disarming smile, "It's rather ironic, considering its potential effect on the victim's lungs, that DCI Spiers chose to administer the paraquat from a cough mixture bottle, don't you think?"

"To be frank, sir, I'm not really surprised," Bob replied, without showing any sign of appreciation for his chief's attempt at humour. "Still," he sighed, a look of relief spreading over his face, "at least we've got our man."

"And no small thanks to you and your little band of mavericks, Sergeant." The Chief Constable grinned openly and offered Bob his hand in a show of geniality that had been distinctly lacking in his greeting thirty minutes earlier.

"Only doing what we're paid to do, sir," Bob said, hoping that the irony of his words wouldn't miss the target. "But, ehm, I'd like to ask one small favour, if I may."

"Anything. Within reason, of course."

"Well, if it's all right with you, I'd like to be the one to charge that bastard Spiers with murder the moment he comes to."

Chief Constable Drinkall's expression darkened. "I'm afraid that won't be possible, Sergeant. You see, Jack Spiers died an hour ago, without ever regaining consciousness."

If Bob felt any emotion at all, it was one of deep regret — not just that an innocent old woman had suffered a needless and horrible death, but also that Jack Spiers had met an easier end than he bloody well deserved. His gaze was drawn to Bill Blackie, who was sitting staring up blankly at the revolving ceiling fan, his eyes moist, and with a look on his face that reminded Bob of a poodle whose favourite butcher had just gone out of business.

Noticing this, Chief Constable George Drinkall cleared his throat loudly. "I think, Inspector Blackie, that we could all do with a cup of coffee, don't you?"

Jolted out of his musings, Blackie stammered, "Uhm, yes — yes, sir. I, uh, I agree, of course. Absolutely."

"Well, why don't *you* go and see if our Spanish colleagues can oblige. There's something I want to discuss with Sergeant Burns — in private." He waited until the deflated Bill Blackie had left the room, then gave Bob a wink. "Now then, Bob," he smiled, ". . . about your prospects in the force."

CHAPTER
NINETEEN

The strains of "*Somethin' Stupid*" blared out from the Bow Bells Lounge as Bob and Julie entered the foyer of the Hotel Santa Catalina.

"Oo-ooh, they're playing our tune!" Julie squealed, in what Bob suspected was a display of genuine excitement, no matter how much she tried to disguise it as tongue-in-cheek. She gave his arm a squeeze and hurried him on, her high heels clattering out a fandango on the polished terrazzo floor like the hooves of a thoroughbred eager for the race.

"Take it easy," Bob grumped, doing his best to slow her down. "What's all the hurry, anyway?"

"Don't be such a torn face," she scolded. "We're late enough as it is, and Pinkie's flinging this party for *you* as much as anybody, remember. So, come on and get with it, Methuselah!"

Bob rolled his shoulders in a way reminiscent of a little boy being dragged reluctantly to school. "Yeah, yeah, but it's just that I feel —"

"I know, like a thistle in a barley field in places like this. Yes, yes, yes, I've heard it all before, so stop your whingeing!" With a good-natured shake of her fist, she hauled him through the swing doors of the lounge.

"BOB-EE-EE! JOO-LEE-EE! YOO-HOO-OO!"

The shrill greeting cut through the amplified music and babble of revellers like a laser through putty. Pinkie was perched on the bar, the centre of attraction in a fluorescent green kimono with vermilion trimmings and a purple lion rampant scaling her left breast. She was waving her pint glass.

"For Pete's sake!" Bob mumbled behind his hand as a sea of grinning faces turned towards them. "What the hell have we let ourselves in for?"

Making their way through the melee towards Pinkie, it became apparent to Bob and Julie that, in addition to all her usual paraphernalia, she was wearing a bouffant hair extension that crowned her head like a rose-coloured, acrylic beehive. Behind her bamboo specs there had been daubed an expanse of raven eye shadow which even Cleopatra would have baulked at.

"Heavens above," Julie giggled, "she looks like Dusty Springfield's granny!"

"Come away in, you pair!" Pinkie called over the milling heads. "Glad ye could make it."

"Wouldn't have missed it for the world," Bob grunted on finally reaching the bar.

"That's right," Julie grinned. She stretched up to give Pinkie a kiss. "I could hardly hold him back."

"Aye, he's got all the hallmarks o' a frantic party animal, right enough," Pinkie tartly observed, while eyeing up Bob's staid blazer and slacks.

Over on his podium, Ian "Juan-The-Organ-Man" Scrabster was now belting out a string of classic sing-along, dance-along and let's-all-do-the-actions

311

punter-pleasers. The present medley comprised such timeless Spanish-holiday gems as *Agadoo*, *The Birdie Song*, and every maiden aunt's favourite, *We're Having A Gang Bang Against The Wall*.

"I wish he'd pack it in," Pinkie shouted in Julie's ear. "Ah'm dyin' tae get the karaoke competition started and everything."

Julie's eyes lit up. "A karaoke competition? Hey, *I'll* be up for that!"

Bob cringed.

"Hiya, skipper! I see you're all dressed up for the old-time dancin'." It was the voice of PC Andy Green, barging his way through the throng with Pinkie's Filipina maid in tow. "No a bad wee party, eh?"

"Yeah," Bob groaned. "No bad."

Green gestured towards the far side of the room. "And you want to see the grub that's laid on over there. Heh, and buckets of free champers as well. Tellin' you, Sarge, it's the dog's ballocks!" Then, noticing Bob coming over all ill-at-ease, he tactfully hazarded, "Champers not your cup of tea, eh, Sarge?"

Julie leaned over and laid a hand on Andy's arm. "It's just that you shouldn't really be calling him 'Sarge'. That's probably what's wrong."

"Oh! Right, got it!" Discreetly pulling down the bottom lid of his left eye with his forefinger, he dropped his voice to a stage a whisper. "Still in the Candlestein mode, are we, Doc?" he confidentially enquired.

Julie laughed and shook her head. "Don't ask me about any of that stuff. No, all I can tell you is that your skipper is now to be addressed as Detective *Inspector*

Robert Burns. Promoted in the field, as it were, by the Chief Constable himself, no less!"

Bob parried the barrage of yelled congratulations from Andy and Pinkie with a coy smile and raised hands.

Pinkie, however, decided that this called for a toast. She turned her head and shouted at the barman, "Heh, Meegwell! A magnum o' the best bubbly and some glasses up here — *por favor*, like!"

"*VIVA THE POLIS!*" she bellowed, clinking glasses with all and sundry, before bending forward to murmur in Bob's ear, "Thanks, laddie. If it wasnae for you and that determined streak o' yours, Ah'd just be food for the fishes by now."

With that, she headed off to get the karaoke session under way, affording Ian welcome escape from his podium.

Bob greeted him with a glass of champagne. "It's a blue do when one of the party's guests of honour has to provide the music as well, Crabbie."

"Yeah, well, I could've put a dep in, right enough, but all the musos that are worse than me are busy tonight."

"And you're not about to draft in anybody that's better than you, correct?"

Ian tapped the side of his nose. "Ya gotta look after the gig, Bobby. Competition's fierce on this island. Anyway, it's good business. The hotel's paying me the usual dough for tonight, and Pinkie's slipping me an extra wee emolument on top." He stroked his moustache wistfully. "Let's face it, man, with another set of wheels to save the deposit for, I need every peseta I can lay my mitts on."

"Hmm, the Merc. What a bloody shame," Bob lamented. "Still, the good news is that you won't have to pick up the tab for the parked cars and the lampposts and things that Spiers walloped with it. My Chief Constable sorted out something with the local Guardia Civil boss about that."

"Yeah?" Ian smiled feebly, displaying all the enthusiasm of a convict who'd just been told that his life sentence had been commuted to twenty years hard labour in the salt mines.

"Yeah. Lothian and Borders Police will cover it somehow, then snatch back as much as they can out of Jack Spiers' assets. Some sort of deal like that."

"And yet they won't cough up for that twat totalling my Merc? And he was one of their own rozzers, too!" Ian was *well* peeved, and he was making no attempt to disguise the fact.

Bob nodded in commiseration. "It's a rough one, I must admit. I think it's just that my mob are trying not to lose any more face out here. They've been acting on advice from the Consul, you see, and he's told them to make sure that no Spanish nationals come out uncompensated for damage caused to their property in the incident."

"And because I just happen to be a British subject, I can go hump myself. Is that it? Land of Hope and bloody Glory, right enough!"

"Yeah," Bob sighed, "it's a real bugger, mate."

"All the same," said Julie, "for their part, the Guardia Civil *have* agreed to quash all charges relating to us stealing boats and things, so it does sort of balance out, I suppose."

"Bloody police nepotism," Ian grumped. "Bloody international Old Bill Mafia!"

"Heh, have they even scrubbed me off the rap sheet for water-skiing in the dark?" Andy Green queried with a surprising hint of anxiety in his voice.

"Certainly have," Bob confirmed. "Of course, the three of us will have to come back to attend the inquest into Jack Spiers' death, when the Spanish authorities eventually get round to holding one, that is. But, in the meantime, you're free to fly home with your pals at the end of your holiday."

"Aw, what a bummer," PC Green moaned. He jerked his thumb in the direction of the Filipina maid, who was staring up at him in open-mouthed admiration. "Just when me and wee Imelda here was startin' to get our act together and that."

"Well, you'd better make the most of the few days you've got left," Bob curtly advised, "because you aren't gonna have much time for all this Randy Andy stuff once you start learning your new job."

PC Green assumed his familiar gormless laddie look. "New . . . *job?*"

"Yep! You can say goodbye to your old mates at the Haddington nick the same day you get back." Bob savoured a moment or two of young Green's obvious puzzlement, then stated bluntly, "You've done your last school crossing patrol, boy. And that's straight from the Chief Constable's mouth."

Andy Green was now standing like a gangly version of Stan Laurel, winding himself up for a whimper. "You mean, they're gonna . . . I mean, the Chief Constable's decided, just because . . . You're trying to tell me I'm gonna be kicked out the force?" His bottom lip started to quiver. "But — but, what'll ma mum say?"

"She'll probably ask you how the blazes you've managed to make it into the CID already, when your poor old dad still hasn't cracked it after twenty-odd years of plodding the pavements."

PC Green scrutinised Bob's poker face. "Nah," he half laughed after a while, "you're pullin' ma plonker, Sarge . . . I mean, ehm, skipper. Like, there's the CID entrance exams and things. Intelligence tests and stuff like that."

"The way the Chief Constable sees it," Bob shrugged, "is that anybody daft enough to do what you did along in the Port of Andratx the other night is daft enough to be admitted into the CID, without need for further assessment. *And,* for my sins, I've been told that you've to be assigned to my squad, *Detective Constable Green.*"

Andy looked first at Julie for some sign that this really might be some kind of cruel mickey-take, then back at Bob. When he received no such reaction, he could hardly contain his delight. "Hey, skipper," he checked, "does this mean I'll be assigned to a lot of *real* C-R-A-P work from now on?"

Bob pursed his lips and nodded sagely. "You better believe it, lad. You'll be up to your nostrils in it for the next ten years at least, I promise you."

"Brilliant!" Green beamed. He punched the air. "Yeah, pure, dead brilliant!"

"Who stole your sweeties?" Pinkie said, poking her finger into Ian's belly on return from launching the karaoke competition. "Ye've got a face like a spanked arse."

Ian summoned up a petted smile. "Never mind me, Pinkie," he whined. "Just you join in with the police back-slappin' celebrations." He inhaled a heavy sigh. "I'll just content myself with memories."

"Aye, well, the older ye get, the more ye'll have to get used to doin' that, son, believe me." Pinkie tapped her lips with her forefinger. "I wonder, though," she murmured pensively, then took Ian by the elbow, wheeling him round. "Just you come wi' me for a minute. There's something I want to ask ye about in the garden."

"No point in asking me," Ian objected. "I know as much about bloody gardening as I do about do-it-yourself brain surgery."

Pinkie turned and called to Bob and the others, "You lot better come as well, then."

"Talking about gardening," Bob said to Julie, "you'll be interested to know that Billy Thomson, the gardener who was arrested for Bertie's murder, has been released from jail — unconditionally, George Drinkall said."

"Glad to hear it. What a nightmare for the guy. What'll become of him now, though? Going back to his old job at the hospital, is he?"

Bob shook his head. "I shouldn't think so. Oh, they've asked him to go back, mind you, but I doubt if Billy'll do it. Small town, some small minds, and a lot of long memories. It would just take a handful of bad-mouthed yobs to make his life hell. No, I think he'll have decided to make a fresh start somewhere else."

"Yeah, *if* the poor gadgie can find a job," Andy Green pointed out. "Easier said than done nowadays, especially if you've just come out o' the slammer."

The more Pinkie listened in to this conversation, the more it caught her interest. "Does he, ehm — does he like a wee natter, this Billy lad?" she asked.

"Used to chat away to Bertie for hours on end, I believe," Bob answered. "Could never hear enough of her gardening stories, he told me."

"My, my, fancy that, now." Pinkie adjusted her bamboo specs. "And, eh, can he drive a car, by any chance?"

"There was a wee pick-up with gardening gear in it outside his shed at Roodlands," Bob recalled. "So, yes, I presume he can at that."

"Well then, there's upwards o' two acres o' gardens and mountainside to look after at my place. Too much for me and wee Imelda here to cope with. Aye, we could do wi' a man about the place, right enough. And there's a nice wee flat above the garage . . ."

318

"Sounds like a good offer," Bob smiled. "Matter of fact, if I hadn't been given this promotion, I might have taken you up on it myself."

There was a wicked glint in Pinkie's eye now. "This Billy lad . . . how would he look in a nice chauffeur's uniform, d'ye think? Ye know the sort o' thing — the black leather ridin' boots and the tight-arsed jodhpurs and everything."

Bob laughed out loud. "Oh, I'm sure he'd look the part OK. He's got a very cultured accent too, by the way, and manners to match. Yes, I'm sure he'd cut the required dash for your Lady Euphemia outings in your pink Jag, or whatever you go for." He opened the door to the hotel garden.

Ian was already standing there, moodily looking at a large cactus. "Right, Pinkie," he grunted, "what was it you wanted to know?"

Pinkie shooed him round the corner of the building. "What I want to know, Crabbie, is what you think of *that*?"

The huffy look on Ian's face dissolved into one of deep hurt as he caught sight of the white Mercedes glittering in the coloured floodlights by the hotel's main entrance. The others started to snigger.

"Very bloody funny," Ian grouched. "Go on, all of you — have a good titter. It's a Merc just like the one I *used* to have." He rounded on Pinkie. "Is that all you needed to know?"

"No. And anyway, it's *not* just like yer old one. It's top o' the range, it's a flashier colour *and* it's two years younger." She dangled a set of keys in his face. "But what I really want to know is how the driver's seat suits yer big, fat jacksy!"

Ian was dumbstruck. He wasn't sure whether to laugh or cry. "You wouldn't just have gone and . . .? Nah, it's gotta be a wind-up." He stared at the keys which Pinkie then stuffed into his hand, then wandered trancelike towards the car. "You mean you've gone and bought this for *me*?"

"Well, it's a small price for a lucky old hoor like me to pay for havin' her life saved, is it no?"

Julie planted a kiss on Pinkie's cheek. "Lucky or not," she smiled, "there could never be a nicer old hoor than you."

"Och, away wi' ye, lassie," Pinkie flustered, "ye'll only go and make ma mascara run wi' all yer nonsense." She dabbed her cheeks with the cuff of her kimono. "And what have *you* got to be so happy about, anyway? You're about the only one that hasnae got anything out o' this whole kerfuffle."

"Don't you believe it," Julie whispered with a sly wink. "I've an idea I'll come out of it quite nicely, if you get my drift."

Pinkie winked back. "Aye, that's what I've been thinkin'. Wummin's intuition — know what Ah mean?" She cupped a hand to Julie's ear. "But now we're on the subject, I thought you said Bobby Burns there had promised you a major prize for catchin' up wi' the rubber boat Jack Spiers shanghaied me in."

"Yes, well, I suppose his mind *has* been on other things since then," Julie conceded. She gave a mischievous little laugh. "But, whether he knows it or not, I aim to collect, and this very night at that!"

"Yer own private Burns Night wi' yer own special haggis, eh?" Pinkie's accompanying chortle was positively filthy.

"A joke we can all share?" Bob enquired.

"Mm-hmm, maybe you'll find out later," Julie cooed. "But in the meantime, I've got something I want you to help me with." She fluttered her eyelashes. "Something that can only be done by a woman *and* a man . . ."

She took Bob's hand and hauled him, protesting gamely, back inside the hotel.

Ian had noticed none of this. He was transfixed, sitting in the Merc and playing with its steering wheel like a kid in a toy car.

Pinkie gave him a playful punch on the shoulder. "Well then, Crabbie, what have ye got to say for yersel' now?"

He looked up at her and grinned. "Aw, Pinkie," he drooled, "this is different class. It makes my other Merc seem like an old banger."

Pinkie went round to the passenger's side. "Well, ye can take *this* old banger for a trial spin round the block while the karaoke competition's still in progress."

"Good idea, missus," Andy Green enthused. He bundled wee Imelda into the back seat and followed her in. He tapped Ian on the back. "Hit the go button, Fats. It's elbows out the windaes time for a nice, posey cruise past the open-air bars and that."

"Hold it!" Pinkie barked. She snatched Ian's hand as he made to turn the ignition key, then craned her head out of the window, listening intently. "What the bloody hell's *that?*"

Andy Green winced.

Wee Imelda squirmed.

Ian grimaced. "Well," he said after it dawned on him what they were hearing, "they're hardly in the Frank and Nancy Sinatra league, are they?"

A contented smile pulled gently at Pinkie's Cupid's bow lips. "Maybe no, but I fancy they'll be a hit tonight for a' that." She chuckled quietly to herself as the bizarre blend of bathtub soprano and mortified baritone reverberated out from the karaoke speakers in the Bow Bells Lounge . . .

> *"And then I go and spoil it all*
> *By sayin' somethin' stupid*
> *Like I love you, I love you, I love you . . ."*

EPILOGUE

Bob got off the bar stool and ambled over with his pint to the corner table where the two old cronies were sitting. He stooped down and patted the collie sitting at their feet. "Good boy," he said, tickling the upturned chin. "Yes, you're a bonny lad, aren't you?"

"She's a bitch!" the owner informed him in tones of high affrontery. "Ye never heard o' a *dog* wi' a name like Nellie, did ye?"

"Sorry, Nellie," Bob said, duly admonished. "You're a bonny *lass*, then, aren't you?" He then addressed the owner with a penitent smile. "I don't suppose she's too fussy about what I call her, anyway — as long as she gets a good run about in Archerfield woods in a wee while, eh?"

Nellie wagged her tail.

Her master scowled over the rim of his whisky glass.

"You know your way about these parts, do you, sir?" the young barman called over, keen to maintain a convivial atmosphere.

"I was born and brought up in Dirleton, as a matter of fact," Bob replied. He cast his eyes round the interior of the bar again. "That said, it must be twenty years since I was last in the Castle Inn here, though. Mmm, and I suppose that would've been the last time I saw Bertie McGregor alive — holding court over by the fireside there."

"Here! wait a minute," the dog's master said. "I know you! I seen yer photie in the paper. You're the Burns lad that's in the polis. Solved Bertie's murder, didn't ye?"

"Aye, well, I was a part of the team," Bob acknowledged modestly.

"Ye done bloody well for yersel' out o' it, though, didn't ye? Promoted up amongst the high heid yins overnight, if I mind right."

"Oh, hardly as quick as that," Bob laughed, trying not to appear too taken aback. "No, no, just a bit of advancement with interest, you might say. Ehm, compensation for having been left to rot at the bottom of the heap for years, maybe. Aye, a late developer, me."

If this self-effacing riposte was intended to win over the two worthies, it failed.

"Never even found out the right truth about yon man that murdered Bertie, did ye?" Nellie's owner jeered. "Some detective you. Hell, I could've done better masel'. Is that no right, Eck?"

His companion chuckled his agreement while peering into his empty glass. "Ye're no wrong, Wattie. Dry, but no wrong."

Bob took the subtle hint. He asked the barman to give the two old boys another whisky apiece, then said to them, "What do you mean the *right* truth? We

324

successfully collared the guilty man, and that's all that matters, surely."

"Aye, maybe so, son," Wattie half acknowledged, his manner mellowing to the sound of the drams being poured, "but ye never found out the really *sensational* bit. That's what I mean, ye see."

"The whole damned case was sensational enough to do me for a while," Bob snapped. "So what are you on about?"

Wattie half shut his eyes, an I-know-something-you-don't know twist to his mouth. "Well, ye never managed to find out who the culprit's mother was, did ye?" he goaded.

Bob took a deep breath and exhaled slowly. What the hell was he doing, he asked himself, getting into a pointless discussion about a closed case with this pair of old codgers? Still, they'd fired his curiosity now, so no harm in playing them along for a bit. "To be frank," he said, "the subject of Jack Spiers' mother did come up in a chat I had with Pinkie Dalrymple in Mallorca. I had a hunch it might've been Pinkie's sister Molly, but Pinkie didn't want to talk about it, and I saw no point in pushing her. Let's face it, it had no bearing on the case, and it's all water under the bridge now anyway."

"Oho! Pinkie never wanted to talk about it, did she no?" Wattie asked, laying the intrigue on thick. He tilted his head towards his pal. "I'm no surprised, are you, Eck?"

"No really," smiled his laconic friend.

Wattie threw Nellie a potato crisp, then looked at Bob, a waggish eyebrow arched. "Ye never heard the story about wee Jocky Archerfield, then?"

"Jocky Archerfield . . . Jocky Archerfield . . . I take it he was one of the whodunnits who were born in the village during the war."

"Aye, that's right."

"Yeah, Angus Forsyth, the old village bobby, mentioned them. The locals called them Archerfield if there was some doubt about the identity of the father, right?"

"Aye, but did Gus tell ye about wee *Jocky* Archerfield?"

Bob shook his head. "No, can't say he did."

"No, because he couldnae, because he didnae even know!" Wattie paused, allowing the tension to build up while he dribbled some water into his dram. His expression was sombre now. "Only ma late wife, God bless her, knew the true story. She was the district midwife in them days, see. Aye, and she brought that bairn into the world one black night in the garden cottage where Pinkie and Bertie lived, along there behind Archerfield big hoose."

"Wait a minute," Bob cut in, "old Gus *did* tell me something about that. Jock King, the caretaker at Roodlands Hospital in Haddington, was supposed to be the father . . . although it might've been his brother Jimmy. Anyway," Bob shrugged, "it turned out that it made no difference either way, because the kid was stillborn."

"Very true. Found in a shallow grave, the bairn was."

Bob looked at his watch and stood up to leave. "Yes, I can see it must have been a big sensation at the time, boys," he said dismissively, "but it's of no interest to the police now."

"Aha, but the deid bairn had a twin brother," Wattie said, timing the revelation with dramatic perfection. "And *it* lived! Oh aye, only ma late wife knew about that, and she took the secret to the grave wi' her . . . apart from tellin' me, that is."

Bob sat down again, his curiosity rekindled. "And this kid, the twin that lived, was the one you call wee Jocky Archerfield, was it?"

Wattie nodded gravely. "And nobody around here knew about that, except Pinkie, Bertie and ma wife. I can tell ye now, son, because it cannae make any difference to anybody any more."

Bob was puzzled. "But why the Archerfield bit? Why didn't they just call him wee Jocky King, if the mother was that sure Jock was the father?"

"Oh, they threatened Jock wi' that, right enough. But then the bairn's existence wouldnae have been a secret, and the truth about his mother bein' pupped out o' wedlock would've been out." Wattie leaned over the table until his nose was almost touching Bob's, then disclosed in a half whisper, "The mother was one o' them lassies that managed to keep her condition disguised, like. Starvation and corsets and things like that, ye ken."

"She was Pinkie's sister," Eck blandly revealed, smiling into his dram.

Bob snapped his fingers. "So I was right! Molly *was* the mother of wee Jocky Archerfield — or Jack A-for-Archerfield Spiers, as his name eventually became."

"And just where would the sensation have been in that, if ye don't mind me askin'?" Wattie snorted.

"Pinkie had another sister," Eck let slip.

"It's me that's bloody well tellin' this story!" Wattie barked. "And anyway, it was a half sister."

"Same mother," Eck went on, unperturbed by Wattie's rebuke. "Different faithers."

"Aye, and I kent the two faithers fine," Wattie proclaimed, reasserting his position as head storyteller. "Up in Perth it was, where I lived as a laddie. Old Donald Dalrymple only snuffed it ten years ago, they say. About ninety-five he must have been. And that old tike Robbie McGregor pegged out just a year or so after him. What a pair o' wild buggers they used to be! And the lassies were just as bad — Pinkie and Bertie, any road. Took after their faithers, and no mistake." He chuckled at the memory. "Mm-hmm, first came to Dirleton frae Perth to work as land girls at the start o' the last war, the pair o' them."

Bob felt the hairs rise on the back of his neck as the significance of what this old fellow had said began to sink in. "Good God almighty!" he muttered, his blood running cold, his eyes staring at the floor.

"Oho! I see ye've got it now at last!" old Wattie bellowed, his face turning puce with pent-up exhilaration. "Some detective you! Aye, that's right," he spluttered, unable to hold back the mocking laughter, "yer man Jack Spiers, the great orphan polisman, only went and murdered his own bloody mother!"

Also available in ISIS Large Print:

The Endings Man

Frederic Lindsay

Praise for Frederic Lindsay: An intriguing and intelligent thriller **Sunday Telegraph**

"Why is it," Barclay Curle grumbles to his agent Jonah, "that all the regional Edinburgh detectives have monosyllabic first names like Jack and Bob?"

Then Curle publishes his newest book — about an Edinburgh detective called Doug — inciting a letter from an anonymous admirer accusing him of stealing the murders she's committed. Fact and fiction become increasingly inseparable when a dead woman is found, murdered by the method favoured by the serial killer in Curle's novel. For Detective Inspector Meldrum — first name Jim — Curle seems the most obvious suspect. Faced with a second murder and a darkening cloud of suspicion, Curle decides to take action. After all, who has more experience of solving murder mysteries than a crime novelist?

ISBN 978-0-7531-7800-3 (hb)
ISBN 978-0-7531-7801-0 (pb)

The Act of Roger Murgatroyd

Gilbert Adair

A wonderfully witty novel that plays with the Golden Age crime genre

A good period detective story   **The Times**

Boxing Day, 1935. A snowed-in manor on the very edge of Dartmoor. A Christmas house party. And overhead, in the attic, the dead body of Raymond Gentry, gossip columnist and blackmailer, shot through the heart. But the attic door is locked from the inside, its sole window is traversed by thick iron bars and naturally, there is no sign of a murderer or a murder weapon.

Fortunately (though not for the murderer), one of the guests is the formidable Evadne Mount, the bestselling author of countless classic whodunnits. In fact, were she not its presiding sleuth, *The Act of Roger Murgatroyd* is exactly the type of whodunnit she herself might have written.

ISBN 978-0-7531-7740-2 (hb)
ISBN 978-0-7531-7741-9 (pb)